Praise for *I Want Everything*

'*I Want Everything* is a book about literature that feels like a bank heist. It's salacious and funny and fun, and has a stay-up-all-night, can't-look-away energy that I adore. I loved it!'

Rita Bullwinkel, Booker Prize-longlisted author of *Headshot*

'Composed with stylistic brilliance and structural ingenuity, *I Want Everything* is that rare thing, a great contemporary novel. While it is first and foremost a hilarious, complex, and profound reflection on the relationship between life and writing, it is also fun to read, entertaining and populated by rich, real characters. Dominic Amerena is a fantastic writer. (Seriously.)'

Lauren Oyler, author of *Fake Accounts* and *No Judgement*

'This novel is that most exquisite rarity: a brilliant concept, brilliantly executed. Amerena has so precisely rendered and skewered Australian literary culture that I was shrieking with delight while I squirmed in recognition. The tease of a mystery plot had me turning the pages non-stop, but there were real gem-like sentences in here too. And on top of that, he can write women. And on top of that, he can write writing! This book is a rollicking laugh through the ego until the bill of the id comes due. I adored it. I wish I could go back and savour it again for the first time. I'll read anything and everything Amerena does next.'

Bri Lee, author of *Eggshell Skull* and *The Work*

'A twisty-turny, deliciously sneaky and bitingly insightful literary mystery. I laughed, cringed, squirmed, clapped and cheered.'

Emily Maguire, author of *Rapture*

'*I Want Everything* is a Russian doll of a novel set largely in an Australian city. It is a layered mystery. It is an enigma wrapped inside an enigma possibly wrapped inside an enigma. It is a book about the complexities of storytelling and idiosyncrasies of writers. *I Want Everything* is also a debut novel by Dominic Amerena, a writer of such talent we can only hope he doesn't vanish on us.'

Tony Birch, author of *Women and Children*

'How I loved this novel about books, writing, and the literary life – in all its corrupted glory. Seamlessly crafted, confident and original, *I Want Everything* took my breath away.'

Sofie Laguna, Miles Franklin-winning author of *The Eye of the Sheep*

'A fun, engaging novel about the disastrous consequences of riding a deception to its fateful end, and of one man's ruthless hunger for literary fame. I loved the reflections on writing, the nature of it, the difficulty, the mystery of it. Amerena has written an engrossing take on the precarity of the writing life, while exploring the ethical dilemmas faced by a novelist.'

Jessie Tu, author of *A Lonely Girl is a Dangerous Thing*

'A delightful literary puzzle, posed to the reader in vibrant and clear-cut prose. "Authenticity", the demonic past and the treacherous body come under wry examination. It's rare for a writer to be this good both at crafting a sentence and at making you want to read the next one.'

Naoise Dolan, author of *Exciting Times* and *The Happy Couple*

I WANT EVERYTHING
DOMINIC AMERENA

Thanks for reading.
Enjoy!!!

Summit
Books
Australia

Summit
Books
Australia

I WANT EVERYTHING
First published in Australia in 2025 by Summit Books Australia,
an imprint of Simon & Schuster (Australia) Pty Limited
Level 4, 32 York Street, Sydney NSW 2000

Summit Books and colophon are trademarks of Simon & Schuster, LLC

10 9 8 7 6 5 4 3 2 1

Sydney New York Amsterdam/Antwerp London Toronto New Delhi
Visit our website at www.simonandschuster.com.au

© Dominic Amerena 2025

All rights reserved. No part of this publication may be reproduced,
stored in a retrieval system, or transmitted in any form or by any means,
electronic, mechanical, photocopying, recording or otherwise,
without prior permission of the publisher.

 A catalogue record for this book is available from the National Library of Australia

ISBN: 9781761631733

Cover design by Sandy Cull
Typeset by Midland Typesetters, Australia
Printed and bound in Australia by Griffin Press

 The paper this book is printed on is certified against the Forest Stewardship Council® Standards. Griffin Press holds chain of custody certification SCS-COC-001185. FSC® promotes environmentally responsible, socially beneficial and economically viable management of the world's forests.

Australian Government

This project has been assisted by the Australian Government through
Creative Australia, its principal arts investment and advisory body.

For Ellena, of course …

PART ONE

ONE

An innocent mistake. Innocent, then progressively less so. I acted immorally, but what did literature have to do with morality? Looking back, it all seemed inevitable, the first mistaken identity leading to the second, leading me to the bedside of the last, great Australian writer, observing her in her natural habitat: captivity. It had nothing to do with me – the deception, the slip of the tongue I couldn't take back. At least, that's what I told myself, until it was all too late.

It began after my discharge from the Alfred Hospital in the first week of February. The tests proved there was nothing wrong with me, yet I felt anything but fine as I waited for my Uber on Commercial Road. I'd been in and out of the hospital many times over the years. I'd learnt to rate my negative feelings on a scale of one to ten, be they discomfort and numbness, dizziness and flatulence. That day my stomach ache was a six going on seven, growing more acute the closer I got to Footscray and home.

We hit the Bolte Bridge, the cranes and crates of the Port of Melbourne visible far below through the suicide fence, the sluggish Yarra and the skyscrapers scattered with coins of light from the late-afternoon sun. I realised then what was causing the ache: shame. For the incident with the night nurse and, more than that, for who I'd let myself become: an unpublished, barely solvent pig. Impossible I should allow my girlfriend, Ruth, to see me like that, achingly myself, so I took evasive action. In a snarl of traffic on Racecourse Road, I cleared my throat and addressed the driver.

—I want to change where I'm going.

The pool was in the complex of buildings at Victoria University, overlooking Footscray Park, sloping down to the Maribyrnong River. Clouds of bushfire smoke were flocked above Melbourne's skyline, which seemed slightly unreal through the pool's main window. I bought goggles and budgie smugglers from the pustular attendant and descended into the change rooms, hoping they would live up to their name. In the mirror I was shocked by what I saw: myself, whippet-thin from three weeks of calorie restriction, looking every inch the emerging writer I still unfortunately was. I had lost a lot of blood in the hospital – a lot of time, too – and I vowed to do something, anything, to ensure I never returned there.

I hacked through the first ten laps until I fell into rhythm. Perhaps the doctor had been right and I was going to be okay, relatively speaking. By the time the cramps set in, my discharge seemed a distant memory. I almost felt good. I wallowed through the last few metres, levered myself onto the lip of the fast lane, where an aquarobics class was in full swing, to the strains of Kylie's 'Locomotion'. I waited to catch my breath, my eyes drawn to the face of a woman with sharply chiselled cheekbones, like the bust of a deposed dictator. She must have been eighty, maybe even older, but there was something about her that was maddeningly familiar: the eyes that were all pupil, the grim hyphen of a mouth. I knew her from somewhere, I was sure of it.

It was still sweltering when I emerged onto Ballarat Road, a northerly blasting up from the Maribyrnong, the sun reluctantly setting. I was waiting at the pedestrian crossing, feeling butch and pleasurably sluggish when I saw a line of oldies, bedraggled from their swim, being escorted by a nurse (how I now loathed *them*!) into a minivan parked in an access road. The van had bald tyres and its windows were caked in dust. Words were emblazoned on its side, in capitals so faded I could only make out the first: MERCY. Fitting, as it was a quality in short supply, especially in myself.

The woman with the cheekbones was at the back of the line, trying to get a cigarette lit. She was slight and wiry, barely up to the bus's window, wearing a grey singlet, straight-cut jeans and workboots too hot for the weather. They were the clothes of a shearer, a wharfie, a Melbournian prose poet. Despite its dampness, her hair sprang up from her scalp. Again I had the feeling I knew this woman, but this time the feeling was more acute. I couldn't look away. Finally, she puffed a plume of smoke, eyes closed in contentment. When she opened them, it seemed she was staring back at me. Without stopping to think what I was doing, I snapped her photo with my phone.

My hair dried in the ten-minute walk home to our tin-roofed weatherboard on Stirling Street, with its peeling ceilings and the gaps between the joists housing huntsmen and other scuttling things. The front door had expanded in the heat and was stuck fast in the frame, but with some very vigorous jiggling, I managed to prise it open.

The living room was trashed, the air close, reeking of body odour and the noxious chop-chop Ruth smoked when she was broke. Clearly she'd made the most of my hospital stay. Each time I returned from the ward, I worried I'd find that Ruth had fallen out of love with me. That in my absence she'd have realised I was the cane toad to her frog, the skin tag to her beauty spot, and she'd sit me down and give me the talk.

She wasn't in the living room or kitchen, but eventually I spied her watering the roses by the sagging back fence. She'd just clocked off from online teaching, though in a black satin smock she looked like she was on her way to a publishing party. She despised the garb of the teleworker – uggs and lunch-spattered trackies – resisted easy comforts in all aspects of her life.

I felt a premonition of doom, as if watching her from some depleted future. Ruth had refused to visit me in the hospital; she said it made her feel ashamed to see me in such a wretched state, cannulated and exsanguinated. Shame. There was that word again. In the three weeks we'd been apart, I'd thought of little other than our reunion, imagining the new flecks of grey in her roan hair (*I tend to have that effect on women*: a joke I'd made one too many times), her character actor's nose, which whistled when she slept. Approaching her from behind, I leant in to peck her neck, but as soon as my lips made contact Ruth yelped and spun around, the hose splashing down my front.

—It's you! she said, removing an AirPod.

We hugged, and her fingers went straight for my rib cage.

—I feel like I could snap you in half. What did they do to you in there? You really shouldn't sneak up on me when I'm listening to my murder podcast. This one has to be heard to be believed. Our fearless interlocutor convenes panel discussions between the daughter of a serial killer and the family members of her father's victims.

—Progeny of the missing and murdered unite, I said, taking the hose.

I soaked the flowers until the soil sluiced onto the concrete, as Ruth spoke about the gentrification of true crime, replete with narrators forever second-guessing themselves. *Who should be speaking and why? Was it their story to tell?*

—I just wish they'd own their desire to titillate and appal. To give us what we've always wanted: white women's mysterious disappearances. Do you want to do the honours?

Ruth brandished her phone and I vogued before the rosebush as she snapped away. Our landlord, Luong, believed the flowers gave the backyard a certain old-world charm, distracting from the tract of concrete that stretched from fence to fence. In our two years living there, Luong hadn't raised the rent, in part because we didn't bother him for upkeep; we let the ceilings leak, scrubbed black mould where it bloomed. He was decent as far as landlords went so we obliged when he asked for evidence the roses were surviving the heatwave, though we had fun with the brief, deadpanning as if for fashion mag spreads or ransom photos.

—My tender button, Ruth said, inspecting the photos. My sodden, tender button. I wish you didn't keep leaving me like this.

*

I sat at the garden table, the warm evening air delicious on my skin, the sky a violent pink through the smoke clouds. Hammered from a half-glass of chianti, I debated whether to tell Ruth about my shameful discharge. Nothing had happened *exactly*, and yet I still felt too clammy and abased to bring it up. So when Ruth asked how I was feeling, I bit my tongue and did a bit about my toxic masculinity.

—Nothing to report. No growths or deformities. But the doctors say I can't procreate for the time being. The drugs I'm on aren't good for foetal matter.

Ruth updated me on her progress with the book, but I found myself zoning out, zonked from wine and exercise; I was still struggling to reacclimatise to the real world, as it were, in all its vicious intensity. Lately, Ruth had been pulling ten-hour writing days, finalising the manuscript for her debut book of essays, *Between the Lines*.

—I have hope that it's finally coming together, Ruth said. Hope without optimism, to borrow a phrase from the erstwhile Marxists we know and love.

Ruth was Melbourne-famous, but unlike the other writers with whom we occasionally commiserated, mourned, kvetched, whined, bitched and bloviated, Ruth had a plausible chance of making it. She was made for making it, as I was wont to remind her. It was only a matter of time.

—What else have you missed? Ruth said. Ella and Ahmed are trying for a kid. Nataliya is 'saving' for a deposit, though as far as I know she's still a poet. I suppose her parents are stumping up. Oh and Ben and Michaela's experiment with throupledom was a resounding failure. Shocker! Everyone's reaching the point of no return. Getting hitched, chucking long-term partners, choosing an unknown future over an imperfect present.

My body tensed as if for the midnight blood round, waiting for the night nurse to stick the needle in. But thankfully, Ruth didn't have any modern ideas about the structure of our relationship. Instead, she'd moved on to news of Australia's manifold crises of the day: the fires in the east of the state; a rare earth mine breaking ground near Swan Hill. Tim Winton's new novel – apparently not without its charms – about alt-right pyromaniac BMX riders. But my mind was decidedly elsewhere; it kept returning to the woman from the pool. I could see every line of her face, could feel the force of her gaze on mine. I knew I knew her – but how? And also: so what? The answers continued to elude me.

—Disaster has become quotidian, Ruth was saying. It doesn't leave a mark, except in art. Now we're all first responders writing triage narratives, the most pressing problem told in the most pressing way. A lot to live up to.

—It's all a bit dour, isn't it? I said, more loudly than I'd intended. These books predicting precisely in which way the world is going to end. Who are they for? The farmers tilling the grain tables being burnt off the map? The villagers in low-lying island nations? The future generations who might look back and say, *Well, at least our novelists saw it coming.* Climate is clichéd, old hat, tedious beyond words.

—The sky above your head would beg to differ.

—We know what's wrong with the world, and who's to blame. A condition of informed helplessness, and one we should resist – just not with our fiction. Let our politics be moral and principled. But fiction should be about murkiness, complexity, problems with no solutions, jokes with no punchlines. You get the picture. When we sit at our desks, we should remember that our real purpose is to be engineers of the soul.

This was what I'd been missing: the texture of how Ruth and I spent our days. This talk of form and content was as old as our relationship. In our first week as a couple I'd sent Ruth the late-onset juvenilia of my twenties, stories about sad suburbanites who fell apart in the usual literary ways.

—Your sentences are clean enough to eat off, she'd said.

She didn't mean it as a compliment. I was a style machine with no substance, flexing my empathetic dexterity. And she was right, though those stories were published, won prizes, made people think (wrongly) that I was a talent on the rise.

—I can't see any of *you* in these, Ruth had said. They could have been written by anyone.

After that, I tried to put myself at the centre of things, in my writing at least. I attempted a thinly veiled autofiction, a novel about novel-making, like all the other novels being made that year. But more often than not the words didn't come. I chored and pottered, scrubbing this and wiping that, brewing pots of coffee, forever checking in on Ruth to see if she needed anything. The pool saved us. Instead of shuffling about the house like some demonic butler, I could swim away my frustration at myself and my sentences, return home in somewhat working order.

Since we got together, I hadn't written a sentence fit to print. Despite my fine words to Ruth, writing now felt like passing a kidney stone. I still remembered what it felt like to enjoy writing, the sheer thrill and risk, a key turned in the lock of the soul. But that was long in the past. One thing I loved about Ruth was her belief in her work and the world. That the latter could change, and not only for the worse. Was faith something you could catch, like all those diseases I'd been treated for over the years? I'd been waiting two years to find out.

—Do you know who said that? Ruth said, fiddling with her phone, as possums screeched on the roof. The bit about engineers of the soul? One Joseph Stalin.

I stood, bilious and bloated. Sensing my unsteadiness, Ruth let me lean on her as we walked back into the house. Fitting because she worked with guts and grit, while I was so ephemeral I often felt like I'd float away. Her work said true things about power and people and politics. Mine did not. We went through the kitchen and the living room, past the rattan couch salvaged from hard rubbish. She was breathing heavily when we made it to the bedroom, where she deposited me on our posturepedic mattress, the brand of choice for the hosts of her true crime podcasts.

—To be continued, she said, heading to the toilet.

My hand shot to my pocket, slid out my phone, found the picture I'd taken earlier. The woman looked exactly as I remembered, the answer to a question I hadn't known to ask. But who was she, and why couldn't I get her out of my mind? When I heard Ruth's footsteps in the corridor, I swiped away from the photo, as if I had something to hide.

One thing led to another. Nice to know the connection hadn't been severed, the red thread that bound our bodies together. Ruth was behind me, and I was trying to forget the woman's face, while Ruth hissed hot and wet in my ear.

—I know what you did. The mess you made. You're such a disappointment. You should be ashamed.

TWO

I wasn't stalking the woman from the pool, that much was for sure. I didn't even know her name, nor why I felt so drawn to her. Stalking implied a certain level of intention, which frankly I didn't have. Stalking required knowledge. But there was no denying I wasn't at the pool to swim; I was still too sore from yesterday's sixty leaden laps, a limbless invertebrate barely capable of pulling on my bathers. The hangover didn't help.

I arrived at the same time as the day before, when the aquarobics class had commenced. Stuffing my clothes in the locker, I felt nervous, borderline giddy for no good reason; I knew intuitively that something was going to happen. Just before I closed my gym bag, I got a text from Siobhan, the Galwegian night nurse: *I'm so sorry. I hope you're alright. Call me anytime.* My stomach gave a sickening lurch. I deleted the message, blocked her number.

The school day had just finished, and the pool was pandemonium. The water boiled with sprogs and sprats, whooping in triumph, waving to mothers on bleachers. We civilians were garrisoned to the slow lane. I breaststroked at a glacial pace, inspecting each wader and paddler through my tinted goggles. Two women lolled on the lane ropes, chatting in what sounded like Greek. A football player I vaguely recognised did lunges at the shallow end. But the woman from yesterday was nowhere to be seen. There was nothing to do but float and watch and wait. Felt strange to keep thinking of her as 'the woman'. But what other label would fit the bill? Prey and quarry seemed a little extreme. The subject of my literary attention?

That subject was usually Ruth. She'd published a piece about pools while I was in the hospital. I'd watched from my gurney, dizzy from the blood round, as the hearts flooded in on her Instagram. Her essay examined the strange and troubling history of Melburnian pools and public baths. Long before Federation, when Melbourne was little more than a stolen swamp, baths were built to discourage white citizens from swimming in the Yarra, which back then was a typhoid-ridden dumping ground for the refuse of the city being wrenched into being, emitting a stench so bad the newborn city was nicknamed 'Smellbourne' until plumbing was introduced at the turn of the twentieth century. The rich paid a premium to bathe first, the price dropping as the water grew dirtier, until the poorest were left with the silty grime of their betters. For Ruth, the public baths represented the workings of the colonial project, bringing the land into line, creating a space delimited for health and hygiene where new arrivals could wash away the taint of a country they knew wasn't theirs. They also presented a possible future, when there wasn't enough water to go around, and we, the great unwashed, would look back with nostalgia at the monstrous excess of the age of showering.

Pride, with the teensiest tinge of envy, call it a two out of ten; I was the swimmer in this relationship, after all. Even at the height of what might be generously called my success, my writing had never received the same attention as Ruth's. The prize-winning stories barely made a splash, disappearing into the maw of journal back issues or defunct websites. Not that I was in it for external validation, that's what I told myself anyway. But a like or two wouldn't have gone astray. I wanted what Ruth had and what she had coming, but I wanted her to have it too.

The children were trooping to the change room now, replaced by a pre-teen swim team who looked like they meant business, stretching on the starting blocks. Judging by the state of my fingers, I'd been submerged for quite some time. The woman wasn't coming back; at least, not today. Hauling my aching body out the pool, my disappointment was completely outsize, a grief for something I'd never had nor lost. Where was this coming from?

And then suddenly I knew.

Ruth and I had met at a dinner party in Northcote two years prior, the other guests all writers, upright literary citizens, who together were a bitchy bunch, venting attention-starved spleens over jackfruit quesadillas and citronella candles, griping about who was getting what grant and why they didn't deserve it, whose middling Oz Lit novel was most worthy of contempt. I had been invited by Linh, my fellow *Tailspin* editor, who was dating the host, a soon-to-be-failed novelist named Simon.

That night I was fresh from the hospital, bank account swollen like a blood-filled tick. The other guests were impressed by my war wounds, the track marks and bruises, though I'd been deliberately vague about what was wrong with me. The sick man of Footscray, in my first and only flush of minor literary celebrity, thanks to that peck of prize-placing short stories. My little journal, *Tailspin*, was also kicking goals, though more for the quality of the parties we threw than the writing we commissioned. An indie publisher had been sniffing out whether I had a collection or, better yet, a novel. Things were briefly coalescing around me.

Though I had never met her in the flesh, I had read a lot of Ruth's writing, essays full of politics, sex and ideas, rounding the edges of her obvious intelligence with a withering humour. She was cool, not just for a writer but by the standards of a non-literary creative practitioner working on stolen lands. All that night I bent the arc of my conversation towards her, my jokes and political blandishments calibrated to get her attention.

Later, we crossed paths outside the house, waiting for our respective Ubers.

—What's the collective noun for a group of writers? I asked. I was thinking a plop. Or a sigh.

—A VHS, Ruth said. A vestigial.

We bitched about writers bitching, agreeing it was the reasonable response to the situation we all found ourselves in: a fight to the death for attention and scraps of institutional support. But at least we weren't poets, zine makers or drama freaks, living like trolls and trollops under a bridge. We rolled a cigarette, then another, talking in the dulcet tones of the future-pashing. I cancelled my Uber.

From that first night, my love was a bright, red ball bouncing down the stairs. Over the course of the next week, we barely left

Ruth's room, except to expel liquids and stuff huge tips in the fists of delivery people, dodging the glares of Ruth's appalled housemate as we scampered back to our lair. Days in, I found myself completely insensible, suffused with savage love, a bloody thing that made me sick with fear that it would end. So this was kissing. This was touch and trembling. The love radiated from me, it was smeared all over my face, letting me live like a billionaire. Bartenders plied us with free drinks, strangers grinned at us on the street. We fucked like the whole world was watching, our bodies fused together, like my cock was hers and she was thrusting it deep into a red centre of feeling. Her housemate moved out and I in, the two of us chanting, *No pets no debt no jobs no kids*, as we unpacked my belongings – a nice word, it seemed to me then: things that tied one to a place or person.

Ruth. That's who the woman in the pool had reminded me of. Actually, the feeling of first seeing Ruth, a sort of bodily knowledge that something momentous was in the offing. That my life was about to change. I stood, frozen in the throng of young bodies at the pool's edge, desperate to understand why I'd made such a connection, if only for my peace of mind. And then, just as swiftly, repulsion. Why was I obsessing over this stranger? I needed to snap out of it, return home and get my shit together. Apply for a job. Write my novel or write a different one.

The whiteboard was propped against the bleachers by the lifeguard's chair. She was a girl in her early twenties, green zinc smeared across the bridge of her nose. Heart pounding, I leant close to the board, which showed the pool's schedule for the week. The classes for the previous day had been erased, but I could just make out the ghost of the words: MERCY HOUSE.

—Can I help you?

The lifeguard was glaring. Then I registered the optics. An emaciated white guy the wrong side of thirty, grinning like a lunatic among a group of children. I hightailed it out of there, not wanting to find out what would happen next.

Mercy House: I had something to go on now. When I got home from the pool, Ruth was still teaching, laptop set up in in the living room where the wi-fi was strongest. She winked as I passed her on my way to the kitchen, where I hoed into a punnet of day-old rice. After the hospital food, simple starch was all my stomach could take.

—Yes, Bradley, Ruth said from the living room. But you need to consider what the fisting is a metaphor for.

I made sure to swallow before I googled Mercy House. And there it was: a state-run nursing home, on the border of Yarraville and Spotswood, a 'vibrant community, offering comfort and care', according to its website. Photos of septuagenarians, grinning with their captors. (I was in a similar photo on the hospital's website, I recalled with a shudder, giving a thumbs-up from the gurney.) The woman had to be one of the residents. And what was I going to do with that info? Stake out the nursing home? Show my pap snap to the staff, ask: *Have you seen this woman?* And what if I did wring up the courage to speak to her? What on earth would I say? *I know you from somewhere. You remind me of my girlfriend.*

It didn't make sense, didn't knit together. I was the shittiest detective in the world.

My phone dinged. A voice note from my mother. She had tennis elbow, wrist and everything else, used her voice to protect her thumbs. She was reminding me about the rally the following day, hoping we could march together, her tone terse, as if I'd already stood her up.

—I'm aware you just got out of the hospital. But frankly that's no excuse.

A memory then: sitting at the foot of her bed on a hot summer's night, my mother snoring softly, a sheet pulled over her head like a shroud, while I read aloud from a novel I'd happened upon in her chaotic bookshelf. My mother seemed to slip out of slumber as soon as I stopped reading; she needed the sound, though I could have been reciting anything. I read the book from cover to cover as my mother slept and the sky grew light over the treetops of Geelong, until it was time for me to get ready for school.

In a daze, I stumbled to the living room bookshelf and began thumbing through the titles. Behind me I heard Ruth's voice, as if from very far away:

—Now, my little engineers of the soul, that's about all we have time for. I'll see you tomorrow.

Finally I found the book I was looking for, on our shelf of difficult women. I'd have known the author photo anywhere: shot from the ground, the author peering impassively down at the lens, the toe of her boot creeping into the frame, as if preparing to crush the reader beneath her foot. It was the woman from the pool. It was Brenda Shales.

*

I must have looked strange to Ruth, cavorting before her with the book in one hand, my phone in the other.

—What's happened? You look like a pig in shit. Did they find an unpublished manuscript by David Foster Wallace?

I showed her the photo of the woman from the pool.

—Who's that? she said.

—Don't you think she looks like Brenda Shales?

I thrust the copy of *Anchoress* towards her.

—The writer? Ruth squinted at the pictures. I suppose she does. It's hard to say.

—It's Brenda Shales! The artist as a much older woman. The best Australian writer living or dead, present company excepted.

—Where did you get this photo?

I briefly explained how I'd noticed the woman at the pool, the face I couldn't place.

—I'd always presumed she was dead, but it seems she's very much alive. And she's here, right under our noses.

—Maybe, Ruth said. I'm not sure what you want me to do with this information. Why don't you sit down and tell me a bedtime story about Brenda Shales? I confess I'm fuzzy on the details.

I moved her laptop to make room on the couch, while a cool breeze blew up from the Maribyrnong through the open window.

—To make a long story short, Brenda Shales wrote two highly successful, controversial novels in the 1970s, and then disappeared from the public eye.

—She was a recluse, right? Ruth said. Which is merely code for a writer who doesn't scrape and bow for publicity, I might add.

—The recluse to end all recluses. Think Pynchon, Salinger, Ferrante. She never gave an interview, never wrote a word besides her two novels. That author portrait is the only known photograph.

—You say she disappeared, but it sounds like she was barely there to begin with. What do we find so disquieting about artists who keep a low profile? Perhaps in their reclusivity we perceive our own need for validation. There are few things more powerful than refusal – and few things more contemptible in the eyes of others. We hate the recluses. Perhaps not at a conscious level, but we hate them nonetheless. And so we scrutinise and demystify. Biography abhors a vacuum.

The cover of *Anchoress* showed a charcoal sketch of a woman at a desk, presumably the narrator of the diary entries within, written by a girl, age unknown, locked in a spartan room. As I began to read out loud, I felt the noose of Shales's prose tighten around my neck.

> *I spent the first day of my imprisonment with my head in the latrine, observing my sickly excretions, looking for something to portend my fate. My kingdom for a lamb to slaughter, entrails to dunk my aching wrists in. But I worked with what I had, prodding my turd with a toilet brush, and then my finger, but it would not divulge its secrets. I paced the cardinal points of the room. The bed the desk the chair the book the door the pen the paper. I screamed into a pillow.*
> *I washed my hands.*

—A bold opening gambit, Ruth said, for a female writer. Even by today's standards.

—It sets the scene for her whole body of work, I said. The banal primed with black magic, violence lurking beneath every word.

Look down, Shales seemed to be urging, to see the abyss beneath.

—I must admit, I'm intrigued by this author photo, Ruth said.

The portrait was black and white, shot from a worm's-eye view, the photographer lying flat on their back, and Brenda Shales dangling a boot over the lens. The angle made her body appear foreshortened, though her face loomed large, those heavy lidded eyes, a mouth which gave nothing away. She must have been craning hard.

—One's not supposed to say this about women writers, Ruth said, but she's alluring, isn't she? Real girl boss energy, snapping necks and cashing cheques.

It took us ages to get the photo right. We were laughing too hard. I lay on the bedroom floor, trying to keep the phone steady while Ruth tottered above me, dressed in an approximation of Shales's outfit, cursing that Brenda must have had legs of iron. By the end she wore an expression of pure enervation, verging on contempt.

—Do you have everything that you want?

Lying there on the filthy floor, I thought of the web of connections which had led me there: Brenda's face in the water, the memory of Ruth and my mother – the unconscious mind doing its thing . . . or maybe, just maybe, other forces were at work. I had been waiting for this for a long time.

Something to do.

Something to write about.

THREE

Brenda Shales could wait, but I couldn't. She hadn't been heard from for fifty years, so what was the harm in giving it another few days, or even hours? I was due to meet my mother at the rally, but at 9.45 am – hideously early for me – I found myself on the steps of the State Library, waiting for it to open. I was still reeling from what I'd learnt. Brenda Shales was alive. This woman, whose books I'd read countless times, was living at Mercy House, just down the road from me. If that wasn't meant to be, what was?

On Swanston Street, people in high-vis were preparing for the rally. One woman was speaking animatedly to a police officer, wearing a black YES! t-shirt. Too far away to tell for sure, but it could well have been my mother. I read about the mine on my phone: the largest in the southern hemisphere, covering thousands of hectares of arable land, wetlands on the Murray River floodplains, sacred sites of the traditional owners. So far, so bad – a straightforward story of pillage and greed. Except this mine was for certain rare earth minerals essential to produce solar panels, batteries for electric vehicles. A green mine, a virtuous mine, according to the powers that were (though, if the polls were to be believed, not for much longer). The jokes wrote themselves. We'd mine our way out of the climate crisis, even if it killed us. We'd found ourselves in the deepest of holes, and all there was left to do was keep digging.

The crowd was forming: students, mostly, and a few leftie lifers, wearing medical masks and balaclavas. More messages from my mother for me to not reply to, asking where I was. I should have been performing my civic and filial duties, have a latte and a chant, vegetables before dessert, but I was itching to get inside the library – a first time for everything.

I admired my mother's empty-nest swerve to the left, though it wore me out. She prosecuted her positions with such venom, haranguing me as if I disagreed with her about the ills of global capitalism and settler colonialism, when I was the one who had done an arts degree. In truth she was lonely, despite all the demos and sit-ins and solidarity events. Her transformation had been all the more surprising because she'd been almost wilfully apolitical when I was growing up, refusing even to watch the news, as she'd found it too depressing. Over Korean barbecue one night a few years back, she'd told me her newfound conviction was actually a return of sorts to her days in the nursing union in the seventies, picketing and striking, when all her friends were part of the movement. She was a revert rather than convert.

—I feel young again, she'd said, her face shining with conviction and bulgogi sauce. I feel alive.

Implication being: she'd felt dead those years she'd spent raising me. They'd been an interruption to an otherwise engaged life. Motherhood had made her apathetic. As had I. Throughout my life, I've tended to disappear into women like a fart in the wind, becoming who I presumed they wanted me to be. With my mother, I was bartender and bedtime storyteller. With my first girlfriend, Michelle, I was the man she loved to hate, anhedonic, passive to the point of catatonia, shuffling around our flat while she tore strips off me. *Where are you? You're a ghost. You're dead. Say something. Fight back.*

Even in the hospital, there was Siobhan, the Irish night nurse, my closest thing to a friend in the ward, though in truth it wasn't close at all. When I couldn't sleep from the drugs, I sometimes sat with her in the rec room overlooking Commercial Road, dark spaces between the buildings where Port Phillip Bay must have been. *You'll* understand, she'd say, before launching into detailed war stories about the men she'd been dating. Drug pigs with enlightened ideas about consensual non-consent and ethical non-monogamy. Porn-warped socialists, sexual enfants terribles. She was a consummate natterer, a national cliché, the height of unprofessionalism. Eventually I'd realised Siobhan was so candid because she thought I was gay. I'd been often read that way in the past, though I couldn't say quite why. More interesting was that, in the countless hours we'd spent together on the hospital ward, she hadn't asked me a single question about my life on the outside.

My life with Ruth fit me like a second skin. Time for reading and, in theory, writing; time, too, to resist the imprimatur of productivity that our generation had subscribed to, willingly or otherwise. The tattoo on Ruth's bicep was a line from Melville: *I'd prefer not to* – a credo describing her refusal to professionalise, her rejection of new furniture and clothing, savings and super. In that negative space she'd made her life, and she'd welcomed me into it, let me burrow, mite-like, beneath her skin. With her I ate like a monk, drank like a priest and fucked – or rather was fucked – like a catamite until I squealed my safe word du jour: *Trump, Trump, Truuump*. Dumb luck, how it all panned out. A sort of miracle. A less charitable idea, which occasionally kept me up at night (among other things): I'd attached myself to Ruth in order to learn how to possess the things I lacked; i.e. courage, conviction and a functional career. But now there was Brenda Shales.

—Shame! Shame! Shame!

The crowd was already in fine fettle, directing their ire at the cops, the government, the whole web of consumption and corruption in which we were all enmeshed. Mercifully, the sound began to fade the deeper I travelled into the building, power walking past a man on crutches to the reception desk, so I was the first one served.

—I want everything you have on Brenda Shales.

—Oh, you're one of those? The librarian raised an eyebrow. Searching for El Dorado.

She led me into the Reading Room, that wonderful, vaulted space, a panopticon of knowledge.

—Everything on Mrs Shales is in there, she said with a disdainful sniff, indicating a green filing cabinet. If you don't find what you're looking for, it probably doesn't exist.

I wasn't the first to try to crack the code of Brenda Shales: who she was, what her books meant and why she disappeared. But maybe I would be the last. The drawer was full of academic and literary journals, and monographs, all with the appropriate pages marked. I removed the lot and stacked them on a desk, walled myself in.

I began at the beginning, with Brenda Shales's anorectic body of work: two novels, published in quick succession in the 1970s, unlike any others written in Australia before or since. *Anchoress* first, and then *The Widowers*, which was about women disappearing from an unnamed country town. The latter was Shales's masterpiece, enshrining her reputation as an important but difficult writer. Both were novels of controlled fury, steam pipes forever on the verge of bursting. They were mercifully short; any more time spent in the worlds of those books would have been dangerous to a reader's health. The prose was easy on the eye, but just a few pages was enough to create a feeling of deep unease.

They had caused a sensation when they were first published. Critics called Shales every name under the sun. Most memorably, she was 'la belle dame sans merci of the Antipodes' – the woman without mercy – who had written two novels of 'mendacious trash'. To feminist writers of the time, Shales was a symbol of resistance against the 'conservative, sexually repressive establishment' of White Australia in the seventies. Her novels were inextricably linked with the social upheaval of the Whitlam era, and she became a figurehead of sorts for a new form of women's writing which was resolutely against men, marriage and the family.

Shales herself never said a word about the books, even when they won an obscure but lucrative Swiss prize for her contribution to 'World Literature' – the award accepted in absentia by her publisher. After that, total radio silence, decades of nothing. Shales's refusal of her public position was read as a metaphor for the voicelessness of women in society, while others surmised Brenda Shales was a pen name for a famous (perhaps male) contemporary, allowing them to plumb the depths of Australia's psyche, to say the most unimaginable things. Who but a man could have dreamt up all that horror?

Despite this lack of an authoritative reading, or perhaps because of it, the meaning of Shales's work was endlessly rehashed over the next half-century. Her novels were frequently mentioned in interviews by notable contemporaries – Helen Garner, Janet Frame, Germaine Greer – who described Shales's work as a mirror, allowing the reader to project whatever she wanted onto that taut surface of text. There were Shaleophiles in the academy and the general reading public, strangely formatted websites collating every word written about Brenda Shales. I scanned the list of journal articles, looking for patterns, something to hold on to:

'What's in a Name? Brenda Shales and the Power of the Author in the Public Domain'

'On Hating Men and Women: The Gendered Literary Landscapes of Brenda Shales'

'The Father Speaks: Psychoanalytic Receptivity in Brenda Shales's "Confessions"'

'"Buildings Hewn From Bone": Outsider Architecture and the Settler Unconscious'

'Dis(embodied) (Mis)readings: Brenda Shales and the Affect of Reclusivity'

'Masks and Myths: Withholding as a Form of Textual Resistance'

I couldn't imagine such literary books making a similar splash nowadays. Literature had become niche; it was knitting. But Brenda Shales's books were different. They were windows into the real, sculptures of glistening flesh. Her books were revered and reviled in equal measure, and even the literary world's more sanguine members didn't know what to do with *Anchoress* or *The Widowers*. The prose was simple enough to parse, but the meaning behind it wasn't. What were these books saying about men and women? About Australia and its bloody history? Were they saying anything at all? Nobody knew for sure, but I knew just the person to ask.

The Reading Room was filling, groups of VCE students studying loudly, sallow men with nowhere else to go. Libraries. The last place in Australia where you could sit indoors without spending money. A series of pops from the street, the festivities had clearly started. I thought of my mother crushed in a swirl of bodies. But even then I couldn't drag myself away, not now that I was getting somewhere.

Even today, fresh readings were still appearing. No-one knew Shales's true identity, but there was never any suggestion she was anything other than white. Earlier this year, though, a prominent Indigenous novelist read Shales's work through a decolonial lens, even though it never directly addressed either race or settlement. The title of the piece, 'We Can't Forgive Them for What We've Done', was a line repeated in both of Shales's novels, and the novelist claimed it could be used to decode Shales's literary project. Shales had tapped into the racial unconscious of White Australia; she was the mouthpiece for a nation of guilt-ridden repressives.

Then there was the strange exclamation point on Brenda's writing career, which still provoked fixation and consternation: the Shales Ruling, re-examined in a recent *Monthly* article.

It concerned a 1978 lawsuit brought by a group of men who claimed Shales had stolen their life stories, resulting in an out-of-court settlement still shrouded in secrecy all these years later. At the time, the ruling was interpreted as a repudiation of Shales's work, and indeed of the women's movement itself. But strangely, though the case had finished almost half a century ago, the principal testimonies were still sealed, despite any amount of FOI requests. In all that time, no-one had shed any light on the identity of these men and what Brenda had to do with them, the sort of non-story typical of pieces about Brenda Shales, speculations upon speculations, dead ends and blind alleys.

All this I knew more or less by heart, but in all those thousands of words, no-one had come any closer to discovering who Brenda Shales was. Writers took it as read that Shales was dead or else living in willed obscurity. None of them knew what I knew: she was alive and kicking, a smoker and a swimmer, hiding in plain sight just down the Princes Highway.

A moment of doubt – worry that I might be making too much of the situation. For what did I have to go on besides a single photo, taken on my ancient android? (I'd never been much of a photographer, as per every ex I'd ever had.) But looking at the picture again, I knew my intuition was right, as the light streamed beatific through the glass ceiling. It had been real, that shock of recognition when I'd first seen her face. It was her. For my sake, it *had* to be her.

I was all caught up with the endless fascination and frustration Shales's career and disappearance. I'd caught up too with the rally, which was approaching Parliament House along Collins Street. OURS, NOT MINE, proclaimed one sign. ME TOO, SAID MOTHER EARTH. The crowd was packed tight, and still in strong voice despite the heat. I was going to have a hard time finding my mother.

It had been *Anchoress* that I'd read to her, a few days after my father left. That night I hadn't registered the words, though the novel's melancholia had lingered with me for days (my mother's demeanour might also have also had something to do with it). I'd returned to Shales's novels as an undergrad, reading *Anchoress* and *The Widowers* in a single marathon sitting in a carrel overlooking the South Lawn, shadows lengthening on the grass. My mind kept returning to them during the next few days, weeks and years, often at the strangest moments: in the shower or on the train, lying on the hospital ward. Her books attuned me to the violent mystery of the world, made me yearn for something lost which might be called literature, that eyrie of difficult thinking.

When Linh and I had first started *Tailspin*, a few years after graduation, we had not been thinking consciously about Brenda Shales, though in hindsight her influence was clear. The entire magazine was anonymous, from the fiction we published (predictably gruesome) to the reviews (unhinged in their savagery), a gimmick to give writers a sense of freedom, which it did: the freedom to be cruel. Still, for a time we believed we were doing something important, even radical, thumbing our noses at our literary betters.

When I met Ruth, I'd been working on a piece for the journal. It began with the line, 'When I was young I believed literature kept women alive and asleep', before detailing my relationship with

Brenda's books, the way they'd followed me around throughout my shambolic twenties. I'd wanted, too, to write about my mother, our uneasy dynamic, though loving in its way; the irony in the fact that, up until she retired, my mother had put people to sleep literally, as an anaesthetist's nurse for Barwon Health, pecking at cryptic crosswords in a corner of the theatre while the surgeons sliced and fiddled. She used to text me clues at all hours of the night, thinking I knew better than her how words worked, though I never had the answers.

Even though the essay would be anonymous, the disclosure was too much; I felt naked on the page, and not in a good way. I tinkered endlessly, then left the piece to rot, eventually losing it, along with all my other unpublished writing, in a laptop snafu involving a wobbly table and a bottle of red.

The black bloc was at the front of the crowd, gangly men in motorcycle helmets eyeing off the cops on horseback arrayed before the steps of state parliament. A tinge of menace in the air. If things were going to get ugly, now was the time. I turned and began walking back in the direction I'd come, looking for my mother or Ruth. It felt good to move against the flow of bodies, with purpose and direction. To be going my own way. I knew now what I had to do.

FOUR

Even then I had a plan, though I didn't want to admit it, a part of me dimly aware of what was at stake, and what I'd do to make sure things went my way. Ruth was already at work when I left the house, and I didn't feel inclined to disturb her; I had bigger things on my mind. I was still in a state of wonder at all that had happened over the past three days, how much things had changed. What luck. What happenstance. Fate (I wasn't ashamed to use the word): that's what it felt like, and it felt great.

I would present myself to Brenda Shales, gush and kiss the ring. At worst, I'd have fodder for an essay on my literary pilgrimage, my once-in-a-lifetime scoop. But I knew already that wouldn't satisfy me. I wanted more.

I trudged through the back streets of Footscray, keeping in the shade where I could. I bought cannoli from Cavallaro's on Hopkins Street, but by the time I'd arrived at Yarraville the filling had begun to run, and I was forced to dump them in the bins behind the theatre. Panting slightly, I arrived finally in the industrial zone backing onto Coode Canal, with its sugar refinery and oil terminal, opening out into a series of vacant lots, across which I saw the jaundiced Yarra, and the Westgate Bridge looming downriver. My mind was ablaze with questions. What if Brenda Shales decided to reveal her secrets? What if she took me under her wizened wing? What if this woman wasn't Brenda Shales at all?

Mercy House seemed the steepest of steps down, for a writer of Brenda's talent. It was on Beverley Street, spitting distance to the Docklands Highway, a complex of squat red-brick buildings backing onto Stony Creek Reserve, the marshland leading down to the Yarra, the smell of brackish water mingling with truck exhaust which hung in the noonday air.

—I'm here to see Brenda Shales.

The nurse behind the reception desk didn't seem to understand the import of my statement. She had a purple cast on her wrist, thin, frizzy hair, a crucifix nestled at her throat.

—How do I spell that?

—Like the sedimentary rock. S-H-A—

—Oh yes, here we are. Brenda Shales. Room twenty-seven.

The blood in my ears was very loud.

—And who shall I say is calling?

I told myself I was a literary well-wisher, but the truth was more sinister. I was there to gawk at a once-great talent, discover how *the* Brenda Shales had ended up in this hovel smelling of refried canola. I was just about to tell the woman my name when a klaxon blared.

—Someone's had an accident, the nurse sighed, beaten down rather than alarmed. I'd better go. Come on.

She bustled me down a corridor lined with footy tip scorecards, the carpet a swirl of orange and green, all the way to a door hung with a Do Not Disturb sign. The nurse rapped on it and yelled:

—Mrs Shales, your grandson's here to see you.

Before I had time to protest, she was gone.

It was the woman from the pool, the woman from the back cover of *Anchoress*, Brenda Shales, eyes boring holes through the back of my skull. She was hunched forward as if she could barely hold the weight of her head, wearing the same singlet and faded jeans from when I'd seen her by the Mercy House van, three days prior.

She stepped back and allowed me to enter. The blinds were drawn and there wasn't much to see in the room: a single bed, a chest of drawers, a TV bracketed to the ceiling, towel thrown over the screen. There wasn't a book in sight. She shuffled back to the bed, and I stood in the middle of the room, hideously exposed. Why hadn't she corrected the nurse's mistake, asked who I was, what I was doing there? She clearly hadn't recognised me as the man who'd snapped her photo the other day – or if she had, she wasn't letting on.

—I was just in the middle of clipping my toenails.

She resumed the operation and I watched the white crescents drop, felt a mad desire to put them in my mouth, fragments of the body that had written the body of work I so admired.

—I'm running out of digits. So tell me what you're doing here. I presume your father sent you. If it's money he's after, please tell him I'm skinter than skint.

Just how long had it been since she'd seen her family? How had she mistaken me for someone she was related to? There was no way to verify without giving the game away. But there was no game to give away! I hadn't done or said anything; I'd just stood there looking at the floor.

—Your father was clear in his letter he wanted nothing to do with me. That was a long time ago, but you must know that. He never mentioned anything about you, though. I suppose he didn't think I deserved to know. I won't ask how you tracked me down. I'm just glad you're here.

Brenda Shales clapped her hands.

—Now, let's dispense with the mushy stuff. Sit beside me; I want to get a better look at you.

I perched on the end of the mattress, feeling decidedly queasy.

—Closer, please. My rods and cones aren't what they used to be.

I shuffled closer, until the sides of our legs were touching. Though her eyes were fixed on mine, she seemed elsewhere entirely. In those infinite seconds I prepared to explain myself, but instead found myself saying:

—So, how are you, Brenda?

—Yes, that's it, pleasantries! Well, since you ask, I am the embodiment of the worst sentence in the English language: *I used to be able to.* I used to be able to do the splits and now my hip seizes up. My bowel used to be merely irritable, now it's apoplectic. My lover - Miralem; my Bulgarian brickie - is losing the plot. He thinks I'm his wife, and he loathes his wife, so I'm steering clear of him for the time being. The food is only fit for POWs and Liberal voters. The nurses do their best, but I caught one of them screaming into a pillow yesterday. My fellow inmates have brains like Swiss cheese and bodies to match. Does that about cover it?

Brenda slumped back on the bed. It was all too much, too *strange*. But it wasn't my fault; any thinking person would have to agree. The nurse had mistaken me for someone else and, curiously, Brenda had too. There'd been a small window in which to clear things up, and unfortunately I'd missed it.

—Maybe I should get out of your hair, I suggested.

—Yes, by all means, she said, an edge in her voice. Time you toddled off. I have a packed schedule too, you know.

I was almost at the door when Brenda called out:

—You'll come back, won't you?

And that was my undoing.

Even on that first walk of shame – from Mercy House to Bar Josephine, where Ruth had consented to meet me – I was dreading the moment of disclosure, when I'd tell Brenda the truth, when she'd see me for who I was: namely, a nobody. It all seemed unreal, and perhaps, in a way, it was. Perhaps Brenda's mind had gone the way of her literary career; maybe in me she saw someone who'd never existed. But Brenda had seemed altogether there, scalpel-sharp, staring at me like the woman on the dust jacket of *Anchoress*, imperious and inscrutable. I'd heard the prologue, read by the author at 0.5x speed, and now I wanted to find out what happened next.

Ruth had set aside this time for writing. Giving it to me instead of her book was an act of great love. She was sitting in the beer garden, pint already half-drunk, nose buried in *Anchoress*. When she saw me she grinned.

—I can tell from your face it's her, the recluse of your dreams. So, how is Brenda? Is that what you call her? Or is it Mrs Shales? Though she doesn't strike me as the matrimonial type.

Was there an edge to Ruth's voice? Something sheathed? No, I was projecting. Ruth was making an effort, taking an interest, but the strange encounter with Brenda was the last thing I felt like talking about.

—It was weird, I said. She didn't seem very pleased to see me. But she asked me to come back. It's sad, our worst fears realised. This woman, who's done as much for Australian letters as anyone, is in the arthritic hands of the state. What hope is there for the rest of us?

I hadn't told Ruth that Brenda thought I was her grandson, I noticed with mild interest. But since it was only a temporary deception, it was beside the point.

—Can you imagine the tides of shit women swam through back then? Ruth asked. Women like Brenda were made of truly stern stuff. But who knows? Maybe she never wanted the accolades and visiting professorships. Maybe she's happy.

I took a sip of Ruth's beer.

—Happy is not the word I would have chosen. Terse. Chippy. Vaguely menacing. But still, chances like this don't come around very often. To meet someone who's sacrificed everything for their art: family, friends, fortune. Not that that's a good thing. Not necessarily. But it is noteworthy.

—Chances for what? Ruth asked. Maybe I've missed something, but what exactly have you got planned for Brenda?

—I want to find out what she's been doing all this time, what she did back then.

An awkward pause, Ruth clearly waiting for me to go on, but I'd said all I wanted on the subject. I went to the bar to order a jug, tapping my feet to the music, 'Casanova' by Bryan Ferry sliding into Shouse's 'Love Tonight'.

—It's a strange novel, Ruth said when I returned, waving *Anchoress* as if wafting away an unpleasant odour. It's brilliant, but god it's grim. While you were at the bar, I had an idea. We should do a dummy run for your pitch to Brenda. You be you and I'll be her. Lay on it on thick. Seduce me.

I was a firm believer in the power of workshopping, but this felt off. My mind might have been playing tricks on me, but Ruth's ironic smile reminded me of Brenda's expression when I'd first taken her photo.

—I want to fill in the blanks in Brenda's story, I said.

—Don't you mean *my* story? Ruth's grin grew wider.

—Yours, of course. I want to know the things you've kept hidden all these years.

—I'll start making a list. Do you have a pen?

I tried to be a good sport, match Ruth's laugh with mine. But her quip revealed just how thin my pitch was. What *was* I going to say to convince Brenda? It was probably moot, because once Brenda knew who I was – or who I wasn't – that would be the end of things. It didn't really matter what I said, because I was, in a sense, already dead.

—I want to write a biography structured around your life and career. I want you to spill your guts and let me sculpt them into a marketable commodity. I want to put you back on the map, in the public eye, where you belong. And I want to be right there with you.

—Lady Lazarus's tell-all sensation? Ruth said. Mapping the uncharted territory of the Australian literary landscape. Your very own plot of terra nullius.

—Are you being Ruth or Brenda?

—I jest. Mostly. I think you're really on to something here. This could be big.

Pathetic how relieved I felt when Ruth gave me her approval; I should probably never let her know quite how much it meant to me.

—Anyway, there's almost no chance Brenda, I mean you, will talk to me, but I have to try. Nothing ventured et cetera.

—You know, you sound like one of those true crime podcasters, poking around in other people's unmentionables. What about your novel?

—It's going nowhere fast, Ruth. Or should I say slow. I think I need some time away from it.

—Well, you'll get no argument from me. I'm just happy to see you so *energised*. Maybe things are finally breaking your way.

Ruth excused herself to go to the toilet, and while she was gone I permitted myself to feel excited, daydreaming about all the terrible things Brenda would tell me. Of course there was the small detail of my true identity, which needed to be – *would be* – ironed out. I hadn't done anything wrong. Yet.

FIVE

I finally had something to write about, though probably not for much longer. Before I asked her any questions, I would tell Brenda, I told myself as I cycled through the evening towards Mercy House, I would make my confession with no expectation of forgiveness. The air smelt like burnt sugar as I passed the CSR refinery. It smelt like an oncoming stroke. In the last few days I'd careened from frustration to elation and now to despair, for I knew this was likely the last time I'd see Brenda Shales. A shame all my brilliant detection would go to waste.

Locking my bike, I was surprised to see Brenda sitting at a bus stop overlooking Stony Creek, a dole queue of bulrushes lining the bank. She looked demonic beneath the streetlamp, a plume of smoke hanging above her head. My resolve evaporated like savings as I loped across the road.

—I was beginning to think you were a phantasm of my dying brain, she said. But here you are again. You are real, aren't you? I only ask because I've just had my happy pills, which tend to make everything blurry around the edges.

—Real as I'll ever be, I said, taking a seat and a cigarette. What is in those pills? You look like you're about to blast off.

—The waters of the Lethe, my dear, Brenda said, shaking the bottle. I pinched them from a nurse who pinched them from my neighbour, Iphigenia, the poor mite. Don't let the name fool you: Mercy House is a den of iniquity.

—So you're not sick?

—I'm not a well woman; never have been. But these are for souls much further gone than me. I'd offer you one, but they're barely keeping me afloat. I sleep with them under my pillow. Stop me if I'm talking too much. One of their side effects is logorrhoea. Diarrhoea too, though don't fret, I'm wearing my nappy. What am I saying? Be advised secrets may be divulged when I'm high as a kite. God, this light is ghastly; you look like you're about to devour me.

We sat at the bus stop for the better part of an hour, talking about Brenda's recent and not-so-recent past, staring at the water, the lights at the shipping yards on the opposite bank, the cars on the Westgate, the struts lit from below.

—I've been entombed in this wretched place going on four years, each day scratched into my bedroom wall with bloody fingernails. Before that a unit on Droop Street, which lasted two decades, until the state sold it off to developers. *Fear not*, the social worker told me. *There's a bed at Mercy House, one of the finest, nearest, public aged-care facilities.* I could still take care of myself, of course – I was barely eighty – but the decision had been made. If only I'd had some family to take me in, wall me off in a granny flat to while away what little time was left to me.

Her reference to her family set my nerves jangling. Who was this son of hers, whom she clearly hadn't heard from in years, if not decades? Where did he fit into the picture and, within the confines of my deception, where did I? It wasn't like I could ask. No, I had to read between the lines, the cues and clues.

—I had a pension, but it didn't go far enough for a place of my own. You know I even stooped to share house interviews, holding forth on my hobbies and interests to a panel of gawping uni students. Unfortunately none were the literary type, so I never got the gig. Compared to them, Mercy House began to look like a blessing.

—What about your royalty cheques? Your eye-watering advances? That mysterious Swiss prize.

—Oh, I blew it all on hooch and heroin; it was the seventies, after all. I wish I did, anyway. No, in truth there was little to blow. My books have had a longer shelf life than most, but dissertations on crypto-feminist literature do not a utility bill pay. And there was the court case, which was not good for the pocket book ... but you'd best keep that under your hat. Mum's the word – or grandmother, as it were.

Brenda nibbled a pill, swallowed laboriously, and turned to me, her pupils pinpricks.

—Have you told your father you've been seeing me?

I let the question linger, watched a lapwing edging along the creek bank, hoping Brenda would read the silence as trembling with wrenching, unspeakable things. The night was loud, the frogs in the creek, trucks braking on the bridge.

—It's lucky we're not waiting for a bus, I said.

My words seemed to relax Brenda; she laughed and lit another cigarette.

—We'd be waiting a long time. This is a bus stop that leads to nowhere. And speak of the devil, I think I see Iphigenia lurking over there.

At the end of the driveway, a thickset woman in a nightie bristled on the arm of a nurse. With surprising litheness, Brenda bounded over and ushered the woman to the bench with clucks and coos, sat her down between us.

—Iphigenia, this is my grandson. He assures me we're related, though I don't see the resemblance myself.

Iphigenia stared at the road, all restless energy, fists balled, muttering in what I presumed to be Greek, her skin radiating a terrible heat.

—Her dementia is quite advanced, Brenda said, so don't expect sparkling repartee. She's a peerless confessor, though, if you have anything to get off your chest. Funny word 'confessor': both the teller and guarder of secrets. Would you mind?

With shaking hands, Brenda passed me her pouch of tobacco, cheap stuff by the smell of it, and I rolled us each a cigarette.

—The bus stop was erected for residents who want to get back to homes that no longer exist. Not long after I moved in, they found a man in the middle of the Docklands Highway, looking for the bus to take him back to Toowoomba, where he'd lived as a young man. Or take Iphigenia. Back in Greece, she was a goatherd. She's strong as an ox, and when she decides to leave, there's little stopping her. She always made for higher ground – the You Yangs or Dandenong Ranges – looking for her flock. Before the bus stop, the staff had to tie her down or dope her up.

As Brenda settled into her speech, her voice became softer, more composed. I let myself be transported; I felt like I could listen to her talk forever.

—It was strange to see how the dementia patients' sense of self remained, though they had no idea where, or indeed *when*, they were. They were all self, floating free above the world. Who could blame them for bridling at their surrounds? Now when someone begs to go home, a nurse plonks them here and tells them to wait. Sometimes I sit with them, holding their hands as they talk about those primal domestic scenes. There's an indescribable moment when their faces go slack, when the desire passes, and they are finally ready to go back inside, like their lives are starting over again.

It felt natural to sit there in silence while Brenda talked, listening with rapt attention, mentally trying to capture every turn of phrase, knowing that I'd be committing them to paper at some point. My questions could wait; I didn't want to interrupt her.

After a while the nurse shuffled over, bags under her eyes big enough for shopping.

—Thank you, Brenda, she said, taking Iphigenia's hand. What would we do without you?

—Your job, presumably. Now, my grandson is joining me in my room for a nightcap. I know it's past visiting hours, but I won't tell if you won't.

The nurse beamed.

—I didn't know you had a grandson, she said.

—Neither did I. But this is his second visit in a week. Evidently he's keen to make up for lost time.

*

Tea made, we sat on the bed, Brenda tensed against the pillows and me cross-legged at the end of the spongy mattress, the same kind I'd spent many nights on at the Alfred Hospital over the last decade.

—Oh dear, Brenda said, blowing steam from her mug. I've seen that look before. The shifty visage of a man about to ask a woman to do something unseemly. Out with it, then.

The moment sharpened to a point of meaning and decision. It was now or never.

—I'm a writer, I said, and I've been reading your work for years.

—Another writer, just what the world needs. Well, if I had anything to do with it, my sincerest apologies. If it's advice you want, you're pissing on the wrong post. I wouldn't wish my career on anyone, let alone my flesh and blood. But I can see from your face there's something else. So what do you want?

There wasn't enough air in the room. I looked Brenda in the face and drew a deep breath.

I am not your grandson.

I was so close to saying it, I was almost proud of myself. Instead, I said:

—I want everything. I want to write a book about you: the how, the what, the when and, most pertinently, the why. I want to be the next great Australian writer. I want to be you.

I went on to describe the biography in the same way I had to Ruth, surprised how sure of myself I sounded.

—It will give the authoritative reading of your books and career, straight from the horse's mouth. It will shit on all those who shat on you. It will put your name up in lights . . . and maybe mine too.

—You're making me blush. But really, I can't imagine anyone would be interested in what I have to say after all these years.

She looked very small when she said that, as if she'd shrunk in the wash.

—People are still reading your books, I told her. They're still wondering who are you and where you went. You're part of the culture and you deserve your day in the sun. You deserve more than this.

I swept my hand around the room, much like the one where the narrator of *Anchoress* was imprisoned. A sad thought: Brenda Shales consigned to her character's fate.

—You don't mince words, do you? A week ago I didn't know you existed, and now you're here with a list of demands.

I was ready for her to relent, consent. I closed my eyes and waited.

—You strike me as a boy who's used to getting what he wants. But not this time, I'm afraid. Please don't look at me like that. I have nothing for you.

SIX

It was over before it began. Six days of Sturm und Drang, in which I'd glimpsed my salvation, the content that would finally make me content. Cruel to have it snatched away when I was so close; cruel, too, that I'd been forced to pretend to be someone I wasn't and *still* hadn't got the scoop. Even the manner of my deception drove me mad, so passive and lacking in conviction: irreducibly me.

I stewed in bed all morning, as the sky lightened awfully, replaying every word I'd said the day before – and, more pertinently, those I hadn't. Could it ever have gone another way? Now I'd never know.

Mercifully, Ruth had been asleep when I'd arrived home the previous evening, after a crazed walk around the western suburbs. But now I felt her stirring. She nuzzled against my neck, pulled my body to her.

—How did it go last night, my little honey trap?

Her hand shot between my legs.

—What does Brenda make you do in exchange for her story? Tell me the terms of your retainer. Do you have to lick the soles of her boots, like in that author photo? Does she pimp you out to the other residents? Yes, I can see you now, giving palliative care, making the old feel young again.

I lay no claim to an interesting identity or sexuality. I am a sub, like the rest of the world. Before Ruth I'd been a sexual terrorist with a baroque and officious list of demands: insert this, hit that, call me so and so and so and so, my partners toggling around my laundry list of kinks and paraphilias, girlfriends becoming accomodatrixes before becoming exes. Usually I felt so alive when Ruth talked to me like that, when I could enter that space of being perfectly seen and purely sexual and display the parts of myself that felt vivid and precious. Ruth wanted to do things I had longed to have done to me my entire life. It was a crime how well we fit together. She found endless erotic potential in the dailiness of our lives. Even my hospital visits were fair game, Ruth framing me as the patient zero of sluttishness. But that morning, the dirty talk had the opposite effect. It made me feel, well, dirty, like I'd done something terribly wrong.

—I'm not in the mood, I said.

—Message received. Tell me about it when you're ready. What a shame it didn't work out.

That day, we tried to maintain normality. We did Bikram in the sweltering front room. In seconds we were drenched, skin turned an allergenic puce. Under extreme circumstances Ruth caught the slightest of tans, but even at the height of summer I always looked like I'd been dredged from a deep-sea trench. We were white.

Once we tired of the old positions, we invented new ones: the Super Spreader, the Side Hustle, the JobSeeker, until our legs conked out. I tried to tire my body, hoping my mind would follow. When it was my turn to use the shower, I turned the water on full bore then, after checking Ruth was out of earshot, I made a call.

—Mercy House.

The receptionist made it sound like a threat.

—Brenda Shales please.

My note of cheer was pathetically false; surely she could hear it too?

—She's asked not to be disturbed, came the immediate reply. Can I take a message?

Was it the same woman who'd made the first slip of the tongue? Who was, in a way, responsible for everything?

—I'll just leave my number, in case she's misplaced it. My home address too. She can be a bit forgetful, you know.

—Brenda, forgetful? The nurse snorted. Not on your life.

In the afternoon we wrote, or Ruth did, perched on the living room couch, vibrating with rabid energy, pounding the keys as if her laptop had done her mortal harm. Meanwhile, I sat at the kitchen table, determined to sort my life out. I scrolled through the ads for writers. Did I want to edit educational textbooks? Too bad, I'd need five years' industry experience. Could I see myself becoming part of a diverse team of communications professionals for Australia's most beloved 24/7 convenience stores? I couldn't, primarily because I didn't have a Masters in Professional Communications.

I briefly got excited about a listing for a 'literary consultant' at a start-up called Shelf Life. As far as I could make out, the business sold books by the metre to people renovating houses: homeowners with bookshelves to fill, who didn't know what to fill them with. After spending forty-five minutes completing the application, I re-read the criteria and found that Shelf Life were looking for consultants with at least five thousand Twitter followers, which was 4783 more than my long dormant account possessed, bots included. My whinnies of frustration eventually brought Ruth to the table to see what was wrong.

—I want to sell out, I explained, but it seems I've missed my chance.

—Oh yes, Ruth said. You've left it far too late. The smart writers sell out first, become lawyers or chiropractors, before pivoting to writing once their futures are secured.

Have you heard Janet Frame's idea about the two kinds of successful writers? There are the strange ones who can do nothing else, whose work consumes them day in and day out, writers wholly unequipped for the real world. The second kind are successful at everything; they could just as easily have been CFOs or gastroenterologists. There's little room left for the first kind anymore: the sickos and fuck-ups. Art's become the province of the sleek and brilliant.

—And which type of writer am I?

Ruth gave no sign of having heard me. As if in a trance, she returned to the couch, where she resumed her work. Within seconds she was totally absorbed in it, or that's how it seemed from my vantage point. I'd always admired and envied (which for me amounted to much the same thing) the way the world fell away when Ruth wrote. A meteor could strike without her looking up from her screen.

Masochist that I was, I found myself skimming through reviews of *Anchoress*, imagining all the questions I could have asked, dreaming of the book that might have been, thinking hell was other people giving star ratings.

Anchoress (1973) by Brenda Shales — $8.99
Description:
The book that launched the career of one of Australia's strangest writers, *Anchoress* tells the story of a young, unnamed woman trapped in a room. As she grapples with her confinement, the reader must piece together the circumstances which brought her there. Part feminist mystery, part literary thriller, this story of a woman pushed to the brink will appeal to fans of *The Handmaid's Tale* and *My Year of Rest and Relaxation*.

Ratings:
★ The_Jabber_booky
If plotless novels are your thing, this is the book for you. I just couldn't relate. Gave up a third of the way through, and it was the best decision I've ever made.

★★ Fronts_piece_on_earth
This book is a slog. I don't know a thing about Brenda Shales, but she must be a cruel woman, or at least severely depressed. The whole time I got the feeling she was spitting in my face.

★ Decolonise_Amazon
I liked the cover but it's all downhill from there.

Anchoress was a template of sorts for Brenda's masterpiece, *The Widowers*, with the same glowering voice strutting through the pages, daring the reader to put it down. Proper nouns were redacted, descriptions detailed yet generic, the setting an Australia out of time. The sounds of jazz and traffic the woman hears through her boarded-up window connoted modernity, and yet the novel's setting seemed stuck in the past. Meals were delivered via a dumbwaiter rising from the floor below. Occasionally, a man came at night, very drunk, telling her the imprisonment was for her own good, while a woman wept on the other side of the door.

The narrator wrote of her captivity in excruciating detail, but the central question – why she was imprisoned – remained unanswered. It was a novel with an absence at its centre which no amount of analysis could fill, a rejection of closure and revelation. But those descriptions! A sunrise like nuptial bedclothes, the marsupial pouch around the narrator's midriff. Shales was nothing if not a brilliant stylist. What more did those bookworms want?

The reviews were bad, the sales good. The critics said Brenda had abandoned the novelist's central concerns, opting for an opaque, European mode, a mask with which to hide the fact she had nothing to say. But it found a readership in Britain and the States, which infuriated the Australians even more.

According to Wikipedia, anchoresses were a sect of pious women from the Middle Ages, who walled themselves inside cells so small they couldn't stand or lie and thus were forced to kneel, secluded from the world, sometimes for decades at a time. Flagellation was considered a form of self-pleasure, and they were not allowed to speak. The title framed the narrator's imprisonment as voluntary, a way to commune with the divine. But there was no salvation in this novel despite her search for omens in the toilet bowl.

At the kitchen table, I scribbled in my notebook, imagining a reboot of the anchoress conceit, whereby the rich retired to pods for permanent digital detox, forever locked out of their devices. The story had a narrator much like me, whose girlfriend, very much resembling Ruth, had just left for one such pod, never to return. My narrators were always being chucked. They lived in the past perfect; if only I'd done this or that, blah blah would have been different.

Maybe short stories would save me, I thought. I went on a submission rampage, hawking my unpublished wares to prizes, pissing away money on fees and subscriptions for journals I'd prefer to top myself than read. Officially I was against the false meritocracy of blind submissions, which always seemed to reward a particular brand of brutalist Australian kitsch: wood sheds and ghost gums; kangaroos hit on misty, country roads; the swelter of the interior, living room and desert. Characters had bespoke Christian names: Quinn and Milo, Arlo and Astrid. Christian. Skindivers and lighthouse keepers the lot of them, smalltown citizens about to be displaced by a mine, a housing development, a fire forever burning in the background. I was officially against prizes until I started getting shortlisted. But this time around it felt desperate, futile, a total waste of time.

Eventually I felt better, resigned to my fate, the dark arvo of my soul over. There would be no book about Brenda; I'd simply have to shove on. I'd saved myself the hassle of having to come clean, or else performing the requisite world-building for that most unwieldy lie. It was easier this way.

Sometimes Ruth and I got drunk and applied for real jobs: tenure-track postings in flyover states; petrodollar professorships on the Arabian Peninsula. We lied through our teeth on the byzantine application forms, though Ruth had to lie less. We assured our prospective employers we could start work immediately, that nothing was tying us to Australia. We lived on a rolling monthly lease, endlessly grubbing for gigs and grants. The only thing that wasn't disposable was our income.

That evening, a bottle of tempranillo half drunk, it was a position at a technical college in Edinburgh. It was nice to be with Ruth, to cease fretting for a few hours about Brenda.

—They want me to describe my pedagogical practice in five words, Ruth said, kneading a knot in her forearm. So far I have the three Is: inclusive, innovative and interdisciplinary.

—Put something science-y, I suggested. Institutions love it when you make art sound as if it's being conducted by technicians in white lab coats.

—Will you come with me if I get the job?

—Do I even need to dignify that with a response?

—Well, yes, if you wouldn't mind. Dignify away.

I shut my laptop and took her hands.

—I'd come with you to the ends of the earth. I'd come with you to Adelaide. Plus, I've always wanted to be a kept man – if you'll consent to keep me, of course. Should we just chuck it in, this whole writing caper? I feel like we're always living for the future, building a portfolio, waiting for a payday that will never come.

—I'm going to take that as a joke, Ruth said. I know you're disappointed, but now at least you'll have time to work on your novel.

—I'm going to take *that* as a joke.

The call came just as the supermarket was about to close. I was prowling the aisles of the Cheaper Buy Miles on Paisley Street, basket loaded with treats to cheer me up: an iffy smelling wheel of brie, Tim Tams in flavours rightly consigned to the dustbin of history. The call was from an unknown number. I held the phone to my ear.

—What will you do with the things I tell you, Brenda said, her voice barely audible, if I agree to tell you anything? More to the point, how will you become a great writer if you're telling *my* story? Perhaps you think talent is hereditary, but I'm not sure that's how it works; it's more nurture than nature.

Greatness: I'd really said I'd wanted that the last time we met, and if biographers could be great, anyone could. But I knew the secrets of Brenda's novels would be worth the wait. And if my intuition was correct, maybe I would do more than rummage through the drawers of Brenda's life. Maybe it would be my book just as much as hers.

I dropped my basket, walked out of the supermarket onto the stifling street.

—Why would I give you all this? she demanded, sounding almost frantic. What do I get?

—Me.

A low blow, but my presence was my only leverage.

—So that's how it is. Pay for play. Well, I salute you for your honesty, and your ambition too: naked ambition, stripped and whipped until it bleeds.

—I want to hear about *Anchoress*, I said, my voice cool and calm. I want to hear about *The Widowers*. I want to know why you stopped writing. Why you disappeared.

—But surely you know the story of *Anchoress*, Brenda said. It's the story of your father.

Before I could begin to think what her words might mean, she added:

—Come over now, or I'll forever hold my peace.

She told me the story of my father over the next few hours, sitting up in bed while I perched on the end of it, in the same positions as when we'd first met, less than a week before. As she spoke, I focused on the tortured shapes Brenda's hands made, the way she qualified every sentence: *this is just how I remember it, I'm sure it didn't happen quite like this,* as if she were erasing each word as soon as she'd spoken it. Throughout it all she looked at me with a keen and pure resentment, like I was a stranger and a thief. The story of my father was clearly torture to tell, and for this reason I trusted it was the truth. Because it hurt.

FIRST INTERVIEW - MERCY HOUSE - 10 FEBRUARY

If it wasn't for Harold Holt, perhaps things would have turned out differently. The Prime Minister caught in that fateful rip, RIP, *like a leaf being taken out, so quick and final*, in the words of the 'family friend' (Holt's lover, as it later transpired) who'd witnessed it from Cheviot Beach. It felt like the world was going to end, or at least mine did. I was sixteen, pregnant, and had no idea what I was going to do.

I remember my father standing by the wireless when the news came in, half past one on a blustery Sunday in December 1967, the second day of the school holidays, my mother and I in our maidenly swimwear, halfway out the door to St Kilda Beach, where we'd been planning to lie all day, sizzling like bacon on a skillet.

Harold Holt. The swim that needed no towel. What great news it was: the best I'd ever heard. To take my mind off my predicament, as I had begun to think of it, I pored over the reports of the tragedy, lingering over the details, such as the PM's final order from the general store before he entered the water: peanuts, mosquito repellent, the morning newspapers. And his wife! The baleful Zara, with that glamorous hair and a name to match, a name so different from mine. *Brenda*. I never could stand the sound of it: the lowing of a colicky calf with a mouthful of cud.

My father didn't buy the official story. Dark forces were at work, the Russians and Chinese, those thugs in the Labor Party, now under the leadership of the dreaded Gough. A prime minister does not simply disappear. Even before Holt's death, my father had been meeting with other concerned citizens, local burghers and bullyboys, to discuss communism's creep into the community, Reds under the bed and on the 96 tram. And after? Well, he lost the plot.

Or perhaps Holt had nothing to do with it, maybe that's just the way it seems with the passage of years. I'm using history as an excuse, an alibi for the way my father acted. I can see you wriggling in your chair, consulting your notes. Here I am banging on about my salad days in St Kilda, like one of my forgetful brethren. Don't fret. I know what I'm doing.

We lived just off Grey Street, in a terrace too big for the three of us. I had the top floor to myself, an ensuite, my own little world. There was even a dumbwaiter, and a bell to ring downstairs, a remnant from the grand colonial days. My parents had planned to fill the house with brats, but they'd had to settle for me. My mother had something wrong with her womb, it was near impossible for her to conceive, though try the two of them did, with Catholic rigour, every night after dinner on their squeaky, wrought-iron bed. She was a neurasthenic, to use the medical parlance of the times, and during her spells of lassitude the house went to pot, though my father never seemed to mind. He did most of the cooking when he returned from the bar with a couple of longnecks, great slabs of meat fried in a pan or boiled grey. The occasional vegetable. He accepted my mother's reticence with good humour, even sympathy, and I loved him for that, his delicacy with her.

He was the branch manager at the Commonwealth Bank on Acland Street; you couldn't walk two blocks without a customer pumping his great pink flipper. He knew everyone's secrets – who was behind on their mortgage payments, whose cheques had bounced – but he was as indulgent with his clients as he was with my mother, always happy to grant a deferral or an extension. He believed in the bank as a driver of social good, actualising the dreams of the emergent middle class. Offerings were forever appearing at our front door, fresh fruit or fish, in thanks for my father's fiduciary indulgence. On Sundays he passed around the collection plate at the Sacred Heart church, a beautiful red-brick basilica with a white marble altar. The parishioners joked he was collecting on behalf of the bank, and he would hold a finger to his sensuous lips, roll his eyes to the heavens as if to say: *Don't tell the man upstairs.*

Behind closed doors, my father referred to himself as the sin-eater of St Kilda. Do you know the term? In the Dark Ages, whenever a person of means died, the sin-eater performed a cleansing ritual over the body, consuming a piece of bread known as a 'corpse cake' from the breast of the dead, taking on the sins like so much toxic debt. My father, in his morbid imagination, believed he was blessing his clients with financial absolution, taking on their sins for himself. I never thought the image quite right; he was more like a priest, the one who always had the power. When I wrote *Anchoress*, I felt like I was a sin-eater of sorts, absorbing his wrongs, and my mother's too.

My mother was ageing in dog years, while my father was as hale and hearty as ever, bristling with energy, as if feeding off her. He was always at work or at those endless community meetings, thin excuses for the men to keep drinking once the pubs had shut.

In his absence, my mother and I kept out of each other's way, reading at opposite ends of the house. We were voracious readers and devoured whatever we could get our hands on: library remainders and rummage sale cast-offs. My mother had a fondness for histories of the Middle Ages, tracts about saints and martyrs and bookworms, tiny insects akin to silverfish which chewed through parchment and manuscripts. The scourge of knowledge in the ancient world. They had another name too, which I've always adored: *the teeth of time*, not a bad title for a novel, now I come to think of it. I'd never understood quite what attracted my mother to this period of history; perhaps she saw something of herself in the straitened lives of those Middle Agers.

We seldom talked about what we were reading, but if a book took her fancy, she winched it up the dumbwaiter from the kitchen to my bedroom. How exciting it was to hear the clank of that mechanism, to peer down the shaft and see a cover levitating out of the gloom. She scribbled notes in the margins, as if trying to tell me something, though I never quite knew what. She was very clever, though with little formal education and a naive veneration for the classics, and a suspicion of anything written in the twentieth century. But we were never close. I reminded her of a part of herself she didn't much like, an introspection, which had brought her nothing but pain. Now where are my pills?

I was fond of reading on the balcony, from where I could watch the streetwalkers parading along Grey Street. I'm sure there's a different term for them now, but that's what we called them then. They were regal, brilliant, with great thick thighs and laughs like a rifle's report. How full of life they seemed, and how dull mine was by comparison. It – life – seemed to be happening to everyone but me and my mother. A juvenile feeling, though one I've never quite outgrown. I see you nodding along; perhaps you know what I'm talking about.

I was wallpaper at my Catholic school, though I muddled through without much trouble. I wasn't a brilliant student, though far from the worst, part of the fifth form's flabby middle. I was petrified of the other girls' crushes and causes, the brackish love they exuded like cheap perfume. I wasn't interesting enough to bully, and they left me well enough alone for the most part.

Sometimes I went whole days without saying a word, I was silent at school and at home, too. Dinnertime was virtually the only time I saw my parents, and it was my father's time to shine. He was the leakiest of sieves, unburdening himself about the money troubles of the middle class through a gob full of chop.

I read and I watched and I waited, for what I wasn't sure. Something to jolt me out of my torpor, I suppose. It finally arrived in the form of Maria. We fell into friendship the year I fell pregnant. And that's exactly what it felt like: a plunge or a plummet.

*

Maria was a scholarship girl with a woman's body straining against the seams of her school dress, visible even beneath the smocks we wore over the top, a far cry from the rest of us knobby-kneed, Catholic prigs. You can imagine what the girls said about her, and the teachers too. Brazen. Shameless. Other things that don't bear repeating. Though, as she would later tell me, Maria felt nothing but shame about that ill-fitting dress, which her parents, immigrants from Bologna, couldn't afford to replace.

I sat behind her in class, watching her volcanic mop, which was forever getting the better of bobby pins and elastics. Maria was always in trouble with the sisters, getting whacked and screamed at for being late or falling asleep in class, reeking of smoke when she returned from lunch. She held her palm out with a grim, determined smile as they set to with a ruler.

One morning in the dead of winter, I saw Maria talking to two women, around the corner from school. They couldn't have been more than twenty, with flaxen hair and operatic busts, though they looked the height of sophistication in their pencil skirts and bare legs, despite the frigid weather. The women were thrusting pamphlets on every schoolgirl walking past, though none of them seemed interested, save for Maria. God-botherers I thought initially, which was strange, because in our little convent, the nuns were doing a bang-up job of saving our souls.

They stopped me and introduced themselves as Constance and Emily. They wanted to give us girls information to make better informed decisions about our bodies. They were the furthest thing from saintly, they were radicals, emissaries from a world of sin and strangeness that we'd been protected from our entire lives by the trinity of family, school and church. I wanted them to introduce me to Maria, for though we'd been classmates for months, we had never exchanged a word.

The leaflet was a DIY job, about something called the Billings Method. The sisters told us it was a way for women to predict their window of fertility, whatever that meant. Needless to say, we girls never spoke about sex. When menstruation had to be mentioned, it was in code: our periods were the curse, our pads slices of sponge cake. Everything to cloak the fact our bodies were changing in ways we couldn't control. We knew this strange process had something to do with babies, but we didn't have the foggiest what.

Maria and the women already seemed thick as thieves, Maria slipping their Winfields into her smock, nodding along sagely as they made their pitch. The Billings Method had been invented to help married women know the times they were more likely to conceive, but it could be used just as easily to prevent pregnancy. Contraception was one way to take back control of our bodies, they told us. But the pill was hard to procure, and men couldn't be trusted to wear a condom. The Billings Method, icky as it was, was often the only option, short of celibacy, for adventurous women. Of course, this knowledge was kept from girls like us, the ones who needed it most, because the idea that we had a sexuality was too much for the nuns and our parents to bear.

Tell your friends, they told us. *Tell your mothers. Or perhaps best if you don't.*

Maria took a fistful of literature, her face the picture of solemnity, as if she'd accepted orders for a dangerous mission. It wasn't until our next home ec class that I found out what she had planned. We were on a baking tear, sponges and pavs and scones, training for what came next: wifehood. It was Maria's turn to demonstrate her skills for the class. She stood before us with a carton of eggs and two metal bowls, and with great ceremony began separating the yolks from the whites. She asked each girl to come forward and dip her fingers in the egg whites, to remember that telltale tacky consistency. Bemused, we followed her instructions. I saw how tightly the nun at the back of the class was gripping her ruler. Then Maria began to explain about the Billings Method, a new breakthrough in family planning, which would help us to know when we could get pregnant, by tracking the changes in our *womanly fluids*. When they resembled the tacky consistency of egg whites, we were ovulating, and could engage in procreative congress, nothing immaculate about it. She passed the flyers along the rows and returned to the front of the class. She bowed her head and made the sign of the cross, paused to make sure everyone was watching, then began to drink from the bowl. That was when the nun flew at Maria, ruler raised above her head.

Somehow, she managed to avoid expulsion, but she was a marked woman from then on. I was secretly thrilled by her act of defiance, and I resolved to make her my friend. My opportunity came one lunchtime when I went to the toilet and heard crying coming from the adjacent stall. Beneath the partition, I saw a scuffed shoe and a crumpled pair of the lisle stockings we were forced to wear all year round, a shin covered in thick black hair. Maria. She was making quite the racket, and I remember wishing I could cry like that. I'd learn later her depression was so bad she often struggled to drag herself from bed, let alone to school, though drag herself she did, not trusting herself alone in the house when she felt that way.

I racked my brain for something to say. In the end, I settled for her name. *Maria?*

The bawling stopped, just like that.

To this day, I'm still proud of what I said next: *I was wondering if you could give me a hand. My husband's back from his business trip tonight, and I need to check my womanly fluids.*

It's such a relief to hear you laugh. This isn't a victim impact statement, you know.

We were inseparable after that, spending every lunch break together, all our after schools. We prowled St Kilda, which back then was still quite rough, talking about the lives we'd lead once school was behind us, describing trips abroad, cocktails and trysts with long-limbed lovers, processing the erotic charge between us, an outpouring of pure, sensuous feeling that characterises so many adolescent friendships.

Maria was fiercely intelligent and a brilliant liar, two things I've often noticed go hand in hand. She could spin stories out of thin air, full of details so strange and particular it was impossible not to believe her. She was forever talking about sex, though she was just as inexperienced as I was, fashioning a brash and fantastic self, trying things on with me as her witness – and what a witness I was.

One day, when we were walking home from school, she told me she blew a Beatle. She was terrifically droll, bum-puffing an unfiltered Newport. I was thirteen when the Beatles came to Melbourne in 1964. Looking back, the sixties started that day, and they ended with the drowning of Harold Holt, bookends to a few years of great confusion and intensity. It must be hard for you to imagine quite how big a deal this was. When The Beatles touched down at Sydney Airport, a woman actually held her disabled toddler out for Paul to bless, as if he was a holy man.

My parents and I watched their Melbourne appearance on the telly. The Beatles waved from the balcony of the Southern Cross Hotel on a sunny June afternoon. What fervour and fanaticism! A heaving, seething crowd. The journalists compared the scene to the Nuremberg Rally, and John even gave a Sieg Heil from on high, goosestepping along the balcony, Nazi jokes still being rather in vogue at the time. My father held my hand on the couch, his grip growing progressively tighter. As soon as it was over, he stood and strode wordlessly upstairs to my bedroom, my mother and I hot on his heels. He went straight to my chest of drawers, removed the records, and snapped them one by one over his knee, while we watched on from the doorway. Looking back, it must have been shocking for our parents to see their daughters as sexual beings for the first time, baying for Beatle blood.

How Maria snuck into their show at Festival Hall, I'll never know; that wasn't revealed in the story. The set lasted twenty-seven minutes, the screaming so loud she couldn't hear a note. Two songs in, Maria felt liquid on her ankle: a girl in a red mac had wet herself. As the house lights went up, and the harried mothers began to drag their daughters away, Maria fought her way through the crowd to the front of the empty stage, hoping to get one last glimpse. Off to the side, security guards stood before a curtain leading backstage. Eventually a woman emerged, with bleached hair and sunglasses. She pointed out girls in the crowd, beckoned them with a crooked finger. She pointed to Maria.

As Maria told it, the first Beatle was drinking a mug of tea so milky it was almost white, the second Beatle was smoking. The third had a boil on his neck his fingers kept returning to, the fourth an erection visible through his pants. The other girls looked at the floor, while Maria stared at the men's faces, slick with sweat, mop tops matted, indistinguishable from the mods she saw every day around St Kilda. Eventually they made their decisions, and the girls were driven to the service entrance of a Spencer Street hotel in a van with blacked-out windows.

The Beatle was smoking on the end of his bed, curtains drawn, the room lit by a lamp. He had a hairless, concave chest, white legs extending from his Y-fronts. His toenails were terribly long. The Beatle asked Maria questions about Australia, just the usual fare: kangaroos, koalas and sharks. He didn't seem very worldly, let alone godly. Maria began to remove her skirt. *No need for that love*, he said, in his peaty Liverpudlian.

I'll spare you the details, but rest assured details there were, clues for Maria's listener to guess the identity of the Beatle she'd blown. That first time she used clinical terms – glans, urethral orifice, moveable hood – that she'd clearly cadged from textbooks: a dead giveaway, though I didn't know it at the time. She told the story many times over the course of our friendship, positioning herself as a woman who'd been living on the edge since adolescence, a vessel for incident, whom history happened through.

I suppose that's how you see me, or am I putting words in your mouth? The woman scorned by an unforgiving audience, martyr cast on the pyre of public opinion. I wonder if you'll see me differently afterwards.

*

We spent a lot of time at Maria's house, an asbestos-ridden cottage in Balaclava that backed on to the train line. We always had the place to ourselves, as Maria's parents worked long hours in the jam factory on Chapel Street. Nell and Vince – nee Elena and Vincenzo – were Italian leftists who'd seen the Blackshirts coming and got out while they could. I only met them a handful of times, coming home from a shift smelling of overripe fruit, hair still in their netting. They were unfailingly polite, asking me about school and my parents in their formal, perfectly correct English, before retiring to their room.

Maria and I wanted everything, all of it, then and forever. We smoked fags and drank the cheap wine Vince bought from the greengrocer, which turned our vomit the most curious shade of purple. We took turns holding each other's hair as we purged straight onto the train tracks. And then Maria's spells of depression, those sinkholes she plunged into for days at a time. After school I tried on items from her wardrobe, while she sat immobile at the end of her bed, turning to me occasionally to murmur: *I want to disappear, I wish I didn't exist.* I felt for her so keenly then, but I won't deny it felt nice to be needed like that.

My father frequented the saloon bar of the Grand Junction Hotel with the club-footed Catholic publican, though he wasn't above wetting his whistle at the public bar, a man of the people to the last. We spent our time at the Tolarno on Fitzroy Street, the beautiful art deco building rented by George and Mirka Mora, filled of an evening with what passed for an artistic set in 1967: women with short hair in the style of Jean Seberg, men with mutton chops and flowing locks, the smoke so thick it was hard to see five feet in front of you. Maoists and Trots, Wobblies and bolshies, Jacobins and dykes. The bartender, a Croat poof named Ivan, let us nurse our watered-down shandies at the end of the bar, where he made sure we didn't overdo it, though that's all we wanted to do. We were good for business, I realise now, signifying the Tolarno was outside the bounds of polite society.

When I returned home at the end of the night, I'd climb the trellis onto the balcony and slip through my window. Often I was so excited I couldn't sleep, turning over what had happened during the evening. From the end of the bar, we overheard discussions about how the world was changing, the old way of things being swept away. The war in Vietnam, Gough and the Labor leadership, the pill, the referendum on Aboriginal citizenship, the end of the six o'clock swill. Even the Saints had won the premiership the year before, Barry Breen defeating the dreaded Pies with his glorious, eternal miss. We were in the thick of things, the world afire with possibility. Sometimes I wrote down what I'd seen, imagining I was telling the story as Maria, my better, brasher half.

Eventually we fell in with a crowd of dogsbodies and sycophants, minor moons circling the orbit of the real artists who occasionally frequented the place. To us they seemed the height of sophistication, but they were kids really, living in share houses dotted about the suburb, and it was to these we returned once the Tolarno had shut. I am sure you can see where this is going, but they never took advantage of us, though we were more or less there for the taking.

The ringleaders were Constance and Emily, who we'd first met outside school. They remembered Maria, of course, and took us under their wings. They turned out to be sisters, worked at a fish-and-chip shop near the St Kilda Baths and studied psychology at Monash. Their goal in life, they often said, was to help women realise the texture of their immiseration. *The Female Eunuch* wouldn't come out for another three years, but the sisters were already well-versed in the language I'd become so familiar with at uni.

I told the sisters about my parents, as I'm telling you now: my mother's afflictions, my father's dopey satisfaction, which belied a bourgeois suspicion of difference. The game we used to play called Spot the Communist, where we'd sit at the back of the tram, surveying the other passengers. I'd tug my father's coat and point out a man with a swarthy complexion, a woman in a short red skirt. And he would nod and wink and silently mouth: *Communist*. What a thrill it was to throw my parents under the bus, to hear their bourgeois skulls crunch beneath the tread of the tyres of progress!

Maria hammed up the role of the child of war, with a certain ironic distance, recounting her parents' war years as if she'd been there herself, in that time of blacked-out windows and ration books. Suspected as a fascist sympathiser, Maria's father was interned in a labour camp in the Riverina when they first arrived, picking fruit in captivity while her mother was left to fend for herself. She subsisted on pigeons she trapped in the backyard of her tenement flat, cooking them in a watery ragù, with kelp washed up on St Kilda beach. The sisters nodded with great solemnity, Maria's story confirming their idea of Australia as a porcine, colonial backwater.

They were in awe of Maria and tolerated me, a dynamic which suited me perfectly.

One night at the Tolarno, Maria was telling the sisters about the eggs, all of them screaming with delight. I was at the back of our little scrum, called on occasionally to fill in a detail Maria had missed. From where I was sitting, I noticed a table at which three old men sat, and one much younger, beneath a John Brack painting, hatchet-faced commuters rushing up Collins Street. Like me, the young man (though he was older than me) seemed all at sea, an innocent bystander to all the fun going on around him. His eyes were close-set, his features thick and rough, as if hewn from a slab of granite. As the sisters cackled with laughter the young man looked up and caught my eye, gave me the slightest of nods.

It was an October evening, unseasonably warm, and the shops were shuttered along Fitzroy Street. We were booting back to the sisters' house, laden with cans of VB and half-drunk bottles of table wine that Ivan had slipped us. I was trying to light my cigarette when the young man appeared in front of me and asked my name. *Zara*, I told him. *Like the PM's wife*. It was too dark for him to see me blush.

His name was Max, he told me, and he'd just flown in from Paris. He was in St Kilda for a single night, and he wondered if he could spend it with me.

We sauntered behind the rest of the group as Max explained his curious job as assistant to Roger, the old man at the head of Max's table. Roger was an art dealer, renowned for bringing the first Picasso to Australian shores back in the thirties. He owned a small gallery in Sydney, which showed minor works by major figures, winkled out of private collections during Roger's endless overseas trips. Max handled the logistics, booking hotels and restaurants, liaising with the other functionaries of the rich and famous.

We were speaking in conspiratorial whispers – or more accurately, he spoke; I still hadn't said a word, besides giving him my name. I was under the impression, perhaps correctly, that the less I said the better.

A neat description for my career, when you think about it. I've always been surprised at how my silence was interpreted as violence. And look at me now.

Max was quick to assure me his job was not as glamorous as it sounded, that travel had long ago lost its charm. Roger was a demanding boss, a penny pincher who insisted on sleeping in fleabag pensions and youth hostels, supping among the proles at workers' cafeterias. Roger needed his ego constantly massaged, his shoulders too, and every sunspot on the back of the old man's neck was burnt into Max's retinas. What gall to complain of a life like that! As I was beginning to tire of Max's diatribe, I realised the street looked entirely unfamiliar. I'd overshot the turn-off to the sisters' house and had no idea how to get back.

Precisely where are you luring me? Max said, taking my hand.

We smelt Elwood Canal before we saw it, the stench of mouldy laundry coming from the end of the street.

I'm about to lose my virginity, I thought as we descended the embankment and found a spot on the concrete beside the canal. Curiously, the prospect filled me with a terrible fatigue, a desire to get it over with.

Max asked me his third question of the evening. *Do you have a franger?*

I told him I was on the pill, which seemed to greatly excite him. I lay on my back, parallel to the water. In the distance I could see the canal emptying out into Port Phillip Bay, the lights of a ship far out to sea.

I'd have forgotten that night with Max if not for the dire consequences. I was aware of the sharp pain which grew progressively duller, the concrete digging into my hips. But it was Maria I thought of more than anything, her image in my mind's eye the whole time Max and I went at it: Maria's face with an ironic smile, as if about to laugh. I was making love in the third person, and Max must have sensed I wasn't really there, because as he finished he hissed, *Where are you? Where did you go?*

I woke the next morning dreadfully hungover, but besides a certain stiffness in the small of my back, I felt much as I had the day before. Prodding my face in the bathroom mirror, there was no outward sign a threshold had been crossed, and at breakfast my parents seemed as blithely oblivious as ever. I'm not sure what I had been expecting, but certainly not this obdurate sameness.

I had been looking forward to telling Maria, but the minute I saw her waiting at the school gates, I could tell she was in a mood. I could smell wine on her breath when she asked me where I'd gone the previous evening. I began recounting the night's events, but for some reason I stopped at the point when Max and I had got lost. Instead I told Maria we had given up looking and called it a night. I'm still not sure why I lied to her, but I suspect it had something to do with that image of Maria's face that had come to me. People do things for the strangest reasons, for no reason at all, and though Maria never questioned my account, she knew I wasn't telling her everything. I had broken the unspoken pact: Maria withheld, fabulated, while I was consigned to tell the truth. There was only room for one liar in our friendship.

We spent little time together over the next few weeks. Exams were hurtling towards us, and we were in very real danger of failing, which meant repeating the year, or dropping out. We hadn't done a lick of work in those delirious last few months, and I decided to knuckle down, no more Tolarno or messing about after school. I buried myself in my textbooks, plagued by a terrible fatigue; I could barely keep my eyes open, the reason for which I couldn't, or didn't want to, understand. I managed to scrape through while Maria, much to the teachers' chagrin, got top marks.

I want another pill but I shouldn't. I need to keep my wits about me for this next bit, but how tired I feel. I could sleep for week.

When the school holidays started I fell into a steady rhythm of long days spent reading and nights at the Tolarno, though our carousing had begun to feel desultory and mechanical, the drinking heavier, the conversation repetitive. Maria had taken up with Paul, the son of a local politician, who was forever torturing himself about the quality of his socialist beliefs: did Paul yearn for revolution out of love for the working man, or merely to outrage his father? Either way, Paul paid for the drinks, the price he paid for our attention. With Paul, Maria was meekness incarnate, a silence I felt was somehow directed towards me. Old friends are nothing compared to new loves, yet I couldn't help but think Maria was sending me the message that she'd moved on.

To distract myself, from Maria and the lateness of my period, I wrote. Sometimes this took the form of diary entries, written in the collective 'we'; other times I spewed my most closely guarded fears and anxieties, writing off my parents and Maria too, shocking myself with the depths of my cruelty. Writing's very easy when you have nothing nice to say.

One night a light was on when I arrived home from the Tolarno. I shimmied up the trellis and got into my nightdress then padded down the stairs to the living room, where from the doorway I spied my father sleeping shirtless on the couch, his belly lolling over the waistband of his trousers, snoring heavily. There were flecks of red on the collar of the shirt flung over the arm of the couch.

The following morning, on my way to the beach, I found a spade leaning against our front door, the blade rusty, the handle smooth from use, the wood bleached from the sun. I brought the spade inside and presented it to my parents, still at the breakfast table, my father looking the worse for wear behind his newspaper. I speculated that a client must have left the spade as a gift: a farmer, perhaps, and a rather hard up one at that. My father went even paler, though he didn't say a word.

There was another spade the next morning and the one after that. I often heard my parents talking in low voices, stopping as soon as I entered the room, fixing false smiles on their faces. Something had happened but I didn't much care what.

The sisters had begun to tire of us: my excruciating silences, Maria's newfound demureness. They started referring to us as their young charges, talking over our heads about university chums, a trip to

Europe in the new year. One night they left the Tolarno without paying, leaving us to pick up the cheque, which Paul was more than happy to do. Though it was clear our invitation had been rescinded, we made our way to the sisters' house, Maria striding ahead, trembling with fury. I tried to keep pace, trying to dream up something to bridge the gulf that had grown between us, but instead I found myself recounting the story of my father and the spades, though Maria gave no sign of hearing me.

They were all draped about the living room on settees, *Sgt. Pepper's* playing on the stereo. They didn't smile when they saw me standing there, a six-pack tucked under my arm.

You made it, Constance said. *Though I don't seem to remember inviting you. We didn't want to keep you up past your bedtime. But seeing as you were clever enough to find your way here, you might as well join us. Where's Maria?*

I realised then that I was standing there alone. I squeezed in between the sisters on the couch, and they resumed their conversation as if I wasn't there. How small I felt. I turned the feeling over like a pebble in my palm, thinking how I would turn it into words later that evening. 'Getting Better' had just begun when we heard the sounds of sex coming through the walls. Maria was shrieking, cacophonic, far too loud to be believable. After ten excruciating minutes, Maria slunk out of the bedroom wrapped in a lilac sheet, hair artfully tousled, a fag hanging from her lips. The sisters sat there shocked, and Maria, blasé as could be, sat on my lap and flung her arm around my shoulders.

Have you heard what Brenda's father's been up to? Maria said with a leonine purr. She proceeded to tell the group what I'd told her, before filling in the blanks. A few nights ago, Maria had returned from the Tolarno to find her mother holding a packet of frozen peas to her father's eye. Along with a group of immigrant workers, he'd been set upon by men with clubs and bats after a union meeting. One man's nose had been bashed in, another had two broken ribs. Maria's attackers had done nothing to disguise their identities: they were the prominent men of St Kilda, drunk on power and beer. After the attack the workers discussed what could be done. An Irishman came up with the idea, a technique his comrades in the IRA had used during the War of Independence to scare the devil out of their Royalist enemies. Vince and his comrades left spades outside the houses of the men who had attacked them, telling them in not so many words: *You're digging your own grave.*

It's all very Shakespearian, Maria said with a cool laugh. *Two families, both alike in dignity and all that. Well, not that alike.*

Who knew if the story was true? With Maria it was always impossible to tell. But everyone could perceive its intention to humiliate, to distance Maria from me once and for all. She was grinning in triumph, wrapped in that soiled sheet.

I rose and dragged her to the bedroom, shoved her clothes into her hands. She dressed like an automaton, tottering as she pulled her skirt on. She was very drunk. I told her then I was pregnant, my voice thin and small, like the first time I had spoken to her, back in the toilet cubicle. It was a relief to say the words, and as I did their meaning finally hit me. I was pregnant, and I had no idea what I was going to do.

Maria was lying on the mattress, still as a statue, her tights halfway up her thighs, as if she were collecting her thoughts. Finally, she began to laugh.

*

Harold Holt's disappearance coincided with my father's month off, a time we usually spent in Rye, on the Mornington Peninsula, though my father thought it imperative we stayed put this year for the sake of the community. He became a shut-in of sorts, terrorising my mother and me for detailed explanations of where we were going, who we were seeing; in the end it was easier to stay inside with him.

Of course I had bigger things on my mind. My pregnancy was a problem that needed solving; it was too dangerous to think of it any other way. I was dimly aware of shadowy figures who dealt with girls like me, but I barely knew the word 'abortion', let alone how to procure one. Books were no help, all the writers speaking in code: *tampering down there, letting the air in, dealing with the lump*. History was more practical. I read about the plants Aborigines used as abortifacients: the giant boat-lip orchid, or the blue-leaved Mallee, neither of which I'd seen around St Kilda. I read about the old Catholic idea that conception began at ensoulment, or the quickening, the moment when a woman first felt the presence of her child. Before that point, she was free to rid herself of a foetus in whatever way she saw fit. I took matters into my own hands, lying for hours in the sun or in scalding baths, shifting furniture until it felt like my back was going to give. I even considered throwing myself down the stairs.

In desperation I went to my mother, while my father was out buying beer. Instead of the questions I had expected she was brisk and practical. She told me of a doctor who would perform the procedure, what she called a D&C, all of it above board, though expensive, but she promised she'd find the money – it was just a matter of drawing it from the bank without my father noticing. I didn't have to ask her not to tell him. She spoke with authority, almost as if she had first-hand experience. It struck me that perhaps our house was empty by choice; that instead of a miracle, I had been a terrible accident.

Plan hatched, I retired to my bedroom. My mother brought sleeping pills and lay beside me, stroked my taut belly through my shirt, assured me that tomorrow it would all be over.

When I woke, the bedroom bristled with noonday light. My mother must have the money by now, I thought, the appointment made. As the sleeping pills wore off, I perceived the world with the attention of a criminal reprieved: the light felt lighter, the air thick with the smell of the ocean, impressions I rushed to record in my notebook. I sat on the balcony, watching the people rushing along Grey Street, the sun glinting off the cars' fenders. How close I had come to ruin!

It took me a few minutes to notice the balcony trellis had been removed and was lying on its side by the front fence, its joints cut clean through. It was disconcerting, but I read it as a symbol of the life I would be leading from now on; sneaking out would be a thing of the past.

I felt ravenous, as I hadn't eaten since the previous day. But curiously, I found my bedroom door wouldn't open, though the knob turned as normal. It seemed jammed in the frame, and no matter how hard I pulled, it remained stuck fast. It still hadn't occurred to me that something was wrong when I heard the clank of the dumbwaiter as it rose from the floor below. A tray of breakfast appeared, fussily prepared, with a ramekin of butter, cutlery on a folded napkin. Mother had really pushed the boat out, and I felt relief course through me. There was a book beside the tray, a tome about a strange sect of women in the Middle Ages, known as the anchoresses. When I opened the cover, a piece of paper fell out, a letter in my mother's hand, informing me that my parents would be keeping me locked in my bedroom until the child was brought to term, then it would be put up for adoption. My parents didn't want my life ruined by my mistake; they would hide my sin and shame from the world.

This is what you came for, isn't it? You wanted the story of how my novel came to be. Well, here it is.

I spent the next six months locked in that bedroom. Six months in which I didn't speak to another living soul, save for my reluctant captors. My parents couldn't bring themselves to look at me, couldn't forgive me for what they'd done. Moreover they couldn't bear anyone *else* to look at me, not the neighbours or my father's clients. Other girls in my predicament were packed off to places in the country, but my parents wanted to carry that burden themselves. They were sorry, of course. About the state of my soul. About how I'd forced their hands. Sorry their God had got the better of them. They were products of their time, and perhaps it's unfair to judge them for following the script.

My story is not unique, nor particularly harrowing compared to what other women went through. This is just what happened. It was fated, as it was for the anchoresses, for whom my mother seemed to feel a peculiar affection. She urged me to draw inspiration from their fortitude and faith, yet all I could think was how hideous their lives must have been if they would prefer to be walled away rather than become wives and mothers.

In the first few weeks I tried hunger strikes and screaming fits. I bellowed down the dumbwaiter, all the worst words I knew. I smashed the glass of the balcony windows, threatened to slit my wrists. I went mad then sane then mad again. The anger abated eventually, as all things do. I read three books a day, and wrote like my life depended on it, which I suppose it did. A few years later, re-reading what I wrote back then, I was struck by how little of it pertained to my pregnancy. I had written about the changing light in the room, the sky at dawn and dusk. I had written about the anchoresses and the sin-eaters and the teeth of time. I charted the changes in my body like it was someone else's. It was as if I'd made a deliberate choice to excise the pregnancy from the text, as indeed I did, in the novel's final version. Some things are too big to approach head-on, they must be written around, and the novel became about anything, everything, except that.

I've often heard writers liken bringing a book into the world to birthing a child. They are speaking about a deep attachment. They are speaking about love. And indeed, for me, motherhood and authorship were similar. My child was never mine, from the moment I first told my mother until he was taken while I slept. Likewise my books were taken from me, by critics and writers and readers. I wouldn't wish either experience on anyone.

A month before I gave birth, I was woken on a chilly May evening by a tapping on the balcony window. I waddled onto the balcony and saw Maria standing in the front yard, clutching a handful of stones. She looked older than I remembered, thinner too, sporting a pixie cut in the style of Twiggy. How they'd managed to straighten that hair, I'll never know.

You look different, I said.

You do too, she replied.

We both laughed, and for a moment it was as if everything was as before. How long ago it felt that I had first spoken to Maria, though it hadn't even been a year. It really is true that adolescence is the only period in life in which we learn anything.

Maria was there to say goodbye. She was leaving for Sydney the next morning with Paul. His name had been drawn for conscription and they were running away. She entreated me to join them. She had a ladder, and a car. We could all live together in Sydney. Desperate, futile words: Maria's way of apologising. The idea was so ludicrous I didn't have to say no. We promised to call, write, and we did, though it was a long time before I saw Maria again in the flesh. Before she left, she turned to me, and said: *I'm sorry this has happened to you, and I'm sorry I wasn't there to help. I love you, even if I have a funny way of showing it.*

When my water broke, my parents drove me to the Royal Women's. The nurses' contempt was breathtaking, they wouldn't talk to me, look me in the eye, didn't respond to my cries of pain, and what pain I was in, so intense that I thought I was going to lose him, and maybe that would have been for the best. The matron insisted I wear a wedding ring, though it was too big and kept slipping off. Even behind closed doors they were determined to keep the lie alive.

I never saw him. Never held him in my arms. He was taken away just after the cord was cut. Later, once the drugs had worn off, one of the doctors explained they wanted the infants to be clean slates for the new parents. It was probably easier that way. They took the ring back, gave me some forms to sign. They gave me hormones to dry my milk and then they sent me home. I was back at school in time for third term.

So you see, this was never an allegory or a fable. This is something much simpler and nastier. A family story through and through – and who better to tell it to than you?

SEVEN

I'd wanted everything and now I had it. I was a character in Brenda's story, just as she was in mine, and I could make her do and say what I wanted, make her tell the truth, terrible as it was.

It was well after midnight by the time Brenda finished speaking, when she collapsed against the pillows, her breath coming in ragged gasps. I turned off the recorder, said her name once, twice, but it seemed like she'd fallen asleep, or else had nothing more to say to me. I removed her boots, her feet emerging like gleaming, though admittedly quite pungent, jewels. Despite the heat I pulled the sheet to her chin, angled the bedside lamp towards the wall; it pained me to think of her waking in the dark alone. When I turned back from the doorway, Brenda looked dead. She looked like my mother.

When I was thirteen, my mother fell apart for the better part of a year, drinking wine every night on the back patio overlooking the rooftops of Geelong, smoking cigarettes, which her hands shook too much to roll, so she taught me how to. I often had to carry her to bed, where I stroked her back while she wept. She'd held it together for a few weeks after my father left, until it all became too much for her.

My father had always been a chancer, fond of a scheme or a sideline: he shot weddings, groomed pets, installed pink batts. But the only person he reliably sold his wares to was my mother, who always stumped up to square his debts. They fought, but perhaps not as much as they should have. I think a part of her enjoyed being so put upon, so clearly in the right. Despite what she said, she loved his salesman's bluster, enjoyed being forever seduced. It was an inheritance from her QC father that paid for the Freedom Furniture franchise in North Geelong, on the shoulder of the highway to Melbourne. My father was the manager, a role he excelled at, and in no time the store was printing money. Success changed my father, he took to wearing floral shirts, running ultramarathons, developing strong opinions about trickledown economics and border security. And then, after a couple of solid quarters, he was gone, his fortune had changed and he could finally take what he'd always wanted, freedom.

At first my mother's sadness felt like a knife in my guts, but eventually I began to resent my nightly routine; I was merely going through the motions. I felt so powerless back then: I couldn't make my mother feel better, nor could I extricate myself from her clinging, ravenous need. In time, I hardened myself towards her, became very good at keeping a lid on things.

I stumbled home in a daze. This was what journalists did every day, inveigled themselves into the lives of their subjects, trussed up strangers' experiences for all the world to see. People might quibble with my methods, but they couldn't question the results, and what results they were proving to be.

The pubs along Barkly Street had just closed, prides of men prowling the kerbs, punching darts, staring blearily at their phones. I was just passing Sloth Bar when a guy in a Doggies jersey pointed at me, bellowed to his mates.

—Look at this young fellow out for his nightly constitutional. Why didn't anyone tell me the cocksucking convention was in town? This bloke must be the keynote speaker. We're in hallowed company.

I kept my head down while they laughed and jeered. I'd better brace myself for that kind of reaction, for my readers would be even more unforgiving, if they ever found out the truth. It wasn't until I turned onto Irving Street that I realised what I was doing; what I had been doing the whole way back from Mercy House.

I was skipping.

Once the adrenaline had worn off, I felt like I'd swum a thousand laps. It was all I could do to get the front door open. Inside, I found Ruth on the couch, laptop on her knees. When she saw me she made a show of checking a non-existent wristwatch.

—I was about to file a missing person's report. White male with no distinguishing marks, last seen pumping an octogenarian for literary tidbits. I guess the fact you're so late getting back means you got what wanted. Why, then, do you look like you've been punched in the prostate?

After swigging the dregs of Ruth's longneck, I paused to *feel my feelings*, as they say, and quickly discerned that, as usual, Ruth was right. I felt grubby and cringe, though not because Brenda still thought me her grandson. The way I saw it, that had little to do with me; I was merely the happy victim of the nurse's slip of the tongue and Brenda's mistake, which I failed to correct. Some men are born liars, and some have lying thrust upon them. No, the deception, if I had to use such a dramatic term, already felt more comfortable, a pair of new boots broken in.

No, what was giving me the willies was how exposed I'd felt, sitting at the end of Brenda's bed a few nights prior and declaring my desire to be the next great Australian writer, like some wasting disease with no hope of remission. What had Brenda said? *Naked ambition, stripped and whipped until it bleeds.* It was pretty hard to argue with that. I had never thought of myself as ambitious – better to be a slacker than a striver with nothing to show for it – but now there was little point denying it. Tricking the book out of her was going to take an effort I wasn't sure I was cut out for. *I want everything*: I'd said that too. All this rather hard to put into words, so instead I said something more palatable.

—The story Brenda told me was horrible but plenty more than useable. I'm torn about whether I *should* use it, though.

Words for my benefit as much as Ruth's, the necessary hand-wringing to let me do the bad thing while seeing myself as essentially good.

—Well you should be torn. I'd be appalled if you weren't. To use or not to use, the writer's eternal dilemma. Why don't I lend you my ears and we can decide if the ethical ball is in or near your court?

The recording was nearly two hours long, including Brenda's languorous pauses, meaning there were endless opportunities for her to give the game away to Ruth, revealing who she thought I was and why she'd agreed to speak to me. There was only one way to find out.

I paired the speakers with the phone, cutting off the B-52's mid-caterwaul, Brenda filling the room like some crotchety godhead. I heard myself attending to the logistics of the recording, checking the levels, making sure Brenda had enough water and drugs.

Enough! Brenda said. *Stop fussing over me. Just let me talk.*

And I did. She did.

Now what do you want to know? Brenda asked.

Assume I know nothing, I said. *Assume you're speaking to a complete stranger.*

Which, of course, she was. Listening back, I noticed Brenda's reticence to talk, the way the words were ripped out of her, it seemed, like so many rotten teeth, her voice cracked and parched. But I was entranced by the story's scope and sweep, how it stood in for the violence of history, and women's place within it, at least that's what I tried to convince myself. Whenever my heart fluttered with compassion, I imagined the story filling the pages of a hardcover book, in the scenes of a film. I saw myself spotlit on a series of stages. Yes. The book simply had to exist. I resolved to switch off my finer feelings and interpret the story of my father with the sangfroid of a narrative surgeon.

The book. The book. The book. It was the only thing I permitted myself to think about. As Brenda talked, I felt my desire to write as something physical. I was *ravenous*. By the end of the recording, it was clear my alias had remained intact, meaning I should shove on forthwith, consequences be damned. Now I'd learnt the story of *Anchoress* from woe to woe, I would discover the story of *The Widowers* and the secret looming above them all: why Brenda had disappeared.

—My god, said Ruth, once it was over, draining her beer.

Motherhood shouldn't define any woman's story, but poor Brenda. Poor women. I mean, what else can you say? It's terrible. It's brilliant. I can see now why you're so into this.

—So, what should I do?

—Do whatever you have to do. This story needs to be out in the world. I'm amazed she told you all that. Talk about manna from literary heaven.

Did Ruth suspect there was something I wasn't telling her? Of course there *was*, but how could she know that?

—I suppose she's had half a century to stew, Ruth continued. And though I wouldn't have picked you as a natural mouthpiece, she seems to trust you.

I transcribed the interview later that night in the front room, playback slowed so I didn't miss a word, lending Brenda's speech a fraught quality. The pauses were even longer, Brenda's breaths like sheets of torn paper, the dry crunch when she yanked at her hair. And where was I? It seemed impossible I'd held my tongue the entire time, but somehow I had.

Most readers had assumed it a straightforward feminist allegory, the narrator's imprisonment a metaphor for the prison of marriage and motherhood. Instead, it was a story about the original sin of family, the vice-like pressure of church and state, with practically no space between the events of Brenda's life and the diary entries recorded in the novel. Even to call it a novel seemed wrong. It was, as she'd said, a family story, and I was the person to tell it.

Dawn was breaking by the time I'd finished, the clouds hemmed with smoke, the myna birds twittering in the tea-trees on the nature strip. By then, I understood just how deep a hole I'd dug for myself. A mine full of precious materials. Mine. But still, I felt exalted and enchanted, aerated in impossible ways. I could hardly keep the smile off my face. I felt the weight of this terrible secret, decades in the making. And something else, which I'd never felt before with such intensity, a ten out of ten.

Power.

PART TWO

EIGHT

Coming clean was out of the question; the story of my father had seen to that. In a way, it was a relief to cease the charade. Not with Brenda – or Ruth – but rather with myself. I could finally admit that I wasn't going to admit who I was and wasn't. No, I would ride my deception to the bitter end. *Do whatever you have to do*, that's what Ruth had said, giving me permission. I was doing, if not the right thing, then the right thing for me.

I awoke late in the morning, and ran straight to the computer to make sure Brenda's words were still there, reading through the transcript with a smile so wide I felt my cheeks were going to split, perceiving the faint outline of what the book might become. I felt buoyant all that day, every cell fizzing, a dynamo of domestic energy, mopping and wiping, making a lemon yoghurt cake for the dinner at Linh's that evening. Meanwhile, Ruth hammered away at her keyboard, pausing occasionally to tell me to stop my whistling.

*

—So when will I get to meet Brenda?

Ruth sprang the question on me as soon as the cab doors locked, giving me no means of escape. It was impossible, of course, at least until I got my story straight.

—I'm not sure that's the best idea, I said, choosing my words carefully. Too many chefs and all that.

—I'm not trying to steal your scoop, Ruth said, sounding offended. It might surprise you, but I'm actually interested in your life.

Thankfully it wasn't far to Linh's unit in Seddon, easy enough to sit in silence until we arrived. There were obvious practical reasons I didn't want Ruth and Brenda meeting. But also: what if Brenda liked Ruth better? Ruth was cut from Brenda's cloth, fierce and fearless, with a mind like a steel trap and a prose style to match. I hated feeling that I was in competition with Ruth, and that was why I always lost.

My good mood revived when Simon answered the door. He was dressed as if for badger-baiting in a Barbour jacket and chinos, face flushed with grog, an ominous sign.

—They're here, he called mournfully and ushered us inside.

I loved spending time with Simon, because he made me feel good about myself, as both a boyfriend and writer. He'd attached himself to Linh around the same time as I'd met Ruth, and had been feeding on their cultural capital ever since. Simon was even more of a failed novelist than me. For the past year, he'd been shopping his knotty doorstopper about a little-known colonial explorer, thankfully with no success.

—Perfect timing, Linh trilled from the kitchen. The takeaway just arrived.

Linh hugged us as if we'd just returned from war, their whippet Aloysius, named for Sebastian Flyte's teddy from *Brideshead Revisited*, pawing at Linh's thigh, aggrieved at having temporarily lost their attention. Linh's hair was bluer than I remembered, their outfit a little more normcore – shapeless jeans and Hoka trainers, a dour Adidas singlet. Linh was my oldest writing friend and comrade, and the pleasure I felt in seeing them was something physical. Since they left *Tailspin* we hadn't seen much of each other; Linh had been too busy: promoting their book of short stories, *The Morning After*, while working full-time as an arts administrator in the Docklands. They'd moved on, and I was happy for them, had never blamed them for leaving *Tailspin*, even though their departure had precipitated its downfall. But the main reason we didn't see Linh was because Ruth and I hated the way Linh acted around Simon: weirdly demure, an ego masseuse. We'd barely tucked into the Malaysian – roti canai and nasi lemak – when Simon started in:

—Another three agents passed this week, he said with relish. That's two hundred rejections in total, give or take. At least I get an A for persistence.

—It's so good, you guys, Linh said. Great even. A great Australian novel.

It was one of life's great mysteries that Linh, figure of light and intelligence, heavily published public figure, expended so much effort to convince us Simon was the *real* writer in their relationship. They genuinely believed he was destined for acclaim and fortune. Linh had low self-esteem, but *that* low? Perhaps Simon was kinder behind closed doors. Maybe he was a Nobel-level fuck. Shouldn't judge a book by its cover. But still, *Simon*?

—One agent said I didn't have the right *qualities* for her list; we all know what that means. Do you ever feel like you were born at the wrong time? In the wrong body.

—Darling, are you trying to tell us something? Linh rolled their eyes. You sound like you're coming out.

Simon stared at me plaintively, as if begging me to step in and confirm how hard we blokes had it. But I knew where my bread was buttered so I kept my eyes fixed on my laksa until he stood and stomped to the kitchen to fix drinks. Now I understood what Linh saw in Simon: just being in his vicinity made you feel like a saint and a star.

—I know, I know, Linh said, sotto voce. You should hear what he says when we're not in polite company. But the last thing I want to talk about tonight is Simon's novel. Ruth, you said you had some big news?

I looked at Ruth, moved that she'd been sufficiently moved to tell Linh about Brenda, a proud mother singing my praises. But now was not the time. Ruth might not want to steal my scoop, but Simon wouldn't hesitate.

—Nothing's set in stone, I said. But yes, something big's in the pipeline.

—Well, that sounds very intriguing, Linh said. But I was talking about Ruth's commission.

—I didn't get a chance to tell you yet, Ruth said, too quickly, looking at me. You've been really flat out the last few days. But I got asked to write something.

She mentioned the name of a famous American literary journal. From the kitchen a glass smashed. Simon had dropped it, or thrown it in anger.

—The editor liked my piece about pools, god knows why. He asked if I had anything in the drawer.

She looked at me, uncertain, clearly afraid to tell me.

—It's only the online journal, and they pay next to nothing. Plus I heard they're funded by a rabid Zionist.

—Don't be so modest, Linh said. It's a coup. Simon! Where are those drinks?

—I actually have a piece that would be perfect, Ruth continued. It's the best thing I've ever written, but I don't think I can publish it in good conscience. How would you describe my relationship with my mother?

The question caught me off guard, though the look on Ruth's face gave nothing away.

—Toxically close, I said. And distant as the sun. One week you speak on the phone every night for hours, then you're fighting about nothing. You're either sisters or mortal enemies.

—Alright, steady on. But I take your point.

—It's something we've always bonded over, I said to Linh. Complicated mothers and absent fathers.

—My father left when I was little, Ruth explained. Upped stumps to mine the Pilbara before it was a lucrative profession. I only met him a couple of times before he died, but he left me a small nest egg – enough that I've been able to write this book without too much humiliating money work.

Perhaps that was why I hadn't told Ruth about Brenda's misapprehension about my identity, this temporary deception which seemed less temporary every day. Because it would be cruel to invoke my father, Brenda's son, when Ruth didn't have one.

With a thump, Simon deposited a tray of negronis on the table.

—The pool piece originated as a digression from a longer essay about the swimming lessons I was forced to endure as a child. And guess what the name of the pool is? Harold Holt Memorial. In Glen Iris.

Here she gave me a pointed look, and I thought again of Brenda, that strange story which I felt I already knew by heart.

—When I was growing up, my mother, Helen, was afraid of everything. Cars, strangers, and the pool most of all. From a really young age I sensed her need, a thwarted, toxic kind of vulnerability. She wanted me by her side every second, like a pet more than a person; I was supposed to cheer her up and provide entertainment. I felt a huge pressure to perform, which I did, at school but more so at home. We lived on top of each other, sharing a wardrobe and even a bed in our dump in Burwood. It wasn't until I was much older that I realised just how weird our relationship was – not that she would ever acknowledge it.

It was unsettling to hear Ruth talk this way, though the story of her mother was one I knew well. Perhaps it was the fluency of her expression, her ability to talk *in literature*. Maybe, too, it was my memory of the essay I had tried to write about my mother and Brenda Shales, which had never quite come together. Was that where Ruth had got the idea from?

—Every morning my mother drove me to the Harold Holt in our clapped-out Camry, and there she would standing at the edge of the pool, hand covering her mouth, while I swam. I hated those mornings: the frigid bedroom floorboards, the chlorine smell that never went away. In my essay, the lessons were a symbol for my mother's suffocating love, which, in one way or another, I've been trying to escape from my whole adult life. Lately I've been better at keeping her at arm's length, but the boundary between us is still more porous than I'd like it to be. I resent our closeness, which I've never been able to put into words, until I started writing.

—Well, I can't wait to read it, Linh said.

—Me too, I said, charging my glass. You're a genius.

Simon didn't move. He was gazing at the table with a thousand-yard stare, a single tear trickling down his cheek.

I read the piece later that night on Ruth's laptop while she lay in bed beside me, directing her cigarette smoke through the window.

—It's just as good as you thought, I said. It's incredible.

—I'm confident in the quality of the writing, Ruth said, lying so close I could feel the sweat on her thigh. Reading back through it, I think I was trying to transform the pity I feel for Helen into compassion. But perhaps that's just my rationalisation, so I can perform my act of monstrous cruelty.

—You say that as if it's a bad thing. I think literature could do with more cruelty.

—Perhaps it could, but this is a person I'm betraying. I told you to do whatever you needed to do with Brenda, but this is my *mother*. Anyway, despite my fine words, I know I'm going to do it.

—It's helpful to pretend we're better than we are.

Ruth fixed me with the full force of her attention as she picked over what I'd just said.

—The essay feels necessary, she said. The only way to disrupt our dynamic, to make my mother see me as someone separate from her. A scorched-earth strategy, but who knows? Maybe something new will grow from it.

I clasped her hands, kissed them.

—I can't believe *these* wrote *that*.

—We're not supposed to subscribe to the idea of artistic genius, Ruth said, grinning, but flattery will get you everywhere.

—You shouldn't change a word. Now I'm going to sit here while you draft a reply to your new editor friend, but first, nature calls.

When I'd left Brenda at Mercy House, she'd looked completely spent, and my intuition told me to let her be for the time being, allow her to catch her breath. But now I had the sudden urge to talk, to make sure she was still onboard. I was nothing like Simon; I was like Ruth, and Brenda was going to prove it.

—I want to see you, I said, once the receptionist had put me through.

—You took so long to call, I thought you were getting cold feet. Feeling guilty about getting your hooks into a lonely old woman. Using our blood ties to draw blood from a stone. If that's the case, you can set your mind at rest. I, Brenda Shales, of sound mind and body, do make this declaration under my own volition. God, I sound like I'm dying.

—Can I get that on tape?

We arranged for me to visit her at Mercy House the following afternoon. I had to forge ahead, before I lost my nerve. Nothing was guaranteed. Brenda might return to type, the withholding recluse, blankest of slates. That's what she'd been doing these last fifty years, so why change now?

Let me be found out, but not yet, not until I'd got what I came for.

NINE

—How are you feeling?

The hospital. Calling just as I was sitting down to write, whatever that meant. The nurse was following up on my discharge, tallying my side effects and symptoms. At first, I'd thought it must have been Mercy House on the phone, bearing bad news: Brenda had slipped in the shower/into a coma/had found a better biographer. But no, just a bored nurse doing her job. How was I feeling? I'd barely considered it since leaving the hospital, which was strange after everything that had happened.

Self-protection, to stop me from thinking about what I'd done, what I was doing, and what I had to lose. Ruth, for one thing. She was sitting across from me at the dining table, in the thin, blue, morning light, tweaking her essay for the American journal. As I'd answered the call from the nurse, she'd held up a finger for silence, though I hadn't made a sound, except to confirm my name and date of birth. Maybe the drug had affected me more than I'd realised, making me act with wilful disregard. A comforting thought, that what I'd done to Brenda wasn't my fault.

I felt the decade pressing down on me, ten years of nothing much. The nurse said my name, waited for me to respond. I performed sums on my computer's calculator. Roughly five stints in the hospital per year, each lasting an average of twenty-one days, so almost three months per year for eleven years, or 27,720 hours. Appalling. The worst thing I'd ever read. Hospitalised for a third of my adult life. I thought of all the pints of blood I'd given, the dizzy spells and upset stomachs. All the times I'd pissed in a bottle, shat in a cup. A death of sorts, by a thousand hours of small talk with nurses and doctors and pigs. And just to make rent and pretend to write my novel. I had been sick, I could see that now, just not in the way I'd thought. Sick of the life I hadn't yet lived, endlessly deferring the moment I'd have to take myself seriously. Those hospital stays were a continuous disruption to friendships, relationships, jobs. I'd disappear into the Alfred's bowels, and emerge weeks later like one of Plato's prisoners, shielding my eyes from the glare of real life. For a whole long, rotten decade my body hadn't been mine, and neither had my time. A violation of my own volition.

—I want you to delete my name and number, I said into the phone, and hung up. Please never call me again.

I looked at Ruth, waiting for her approval, sure she'd have intuited the momentousness of what I'd done.

—That was the hospital, I said, with great solemnity.

—If you're going to continue to make noise could you please vacate the premises? Some of us have to work.

I apologised and scurried to the front room, face burning with shame. I still had hours to kill before I was due to meet Brenda, so I forced myself to sit at my desk, breathed deeply until my heart stopped racing, tried not to think about what it meant that I'd never return to the hospital. Thankfully I had the book to distract me. After hearing the story of my father I needed to consider what I had, what I needed, and what I would do to get it. I was sure I had the beginnings of a book now, the start of something big, but what exactly would it look like? A straight biography seemed above my pay grade; archivists more dedicated than me had been unable to pick the lock of Brenda's past. What sources could I draw from to verify what she had told me? No, that would be altogether too much work

Perhaps I could fictionalise the whole affair, write a novel about a novelist finding another novelist? But I knew the book's power would come from the knowledge that it was true, that the events described had really happened.

So it was to be non-fiction then, a vessel for Brenda's voice, interspersed with sections from my perspective, telling the story of our meeting. Instead of Brenda's grandson, I would frame myself as a young writer down on his luck, looking for something to fill his pages. Her words true, mine true enough. To Brenda I would be one thing, and to everyone else another. Now I was getting somewhere.

I spent the morning cleaning up the story of my father, removing Brenda's pauses and hesitancies, making her sound more declarative than she'd actually been. Then I turned to this other character, myself at a remove, skimming through old versions of my autobiographical novel, looking for salvageable sections.

In one version I had Parkinson's, in another sickle cell anaemia, in another still a club foot. Erectile dysfunction, bulimia, rickets.

Sometimes I gave myself all of the above. I lurched across the pages of my novel, stinking of vomit, shaking uncontrollably. It was like reading a fever dream, all heat and menace. I was going to have to start again from scratch.

For the last hour, I'd badly needed to piss. I didn't want to disturb Ruth, but things were getting pressing. I sat at my desk, listening for a break in proceedings, Ruth's fingers to cease tapping at her keys. Things felt unbalanced between us, like one leg was longer than the other. Ruth had her nest egg and tutoring job and fame, while I had a little remaining blood money and no prospect of more. Ruth was moving up in the world, and I'd been treading water, shaping my life around hers – which was just the way I liked it, or that's what I'd always told myself. I was forever tiptoeing around her, afraid to disturb or offend. When was the last time she'd asked me how I felt?

I pissed on the rhododendrons out the front of the house, beside the golden orb's web, so close I could reach out and touch it. The sun was behind the smoke clouds, meaning I might just be able to handle the UV. There wouldn't be a better time to leave. I'd thought about my life quite enough.

Brenda was waiting for me in the lobby when I arrived, chatting with the nurse behind the reception desk, the same woman who'd made the first slip of the tongue.

—And here he is, Brenda crowed. The man of the hour. The name on everyone's lips. My fellow inmates are very jealous. Three visits in one week. Must be a record for someone not about to shuffle off.

Strangely, the nurse looked nonplussed, lips pursed as if in disapproval. I found the fixity of her stare unsettling. Maybe she was recalling the circumstances of my arrival, the fact it had been her and not me who'd made me out to be a relative. *It's all my fault.* That's probably what she was thinking. Taking ownership of what she'd done.

—Let's talk in the recreation room, Brenda said. The least apt name in the world.

It smelt like fish fingers, the carpet the same vomitous swirl of orange and green. The other residents were slumped on settees, staring vacantly at the TV showing Andrew Bolt's sneering, rubbery face. It cut to a news report about the encampment at the mine site near Swan Hill. My mother's face didn't appear, though she was there somewhere; she'd been sending me blurry photos all week. A huge Christ hung on the wall, body sheeted in blood, very Mel Gibson, but at least the room got light – perhaps even too much, as it was a sweatbox in there.

Brenda led me to a table on the far side of the room, coated in a thick layer of dust.

—Was the nurse in reception looking at me strangely? I asked, trying to sound offhand.

—You'd probably look that way too if you had a job like hers. But why would she be concerned about you? You haven't done anything wrong.

Her comment seemed pointed, and she was smiling in that infuriating way of hers, as if there was a brilliant joke she refused to share.

—Don't worry, I haven't told them what we get up to behind closed doors. What you're really here for. Your inheritance, as it were.

We took our seats, sending dust motes spiralling into the air. I produced the recorder and began testing the levels.

—Straight down to business.

—Sorry, it's a habit from my days as a literary journalist.

—So this isn't your first rodeo? And here I was thinking I was special.

—Brenda, you're not like any writer I've ever met, and I mean that as a compliment.

After checking the recorder wasn't on, I began to tell Brenda how I'd fallen out of love with fiction – maybe as some kind of proof that I was there for the right reasons, even though I wasn't.

—A couple of years ago, I managed to wrangle an interview with a famous American novelist. A Pulitzer winner and big swinging dick. He was in town to promote his new book, a seven-hundred-page breezeblock about the opioid epidemic, replete with a cast of lavishly mutilated characters. A compelling piece of writing, if a bit of a slog. We met at Jimmy Watson's.

—Is that place still going? Brenda said. I spewed up there, on more than one occasion.

—The writer was dressed like he was about to go the gym, with these forearm tattoos which struck me as faintly Māori. He said he had to stand while we talked, because of a slipped disc from back when he was a furniture delivery man. A bit rich, considering he'd been a university professor for twenty years, but still, a nice detail to include in the article, as he clearly knew I would. In my experience, writers either can't talk about their work to save their lives, or else they're consummate pros, everything clean and clear and in its place.

—And what kind, pray tell, am I?

—Neither. That's the point. That's why I'm telling you this story. Anyway, by the end of the interview, I felt a bit used and sweaty, like a bench press the writer had used without a towel. I had my quotes, my stats about deaths of despair, but it all seemed so frictionless. While he checked out the waitress, he let me buy him a drink, and I told him about the journal I was editing, which was on its last legs, and the great novel I planned to write one day. Eventually he said he had to go. While we were waiting for his cab, he told me about the technique he'd used for his opioid book. With a novel that size, he said, one of the hardest things was differentiating one character from another. He told me a well-chosen disfigurement animated flat characters, made them stick more concretely in the reader's mind. What was the story with the one-eyed love interest? Why did the brother eat through a straw? That sort of thing. I still remember what he said, just as he was stepping into the car: *I don't kill my darlings, but I maim them in cruel and unusual ways. My other piece of advice: lift with your legs.*

Brenda cackled and slapped her thigh.

—Sounds like a real shit, she said.

—The worst part was I listened. I've been trying and failing to write an autobiographical novel for the last two years. I keep giving myself illnesses and conditions, I suppose because I thought my character wasn't working. He seemed so flat, so two-dimensional.

—Don't be so hard on yourself. You contain multitudes. You roll fantastic cigarettes. And you have cheekbones to die for; I wonder who you inherited them from?

—This might sound strange, I continued, but until meeting the novelist, I'd still been naive when it came to writers. I thought people who wrote great books were in some way great themselves.

Speaking to him shattered my illusions. Suddenly everything seemed like a trick or technique. I started to see the same quality in other books. Even ones I used to like began to seem contrived and confected. I guess I want you to know that talking to you has revived something in me. Call it faith. Or love. I want to be a writer, even though it's ruining my life. And I want to write something great, like you did.

—But what makes a book great? Brenda asked. Surely that's a matter of taste.

—This might sound naff, but I've always found the Platonic idea of the tripartite soul to be a useful model for writing fiction. Someone's essence, what makes them human, is a combination of spirit, desire and rationality. The soul must make its great circuit with these three forces in conflict, and all great books are a battle between the head, the heart and the guts. My problem, as you might guess, has always been writing from the heart.

It had been a long time since I'd spoken with such candour, at such great length. Even with Ruth I seldom talked so freely about my doubts and insecurities.

—I greatly enjoyed that little disquisition, Brenda said, with real warmth in her voice. I had been thinking that our project was decidedly one-sided. You sit, I talk. I don't know the first thing about you. Perhaps that's deliberate on your part, but it doesn't sit well with me. I'd like to correct the imbalance. Make things a little more tete-a-tete, tit for tat. You tell me things, and I tell you things. Doesn't that seem fairer?

—Speaking of which, I said, pointing to the *Anchoress* cover, maybe it's time to get this show on the road. Literature waits for no-one.

—It's nearly feeding time, didn't I tell you? And then we're off to the pool. Saying that out loud, it should be the other way around. There's no rush, is there? Besides, there are some people I'd like you to meet.

I tried not to let my disappointment show as Brenda walked me to a table where two people sat: a woman with a fine-boned, ruminant face, and a hulk of a man, white hair swept up in a bouffant. They were playing chess, though the woman seemed to be making moves for the both of them. The man was far away, his eyes registering our approach then sliding off into the distance.

—I told you, didn't I? Brenda said to them. I didn't just make him up. Edna, Miralem, this is my grandson.

I shook the woman's hand, and then the man's, his great paw limp in my palm.

—I *think* I can see the resemblance, Edna said. Perhaps it's the eyes. But Brenda, I thought you told me that you didn't have any family. That's why you were living here.

—I said I'd never *met* my family. But he's here now, and that's the main thing.

—I don't think that *is* what you said, Edna objected. You're exact words were: *I never had anyone except my parents and my one and only friend, and it is the great shame of my life.*

—I think you're having a senior moment, Edna, love. Happens to the best of us.

I don't know how I knew Brenda was lying, but I did. Edna seemed to sense it too, hands clasped in her lap, waiting for Brenda to explain herself.

—Edna used to be a school principal, can you tell? Can't get anything past her. Alright, I might have massaged the truth, but perhaps you can divine the reason why. It was worse to know I had a family I'd never met and who didn't want to meet me. Better to pretend they didn't exist.

Edna nodded, before turning to me, and asking in a voice full of worry instead of accusation:

—Why did it take you so long to find her?

My face must have conveyed how I felt, for the two of them looked concerned. This was the moment where it would all come crumbling down, when Brenda would perceive the truth.

But as I fumbled for an answer, I realised she was looking over my shoulder. The nurse from reception was standing at the rec room entrance, beckoning Brenda over. The way she was looking at me, I knew I wasn't invited.

—It seems I'm being summoned, Brenda said. Let's pick this up tomorrow. Why don't you buy me lunch? Let's say Hao Phong at two.

I'd had a lucky escape, but it had been too close for comfort. I had to get my story straight and stick with it, flesh out this lie, put my writing skills to bad use, gin up some back story and decide once and for all where my father and I fit into things. If I was going to lie, let me lie brilliantly.

TEN

The only way to take what I wanted was to pretend none of it was happening. To think of Brenda as if she were a character in a novel, my novel, pure fiction. Her child had not been taken from her. She hadn't been imprisoned for six months, had not been driven mad by grief and betrayal. All of that was a plotline for a character as invented as mine.

I woke at first light, left Ruth sleeping, made coffee and padded to the front room. The day felt full of promise. The grass on the nature strip glimmered with dew, the neighbour's tabby stalked along our fence line. I felt limber, a machine made for work.

I spent the next few hours rewriting the circumstances of my meeting with Brenda, trying to stick close to what had happened in real life. I narrated my visits to the hospital, my struggles with my autobiographical novel (see above), my relationship with Ruth. These sections would act as a counterpoint to Brenda's story, a frame to give her words more weight. I wrote a character fit for public consumption, the man I pretended I wanted to be, a writer much like me, in love with a woman much like Ruth, in love with literature too, a true believer, who, in a fateful twist of circumstance, stumbles upon an idol from the far-flung past. I had no illnesses or disabilities, visible or otherwise. In this version, Brenda gives him what he wants, the secrets she's been keeping for so long, despite not knowing him from Adam: a straightforward tale of literary archivism, of *activism*, not whatever this was.

When Ruth finally emerged from the bedroom, I was scribbling down questions, though I knew I wouldn't need them. I wasn't interviewing Brenda in any traditional sense; I was more like a witness, or – what was that word Brenda had used? – a *confessor*. But still, it paid to be prepared.

—I thought we could spend the day together, Ruth said, her voice muffled by her bruxism nightguard. We've barely seen each other since you got out of hospital. You've been keeping out of my hair while I work, and I appreciate that, but I'm done now; the essay went live last night.

—That's great, I said, giving her a hug. And what's the response been?

—I have no idea. I've been too scared to check what people are saying. That's beside the point though. I feel sick at what I've done. I know it'll be good for my career, but is that sufficient reason to betray Helen?

—It's payback for decades of shoddy mothering.

—Don't speak about her like that, please. I know you're trying to justify what I've done, but I don't want that.

She closed her eyes and plugged one nostril, breathed deeply through the other, a yogic stress management technique.

—So what do you say? she said. Let's chuck our phones in the river. Go for a walk. See a movie at the Sun. Engage in some sodomitical sex. Whatever. I don't want to think about writing today.

—That all sounds lovely, but I have lunch date with Brenda.

—And I suppose I'm not invited?

—It will only take a couple of hours and then I'll be yours.

—But I want you to be mine now.

She kissed my earlobe, then, feeling the tension in my body, withdrew. Instead she picked up the copy of *The Widowers*.

—You know, I never liked this book. I admire it, sure, in the same way one might admire a virus for its ruthless efficiency. But it's so cold. Like dying of exposure.

—I read once that freezing to death actually feels very warm. But I take your point.

She began flicking through the pages at random, then began to read.

—*If I'd known she'd shut up shop, I never would have married her. She should take it as a compliment that I'm so expressive with my love. I want to express as soon as I wake up, when I get home from work. Love, love, love. That's all I think about. I still want to love her even though she's let herself go. And if she doesn't love me more, I will be forced to love someone else, even if I have to pay for it.* Is that daring? Showing us the worst of men? Telling us what we already know?

—Well, respectfully, yes. Especially for a book of that time. I know you're cross, but there's no need to take it out on Brenda. She hasn't done anything, and to be honest neither have I. You want me to put you before my work. But when have you ever done that for me?

*

To have tension between us was unusual, unbearable, but I was determined not to give in. To distract myself I turned my attention to *The Widowers*, a monolith, which had loomed, sheer-faced, in my mind's eye ever since I met Brenda. *The Widowers* had truly made Brenda's name, creating the kind of controversy that was unimaginable now. The critics of the day had launched a crusade against the book, and then there was the Shales Ruling, when a judge ruled in favour of a group of anonymous men who claimed swathes of the novel had been stolen. In the decades since, no new information had come to light, no-one had come forward to lay claim to the terrible acts recorded in the book. Brenda had never clarified nor justified, which only added to the mystery. Her publisher had admitted fault, though curiously the book remained in print, each new edition beginning with a disclaimer acknowledging the outcome of the trial. I was certain it was the story behind *The Widowers* that would make or break my biography. *Anchoress* had been the appetiser; *The Widowers* would be the main.

The foreword of my copy was written by one of Brenda's contemporaries, a writer whose slow accretion of books and accolades had finally, in her late seventies, earned her a reputation as a writer to be taken seriously:

What else is there to say about Brenda Shales? Enough has been written, too much. Speculating as to who she was, and how she came to write those bedevilling books. I have nothing to add on that score. The story of Brenda Shales reminds one that living as a woman in Australia is like being flogged to death by a leaf of soggy lettuce, to paraphrase one of our odious prime ministers. The controversy – or let's use the proper term, *sex hate* – unleashed upon Brenda Shales's masterpiece, *The Widowers*, obscures, I think, the singular qualities the novel possesses, the clear-eyed brutality of its vision, its obdurate *strangeness*.

I was living in a terrace house in Carlton when *The Widowers* was released. I'd just got hitched to a man I shouldn't have, and my life seemed at a loose end. We passed the book around like some graven object, housemate to housemate, until it fell apart at the seams. It was that sort of book. Even those who professed to hate it could not keep their traps shut about it.

It introduced me to new possibilities of form and voice, style and substance. It taught me the meaning of the word *uncompromising*. Thought looks into the pit of hell and is not afraid, and this book thinks better than all but a few.

From the first paragraph, we know this an Australian book, with its sparse and vivid beauty, its beery, cheery menace. But it's an Australia *unlike*, simultaneously imaginary and grounded in reality.

It was just getting dark as I approached the town, evening like a sheet of torn paper, a rug thrown over the wheatfields. They call this a valley, but I saw no peaks nor minor mountains. In time I would come to learn the names for the weeds flowering on the roadside: caltrop, boneseed, Illyrian thistle, hardhead, ragwort, Paterson's curse. By moonlight, the buildings looked hewn from bone, a post office and a few pubs, all done up in that fussy, colonial style. I wanted to disappear and the town seemed a good place to do it. It had the air of being barely there, of time having passed it by, if it had passed it at all. Over the next few weeks the women began to disappear, first one and then another. Eventually I was the only one left. It was just me and the widowers.

The Widowers describes an unnamed woman's encounters with a series of men whose wives have disappeared into thin air. The cause of the disappearances isn't explained, and is scarcely remarked on by the narrator or the men she meets. The women are there then they aren't, like the rain. The men make a series of pilgrimages to the narrator's ramshackle homestead on the edge of town, where they proceed to confess their most intimate secrets. The novel is essentially a series of monologues, men's voices speaking into the void, ninety-four of them in all. A book of blokes talking: not the greatest advertisement for high art. But Brenda Shales records this litany of terrible deeds with love, care and attention – which is, after all the only antidote to violence.

Who is this strange confessor at the centre of the text? There is something of the analyst in her, whose silences elicit those heart-wrenching confessions. Indeed some people have speculated Shales must have been a shrink, and these testimonies were drawn directly from her case notes. The novel has the quality of a court transcript at a war crimes trial, each speaker essentially begging for his life, throwing himself on the narrator's mercy, though what she could do to help is never made clear. The testimonies are achingly intimate, yet impersonal; they speak for men as a totality. Perhaps, as some critics have surmised, our narrator is a sort of gatekeeper, weighing their souls against the weight of a feather before allowing them to pass into some arid limbo. I've often wondered if she might be that young woman locked in a room in *Anchoress*, if the world of those novels is one and the same.

When the book was released, all the talk, perhaps unsurprisingly, was about the men, and how much Brenda Shales hated them. Shales was showing these men at their most raw and vulnerable, which is seldom a pleasant sight. But what of her disappearing women, who, for me, are the key to this book? In later years, a group of critics read the book literally: Brenda Shales wrote a novel about men telling the secret history of their marriages, confessing their most intimates acts of violence. Their wives had literally disappeared, a sort of textual femicide, women's voices drowned out by the droning of men, who do nothing but complain and explain, who beg for sympathy not just from the narrator but from the reader too. Instead of writing about the silencing of women, Shales was silencing them herself. To them, Shales was worse than a misogynist; she not only hated women, but had made it her mission to rehabilitate men who hated them too.

But women were disappearing. That's what it seemed like to me, living in Melbourne at that time. Disappearing into marriage and motherhood. Being consumed, subsumed, by the burden of history and the body. I left my husband a month after I read *The Widowers*. It is, and always will be, that kind of book.

My book wouldn't be like that, I knew, with a pang of disappointment. What I was concocting was not literature, but the story of a parasite and his perfect host. Or maybe I was the host, infected by Brenda's story. Either way I had to put an end to this.

Without stopping to think about what I was doing, I called Mercy House.

—Please connect me with Brenda Shales. I really need to talk to her.

There was a pause, a muffled sound, as if the nurse was speaking to someone else.

—Before I put you through, I need your name, please. For our records.

She was trying to sound casual, but I could hear the menace in her voice. I hung up.

I'd tried to do the right thing, and now I never would. And besides, was it really fair to abandon Brenda, to have her lose the only family she'd ever known all over again? At this point, wouldn't the truth be more cruel than the lie?

Brenda was already at Hao Phong when I arrived, sitting at a table by the window, hair sticking out at all angles. It was after the lunchtime rush, and the restaurant was empty save for the waiters lolling against the counter.

—This menu's as long as my arm, Brenda said, sliding it across the table. I'll leave the ordering to you.

—Let's get this table groaning, I said. My shout.

I reeled off dish after dish: sizzling tofu hotpots, veggie pho and bún cha. I would put my remaining blood money to good use.

—I suppose you'll make me sing for my supper. Fret not, you'll get your pound of flesh. If you're a good boy. But first let's enjoy this lovely feast.

She ate with sensuous attention, telling me through moans of pleasure that the meal reminded of her of the first time she'd tasted Chinese food. A hole in the wall in St Kilda, little more than a counter and stovetop. The locals would arrive with aluminium saucepans and the chef would fill them straight from the wok, chow mein and fried rice, the spice nothing like she'd ever tasted before.

—I have often wondered if the Australian character, Brenda said, so brittle and mean, was shaped by the poverty of our palate. We live in a country where everything can grow, and yet our diet, up until the past few decades, was limited to grey meat and offal, root veggies boiled to death. A thoroughly British cuisine, a way to make the country our own. Later, food become a sort of citizenship. We absorbed the Greeks and Italians and Lebanese, then the Chinese and Vietnamese, because of what they put on our plates. Yes, the way to a coloniser's heart is through his stomach.

She told me about the food at Mercy House, the slurry that passed for sustenance, *cucina povera* of the worst kind, everything pulsed and pureed, the inmates not being the best chewers.

—I know exactly what you mean, I said.

As I had the day before, I felt the urge to make a confession, though not *the* confession. I wanted to tell Brenda something I held, if not dear, then with fear.

—For more than a decade, I've been in and out of the hospital. I stay for weeks at a time, sometimes months. I loathe it, as you can imagine. The boredom. The blood tests. The fear of what the drugs are doing to me. But it was the food that always got to me: the cardboard quiches and sour salads, bangers and mash, everything boiled the same cirrhotic colour.

—What's wrong with you? Brenda asked, her face suddenly grave.

—Nothing except a chronic aversion to gainful employment. I am a guinea pig for medical trials; I get paid to have experimental drugs tested on me. I've participated in dozens of trials over the years.

I laid my forearms on the table, pumped my fists till the veins popped blue and thick.

—I've been told they sit very close to the skin. They always let the student nurses practise on me. Not very pleasant, especially when their aim isn't true, but I try to grin and bear it, because up until a couple of days ago they were my employers. The nurses always made a big song and dance about how my veins made their job easier. I've always dreamt that one day my writing would receive the same sort of acclaim.

—That sounds like a joke you've told before, Brenda said, rolling her eyes.

—The consent forms were always grisly reading but the side effects were never anything special. All told it was easy money. Deadening too. I started pigging at nineteen, often with friends and housemates. The money gave me time and space to write, though it never felt like I was writing enough. But eventually my friends moved on. Every time, I told myself *this* would be the last time I did it, my real life would start the moment I was released. Sometimes I managed to stay away for months at a time, but I always ended up back there, cap in hand and veins outstretched. I got used to the money, using my body instead of my mind. I needed it too; it's not like there are many jobs out there for an arts graduate with a hundred med trials to his name. I could have tried harder to find one, of course, but mostly it felt like I didn't have any options. At a certain point I stopped telling people what I did for a living – though *living* strikes me now as rather a strong word. Maybe *waiting* is more accurate. When people asked where I'd been, I said the hospital, without filling in the blanks. I let them think there was something wrong with me. I guess there was. Now I should tell you about my discharge.

—Not while I'm eating!

—I mean what happened on the morning of my release from the last trial, a drug for osteoporosis. I did my last blood round and got the cheque from the doctor. He had a print in his office with a quote: *Ever tried. Ever failed. No matter. Try again. Fail again. Fail better.* Who says literature has no practical application?

From Brenda: crickets.

—It's Beckett, I said, my voice as perplexed as her face.

—Ah, *Beckett.* Yes, of course.

Critics had frequently spoken of Brenda and Beckett in the same breath, usually invoking his name to insult hers. I continued with my story.

—When I was leaving the doctor's office I almost ran smack bang into the night nurse, Siobhan, taking a tray of blood to the lab. I'd spent a lot of time with her over the years, though we'd never seen each other on the outside. Anyway, she put the blood and down and gave me a hug and said: *Till next time, Rhys.* Where she got that name from I have no idea, but it certainly wasn't mine. When I pointed this out, she started to apologise in a way that seemed overkill for a slip of the tongue. Given the number of people who came and went from the hospital each day, it would have been ridiculous to think could they keep track of every name. And though I was a return customer – one of the family, as we occasionally joked – the nurses surely didn't think of me more than any other participant. I was a prize pig, but I was still a pig. But Siobhan looked distraught. Eventually she confessed that Rhys was how the other nurses referred to me behind my back. Rhys. As in rhesus. As in the monkeys the drugs were first tested on.

—How very Australian, Brenda said.

—The nurses had other names for me too, apparently. The Trial Bludger. The Side Effect. They kept a running tally of how many hours I'd spent in the ward over the last decade. And all that talk about my excellent veins was apparently a big joke. They were just taking the piss. Siobhan was telling me all this as a way to warn me off returning to the trial ward, and for that I should be grateful. Everyone at the hospital thought I was a loser who had nothing to offer other than my blood and my body. This is the first time I've talked about this. I haven't even told Ruth, that's my girlfriend by the way.

I gestured to the waiter to take our plates, my cheeks burning.

—Anyway, I'm done with all that now. Now I have you.

Brenda grinned at me.

—You poor little pincushion. Much as it pained you to say it, I'm glad that you did. You can trust me with things like this. Now, I'll nip out for a post-prandial fag, and then we can get down to business.

While she was gone I flicked through my copy of *The Widowers*. The cover had a photo of a young white woman in a yellow sundress, barefoot in a wheatfield, shot from behind, her hand running through the winnowing sheafs. A trick of a cover, a dark triumph of marketing, presenting this gruesome novel as a breezy summer read.

—What fresh hell is this? Brenda said when she resumed her seat. Talk about not judging a book by its cover.

I was far away, thinking of that afternoon I'd just described, how Siobhan had led me to Brenda. After her confession, I'd had to swim off my shame. Siobhan had seen me for who I really was, and then I saw Brenda. Perhaps, too, Siobhan's slip of the tongue had stopped me correcting the nurse's at Mercy House. I was grateful to Siobhan. Hateful too, because now there was no way out, I'd have to see my deception all the way through, come what may.

SECOND INTERVIEW - HAO PHONG - 16 FEBRUARY

I've missed you, you know, far more than I expected. You don't want to hear this, but I've spent the last days waiting by the phone, a spotty lass who's lost her you-know-what and wants to take it back. I couldn't help but think you'd had your fun and left me in the lurch. I have largely done a sterling job of not thinking about that time in my life, not thinking about *him*. And now it's all I can think about, thanks to you. Perhaps this will prove cathartic in the end, but so far it has been a mortifying experience. Well, never mind – onwards, into the breach!

My life cleaves neatly into two periods. Before *The Widowers* and after. Fame – though perhaps ignominy is a more appropriate word – made me feel like a footpath and a fugitive, like I belonged to everyone except myself. People wanted to become me or destroy me, to be saved from writing. Wild-faced women sidling up to me in Woolies, ponytailed blokes who looked in need of several hot dinners. They were earnest, ravenous, like you when you first appeared at my door.

You are mistaken, I wanted to say, but I kept my trap shut and let them project, which was nothing less than they expected. The strange part was they thought their attention would make me happy. Why wasn't I swanning around with a grin from ear to ear? Didn't I know how lucky I was to have my face picked out from the crowd? Eventually, though, being recognised was the least of my concerns.

The hardest part about telling a story is knowing when to start. I can impose a shoddy scaffold of narrative, a this then this then that. But that would imply I understand better now than I did back then, when in truth, things seem just as murky as ever. Things don't really ever begin, nor do they truly end, and accordingly *The Widowers* didn't come about in a straightforward manner, but I will try to explain it as best I can. Everyone knows about the aftermath, me up to my eyeballs in debt, regretting ever putting pen to paper, the critics dancing on my grave. But the beginning, well, that's a little trickier.

I suppose my first semester of university in 1971 is as good a place to start as any. I'd wanted to study literature, and I probably would have, had I not been forced to pay for it. I plumped instead for teaching, a profession as sturdy as the rod the nuns whacked us with, at the school I'd not long left. They beat me and I joined them, as there wasn't any other option, save for waiting for Gough Whitlam to abolish tertiary fees, which he eventually did, too late to be much help to me.

I was still living with my parents, an arrangement which felt more untenable by the day, as I explained in the letters I sent to Maria in

Sydney, which mostly went unanswered. In the years following my pregnancy, life continued much the same as before, my mother still turned in on herself, my father turned up to eleven, bloviating at breakfast, lunch and dinner on the manifold ills of the day, Gough Whitlam chief among them. I had to look closely to perceive the signs of strain: my mother was physically incapable of setting foot in my room, while my father brushed his teeth as if he were trying to destroy something. Needless to say my pregnancy was never mentioned, not from the moment they brought me home after the birth, sutured and woozy, until the day I left that house for good. What brilliant secret keepers we were, especially from ourselves, avoiding the topic as if our lives depended on it – and in a sense, they did. Silence allowed us to pretend nothing had changed, which suited me far better than if they'd tried to convince me it had been the right course of action. At some point they adopted a snaggle-toothed bitzer, Romulus, whom they doted on, showering him with a frenzied love they had never shown me. I had to get out of there.

I had become very good at distancing myself from how I felt. I perceived the world as if through a thick plate of glass. My emotions, what few of them I could identify, seemed to occur at a great distance, a storm far out to sea. And then there were these waves of uncontrollable feeling, rage and sadness and a pain so pure it set my teeth on edge. I learnt to deal with these bouts of feeling the only way I knew how, through repression and compart-mentalisation. I could see my life going one of two ways: I could give in to something which felt very much like madness, or I could do my best to forget, walling off that part of myself.

While I waited for my school exam results, I filled my days with writing. I was not born a writer, but I became one through boredom, those endless afternoons tinkering and revising, finding myself returning to those diary entries I'd made while pregnant, for what reason I couldn't say. Writing a book is like assembling a chicken coop in the middle of a tornado. One moment it's a patchwork of jottings, and the next it's a single, unified *thing*. There's no better feeling in the world.

When I was accepted into teachers' college, my parents offered to pay my tuition, but I refused. Instead I took a summer job, cleaning offices in the city at night, after the workers had gone home. One of my regular clients was the publisher that had released the Miles Franklin winner three years running. Once I had finished polishing the floors and emptying the ashtrays, I often wandered the echoing building, snooping through desk drawers, helping myself to liquor in the editors' offices, permitting myself to fantasise that one day I too could be that wondrous thing, a published author.

Sometimes I would place trunk calls to Maria's share house in Glebe. I was jealous of the life Maria seemed to be leading in Sydney. She was always talking over the sound of music, shouting, crockery clattering, the din of real life, so different to the quiet of the office, a neat metaphor for the dynamic which still existed between us, though I have always been suspicious of metaphors. I clung to her friendship with a desperation I tried desperately not to show, feeling she was my last chance to enter the world of adulthood.

Maria was working as a receptionist at Heatherbrae, an abortion referral clinic in Bondi, which had recently become a cause célèbre after a raid by the vice squad. It brought Maria within the orbit of some of Sydney's women's libbers, and her life, as she told it, had become a souped-up version of our Tolarno days, nights spent drinking and smoking pot, parties at the houses of writers, musicians and actors, whose names she dropped with a casual disdain. Privately I wondered why she couldn't mooch about in the same city as me, but I knew better than to complain.

But I could sense all was not well. Maria's stories had always been constructed to appal and entertain, but now they often regressed into diatribes which I found hard to follow, rants about people I'd never heard of, threads which never quite connected, speaking at such a frenetic pace I had to beg her to slow down. And that was when she picked up the phone. Weeks would go by when I couldn't reach her, which I told myself was because she was busy living, truly living, though a part of me remained worried.

I told her about my studies, what little there was to report. The teachers-to-be were for the most part sensible, secretarial types, rejects from more glamorous professions. Or else they were artsy bludgers in it for the short hours and long holidays. But I could tell Maria was tiring of me, and the life she'd left behind. Her silences grew longer, she always seemed on the verge of hanging up. In a desperate bid to impress her, I told her about what I'd been writing, these queer snippets about my imprisonment. Maria listened to me read my manuscript over the phone, over the course of three nights. She never said a word, though I could feel her presence on the other end of the line, the intensity of her attention. For those hours while I read, it felt like the dynamic had shifted between us, as if a current's flow had been reversed.

Maria told me what I should do next. Leave my manuscript on an editor's desk, along with my name and number. I protested, saying it wasn't ready, wasn't good enough, I was too shy to put my name out there.

—So don't, Maria said. Pick a different name.

In the end we settled on Shales, the name of the nun who'd beaten Maria after she'd taught us about our womanly secretions. The question of a forwarding address was more difficult. The last thing I wanted was to involve my parents, so I gave Maria's address instead.

It's good that one of us is doing something with our lives, she said.

It was the last thing I'd ever expected from her, something that sounded like support, like love.

Maria wrangled me an interview at a sprawling share house in Collingwood. The woman who answered the door wore dungarees and gardening gloves, a picture of vitality. She introduced me to the other housemates, and I immediately forgot their names as they led me out to the garden where they'd been planting tomatoes. We drank bitter black tea while chooks and toddlers careened across the grass. One little boy was called Che, an angelic terrorist piffing dirt in our direction. I can still remember his wispy ringlets and ropey musculature. I couldn't keep my eyes off him.

I felt such a dag in my ridiculous bell-bottoms, which I'd bought specially for the occasion, and which pinched my belly terribly, so I was continually holding my breath. My hosts were all involved with the liberation movement, organising consciousness-raising groups and holding community meetings at their office on Little La Trobe Street. To my utter horror Maria had told them about my novel, and they were full of questions, asking how I thought it fit within the emancipatory project. I gaped and gawped. I wished Maria had been there to answer for me, to tell these lovely women what my work was doing and why.

One of them took pity on me, asked about my influences. *Doris Lessing*, I managed to squawk. *Thea Astley*. They looked crestfallen when I admitted I hadn't read *The Female Eunuch*. An entire house of Marias, I thought with dread as I sipped my tepid tea, and the talk mercifully moved on to other topics. It was a relief when I never heard back from them.

Eventually, I found a room at a women's boarding house in Parkville called Cumberland Place, run by a middle-aged widow named Carmel, a remnant from an era that was on its way out. Cumberland Place was populated by working-class wraiths: quiet, young women who'd been cast out of polite society. We were a febrile body politic, ripe for consciousness-raising, but the women of Cumberland Place were a sorry lot for the most part. There was Muriel, who'd been forced to work as a washerwoman at the Abbotsford Convent, after being chucked out by her parents (for what, she never told us), and had somehow escaped their clutches. Cynthia, whose husband of two months had been killed in Vietnam. Alice, who'd been dumped on the steps of the Royal Women's by a backyard abortionist who couldn't stem the bleeding. Their stories, gory as they were, confirmed I'd got off lightly.

Carmel treated us with a queenly reserve, though she was a kind woman, and a feminist to her marrow, though she would have chucked up had I ever called her that. She charged a pittance for rent and let the rooms to the women who needed them most, no questions asked. Though I declined to recount my own sob story, she must have sensed a sadness in me, a certain resignation; she could see, perhaps much better than I could, that I belonged at Cumberland Place.

We kept to ourselves, save for watching telly together in the chintzy living room, whose every surface was bristling with Hummel figurines. We favoured reruns of a popular show from the sixties, *Divorce Court*, which re-enacted scenes drawn from 'real life' court transcripts. Amateur actors committed adultery, battered wives and drank themselves silly – which back then were the only ways to break the bonds of matrimony – and were duly humiliated before a bewigged judge.

We were just as hungry for reality as you lot are today, and those tales from the dark side of matrimony were a particular hit in Cumberland Place, I suspect because it made us believe that, in remaining single, we had avoided a fate far worse than loneliness – namely, being yoked to a bloke who was our legal lord and master.

I ate my meals in my room, a jaffle or tin of baked beans. I plodded through my studies, waited to hear back about my novel. Meanwhile, life seemed to be moving on without me, the world opening up. Whitlam had made everything suddenly seem provisional: no-fault divorce, free university and health care, abolishing the death penalty, equal pay for working women, Aboriginal land rights. My life was just getting started, but my trajectory already seemed set. In those first few months of university I often thought of that Kafka line: *Oh, there is hope, infinite hope, just not for us.* That's what it seemed like: I was living in history's nadir, which would be replaced by something better, though by that point it would be too late for women like me and those I lived with.

One day an envelope arrived from Maria. Inside was a letter from the editor, addressed to Brenda Shales, the name unfamiliar at first, until I remembered it was me. The editor was brusque, matter-of-fact. He had no idea how my book had ended up on his desk, but he was glad it had. He blew smoke up my arse for a few paragraphs, then made a tentative offer. It might be a good fit for a new imprint geared towards women's writing. He proposed a modest advance.

I felt like all my periods had come at once. I felt pregnant. The news was too downright unbelievable to process as anything other than discomfort. I sat like a stunned mullet at the kitchen table of Cumberland Place, until Carmel poked me with the end of her broom.

They're publishing my novel! I managed to squeak.

Carmel clutched me to her lye-smelling bosom, rocked me back and forth. *A novel?* she said. *Well, isn't that lovely.*

I blew a week's wage on a call to Maria from the phone in the hallway. I told her about my good fortune, forgetting it was she who had sent on the letter in the first place. I babbled about what it all meant, what I should do. For some reason, the idea of the book being out in the world, my face on the dust jacket, seemed impossible, struck me as a humiliation of the highest order. I knew I was working myself into knots for no reason, poisoning the moment with my ridiculous anxiety. But still, making myself visible felt like a monstrous proposition, and one I wasn't ready for. Maria was curt, wondering why I sounded like some terrible tragedy had befallen me. Wasn't this what I'd wanted?

The following morning, I opened a post office box in my new name, then spent the rest of the day drafting a letter to the editor, which I scribbled with my brand-new signature and left on his desk. I told him I was thrilled to publish but wasn't willing to meet in person. Brenda Shales was not my real name and I didn't want to become a public figure. Literature, I wrote, should exist only between the pages of a book, unsullied by the business of biography. Fine words, though untrue. I was scared to reveal myself completely, concerned by what people might say. And perhaps my worries were well founded, considering what happened.

Now those waiters are beginning to glare. Perhaps we should pick things up next time?

ELEVEN

Nothing was stopping me now except the truth. I had broken Brenda, in a manner of speaking, worn her down by turning up. I had to quell whatever conscience I had left, excise my passivity like some malignant growth. Threat lurked everywhere: the staff at Mercy House; Brenda's chums (not as senile as I'd have liked); and the two people who worried me the most, Brenda and Ruth. Everything was staked on the book, my actions primed with meaning and consequence. This was life in ALL CAPS, sickly thrilling, but I didn't know how much more of it I could take.

Ruth hadn't been home when I'd returned from lunch with Brenda. It had struck me as a touch theatrical, the phone left on the bedside table, the lack of call or message. But better her absence than another fight. Besides, it gave me time to luxuriate in the excitement of the hunt, the intrepidness of it all. Brenda's story had flowed so elegantly from *Anchoress* to *The Widowers*. I had no idea how it would knit together but I was rapt, even on second listening, sitting in the backyard, watching the fruit bats winging out to feed. I was already itching for the next session.

I was still there, sitting in the dark, when Ruth arrived home, calling my name as she moved from room to room, sounding lost and drunk.

—I didn't think you'd be here, she said, catching sight of me from the back step.

—Here I am.

Ridiculously, I waved. She fixed me with a glare that turned my guts to water.

—That remains to be seen.

The next day, writing was a cinch, as easy as breathing. I told myself true literature (for that is what I was convinced I was writing, or least transcribing) was more important than quotidian questions of ethics and morals. I could worry about the rectitude of my character the moment the book was published. Brenda and I were in a rhythm, and how exciting it felt to be continually on the verge of breakthrough. All I had to do was sit tight and shut my lying trap.

While Ruth slept, I wrote everything up until our meeting at Hao Phong, removing all parts which made me look bad (which I feared would make it a very short book), imagining myself as a nameless interlocutor – much like the narrator of *The Widowers* – whose only role is to listen, a biographer with no biography of his own, his career the last thing on his mind. All in all, a bloody good bloke.

I wrote without revising, without breaks, breakneck. Now I wouldn't be returning to the hospital, the book's success was more vital than ever. Despite its suspect provenance, I was confident in the material, principally because the best parts weren't mine. What Brenda had told me, what she would tell me, would propel her into the limelight, and I'd be right there with her.

Ruth emerged from the bedroom around noon, looking wan and photocopied, just as I was making a fresh pot of coffee. She rifled through the freezer for something to eat, retrieving a package of potato gems.

—I'm sorry about my disappearing act, she said. Blame the essay.

Warily, Ruth offered me her phone, as if it were contagious. She looked so serious that I braced myself for bad news, spectacular rejection, but then I saw the slew of reposts, shares and requests, messages flooding her inbox from people who wanted a piece of her, big fish some of them. It took me minutes to get through all the adulation, the chorus of readers telling Ruth she was the one, pressing the coin of our realm – attention – into her sweaty palm.

—Yes, yes, I know I signed up for it. There are starving kids in Africa who don't get this kind of notice. But still, I can't help feeling icky.

—Could that be the beer?

—Daughter-boarding, Ruth said, as if I hadn't spoken. That's what they're calling it. Hit pieces by young women against their mothers. Apparently it's quite the trend. Yesterday, after you left, I kept imagining her stumbling across it. Helen, I mean. Her face falling as she realised. I had to get that image out of my mind, liver be damned, get away from it all. It's like something from a fairy tale: in order to get what I've always wanted, I have to betray the person I'm closest to – present company not excepted.

As usual, when Ruth said something cruel or crushing, I chose to take her last words as a joke, though she wasn't smiling.

—You know, Brenda said something similar about fame yesterday. It made her feel like a footpath and a fugitive.

—Brenda! That's who I should talk to. What was the name of that nursing home again? Mercy something? Perhaps I'll give her a call.

My stomach gave a violent swerve. Was that a credible threat? I still didn't get why Ruth seemed so stricken, as if something had been taken from her rather than given. Brenda had the same quality: aggrieved by getting what she'd wanted. The two of them were more alike than I cared to admit.

Ruth opened the oven, dumped the barely defrosted gems into a cavernous salad bowl, slathered them with barbecue sauce.

—And speaking of Brenda, Ruth said, I bit your head off yesterday, didn't I? A bit uncalled for. It took me four pints to understand what had got me so worked up.

I braced myself for the punch.

—Let me preface this by saying: your book is going to be great, a big deal. My problem isn't with Brenda or the book, but how easy it's been for you.

—Easy? I spluttered.

What a ridiculous word. I'd never done anything harder; this hairshirt of guilt fit me like a second skin. But deep down, did I feel guilt? Or did I feel guilty about my lack of guilt? A sort of meta-guilt?

—You, Ruth said, recognise a noted recluse, whom no-one has heard boo from in fifty years. You ambush her at her place of residence, and she invites you in for tea and bickies, decides to spill the full, unabridged beans. The great mystery of Australian letters falls right into your lap.

—There were no bickies. But yes, that's about the sum of it.

Our meeting was ancient history. I never wanted to speak of it again. But thankfully Ruth wasn't suspicious about how I'd got the story; she resented that I hadn't suffered sufficiently in the acquisition of it. Oh, how little she knew and would never know.

—You don't think I deserve it.

—Your words, not mine.

She gave the gems a tentative chew, then tucked in with gusto.

—I don't want to fight, I said. Famous last words. But it seems you want me to apologise for working my way out of my writing rut. Do you want me to be a pig the rest of my life?

Ruth pushed the bowl across the table, her face ashen, tender too.

—That was wrong. The food, but also what I said. I'm wrong and you're right, much as it pains me to say it. Perhaps there's a part of me that likes the imbalance between us, if that's not too strong a word, that wants to retain the upper hand. I know it's not a zero-sum game, but I want to be the special one, despite my whinging. Regardless, I'm sorry.

Now was not the time for grinning, and yet I permitted myself one, face mushed into her shoulder as we hugged. That feeling again, burbling inside me, the excitement of control exerted, of things going according to plan.

The rest of the day was a temporary autonomous zone, freed from responsibility, life lived on aeroplane mode. It was pancakes and perusing *The Age*'s ever-thinning books section, which had lately taken on a particularly keening quality, each title described as incredibly necessary *in times like these*.

—Talk about projection, Ruth said. It's like they're trying to prove the value of literature to a productivity commission.

I commandeered Ruth's phone, acting as a sort of secretary, calling out the names of people who'd given a heart or a message of support. Some of it I deleted unread: all caps messages from burner accounts with subject lines like, YOU KNOW WHAT YOU DID – the unfortunate price women writers had to pay to be in the public eye. The essay – published under the title 'Australian Crawl' – had clearly struck a chord with sad sons and fail-daughters the world over, pieces already popping up discussing its merits and problems, writers around the world trying to steal Ruth's attention for themselves, speaking the genre of daughter-boarding into existence, a form of textual matricide. It had officially gone as viral as a piece of literary non-fiction could.

When we woke from our afternoon nap, our bodies were clasped together as if for warmth, though it hadn't dropped below thirty for days. Drowsily, Ruth performed the mating ritual, hissing insults in my ear: *fucking pig* et cetera. But just when things were starting to get interesting she rolled over.

—The flesh is willing, but the spirit is weak. Actually, the flesh is weak as well. I feel like a colostomy bag.

—I can drive, if you'd like?

I spoke in a drawl, wolfish and butch, not like me at all.

Ruth sat up in bed, head cocked in surprise. She shrugged, as if to say, *It's your funeral*. Then she said:

—It's your funeral.

I seldom made the first move in our coupling, nor the second, third or fourth. The few times I'd been on top, I'd been overwhelmed by the pressure to get things right, my touch too soft or hard, my dirty talk canned, an overwhelmingly underwhelming performance. It had always seemed pointless to engage in a power struggle with Ruth, benevolent dictator of my heart. No, I was a first responder and always would be. Sex with Ruth had always felt like sinking into something, bleeding out in a bath. The boundaries between things slowly dissolving, myself most of all. But that afternoon I wanted to try something different, and that would never happen with Ruth staring at me as if trying to recall the punchline to a joke. And then I remembered the eye mask. My ex, Michelle, had made me wear it, so I couldn't see her self-consciousness when she'd consented to top me.

—Put this on and roll over, I said.

Ruth did what I said, lying prone in the middle of the bed, and I knelt above her, taking everything in: the light through the curtain dappling her body, the ends of her hair still damp from the shower, a pimple on her shoulder in sore need of popping. I felt then my duty towards Ruth, my desire to ease her passage through life. The weight of duty and desire, it felt too much to bear. Ruth made to slide her hand between her legs.

—No, I said. Not that. Not yet.

—What's got into you? she said, her voice muffled by the pillow. Who is this man?

—I'm just a fan, I said. I've been reading your work for years.

The moment stretched on, and still I didn't move, didn't touch her, my whole body flexed, full of energy that had been building up my entire life. I felt like running full pelt up a hill, screaming like a madman. I felt like naming an ocean. Procreating. Ruth's nose twitched, she began breathing through her mouth, at first in a regular rhythm and then with great, wet gasps and still I didn't touch her. She tore the mask off and sat, pulled the sheet to her chin.

—What's wrong? What did I do?

I sounded frantic, for that's what I felt, the bill finally due, punishment visited not upon me but on Ruth.

Ruth didn't seem to know quite where she was, giving these long, slow blinks as if trying to work a speck of dust from her eye. Then she started talking:

—The mask reminded me of something. That feeling of opening my eyes and not seeing anything. When I was in my early twenties I dated a boy from Scotch College. Nic. You wouldn't have liked me back then. *I* didn't like me. Nic was even worse. He was sober the whole time we were dating, because at a party one time he'd jumped from the roof, breaking both legs so badly the doctors thought they'd have to amputate.

We fought all the time, never fucked. Never knew how to spend time together. When I got home from my shift at Bimbo's, he was always plying me with grog. Beer, wine, whatever. My glass was never empty. Getting me drunk was the only time he was nice to me. It was a different story when I was hungover. He'd rage about the house, clean aggressively, drag me over the coals. He got to be the adult in the room, and it drove me mad – not just Nic's behaviour, but my inability to change the dynamic. The fighting gave our relationship a sort of texture, a drama which back then I always sought out.

Anyway, one weekend we drove to Nic's family's holiday house in the hills behind Lorne. The first night I let him get me drunk, and the next day we fought. Plates were smashed, things were said that couldn't be taken back. It felt like the end, and good riddance. I walked down the hill to wait for the bus back to Melbourne, which wasn't due until later that evening. I traipsed along the foreshore, ate some fish and chips. It was just getting dark when Nic pulled up beside the tourist centre where I'd been waiting, in his parents' Subaru. He said he was sorry – not just for the fight, but for everything. He said he wanted to make it up to me.

I got into the car because of his face. I'd never seen him look so wounded, so lost. As soon as I sat down Nic passed me an eye mask. He said he had a surprise for me. He must have got the idea from this stupid article called 'Small Acts of Love and Devotion' that I'd sent him a few months before. Blindfold your lover and surprise them with a picnic, that type of thing. When I put the mask on, I remember thinking, *He gets it. He's listening.*

The last thing I saw, before slipping on the mask, was Nic following the road around the coast, heading in the direction of Apollo Bay. I thought he was taking me for dinner at the Wye River pub, or to a lookout to watch the sunset, though it was pretty well dark. I don't know how long we'd been driving when the radio reception started to go. Nic switched it off and I realised I couldn't hear the ocean anymore, just the tyres humming on the bitumen. I felt the car turn onto a gravel road and drive slowly uphill. My mind kept returning to that image of Nic's face during the fight, how he'd glared at me like he wished I didn't exist. I asked him to stop the car, and I took the mask off, and it was just the headlights on the dirt road and the gums and pitch-black all around. It was too dark to see Nic's expression, but I could make out his teeth. He had these straight, white teeth. Presidential teeth. And I could see his teeth in the dark, and it looked like he was smiling.

He finally pulled over onto the shoulder of the road and asked me what was wrong. I'm still not sure why I did it. I have never thought of myself as a vulnerable person, but I was so angry that a man as dull as him could make me feel scared, even for just a few moments, even without meaning to.

Once the car was in park, the engine switched off, I elbowed Nic in the face with all the force I could muster, smashing his nose to smithereens. I told myself it was for self-protection, but even then a part of me knew that wasn't it. I was fed up with our relationship, and my attack was a brutal way to end it. Nic started bawling, blood flowing onto the steering wheel. I opened the door and walked into the trees. After a while I couldn't see the road anymore, I couldn't hear Nic calling my name. Then I came across the lights. Hundreds of tiny, blue lights dotting the trees and ferns, a carpet of stars at my feet. They were glow-worms, thousands of them. Millions. I'd never seen anything so beautiful in my life. This was what Nic must have been trying to show me. I remembered then he'd told me about the glow-worms, back when we first got together. Whoops-a-daisy. Clearly a case of crossed wires, but still: it was telling that Nic hadn't been able to discern the fear in my voice, or if he had, he hadn't done anything to assuage it.

Eventually I wandered into a clearing. There were a few picnic tables, a barbecue and two boys sitting around a camp fire. They didn't seem surprised to see me, blasted as they were, on weed and I don't know what else. They introduced themselves as Jai and Jackson, local boys, who insisted they'd finished high school, though their spotty skin said otherwise. Jai had a rat's tail and wore a cock-covered cast on his arm; Jackson sported a shark's tooth necklace and a harelip which glimmered in the firelight. The bong was strong, and in a few seconds I'd forgotten all about Nic. I talked about my life in Melbourne, I told them I was single. It was chilly and Jackson offered to share his polar fleece. Then in no time at all the three of us were naked, rolling around on their swags. Everyone was a bit sheepish in the morning, but they gave me a ride back into town, waited with me for the bus to arrive. I wrote my number on Jai's cast, though I switched a couple of digits. I never saw those boys again – Nic neither.

As Ruth talked, I felt a disquiet so great it was hard for me to keep track of what she was saying. I was thinking about Brenda, for Ruth's story was Brenda all over: the glaze of her eyes, the expression of excruciation, not the connections my conscious mind wanted to make. I tried to hug her then but she shied away from my touch, pushing my arm away roughly.

—Sorry, she said. But this isn't that kind of story. Despite all outward appearances, this is not some trauma I need to work through. It was just something that happened. I know all that came out of the blue. Clearly writing that article has made me a bit more – how should I put it? – receptive to the past. Things are coming up unbidden, though I wish they wouldn't.

—What can I do to help?

—Help? She gave a sigh of exasperation. Do I look like I need help? Perhaps I do. Well for now, you can leave me alone. And please, *please*, don't look so wounded.

*

We kept out of each other's way, Ruth watching crap on her computer, me brooding in the front room, replaying the afternoon's events on a loop of self-pity, wondering what I could have done differently. Ruth wasn't angry with me, I could see that. But she wasn't happy either.

Surely the story she'd told that afternoon had meant something more than what she'd said. It had referred to a carelessness in my disposition; my inability, like Nic, to give her what she wanted. In the two years we'd been together, she'd been the epitome of control, which was just the way I liked it. Had something slipped between us? I couldn't get it out of my head, the way that Ruth had looked at me, like I was a complete stranger.

I brought up her essay on my computer, hoping to find a clue. 'Australian Crawl' touched upon troubled chapters of Ruth's upbringing I had known about only dimly. She'd had an older sister who died not long before Ruth was born – a late-term miscarriage or a still birth, as far as Ruth knew, though Helen had always been vague about the details, even years later. One of the crucial scenes of the essay revolved around a conversation between Ruth and Helen as they drove to the pool in the black-blue depths of the morning. Helen had told Ruth, apropos of nothing, *You had a sister, Ruth.* Death was an abstract concept to Ruth back then, and to her young ears it had sounded as if this phantom sister, like Ruth's father, had left home and might one day return.

In later years, Helen had refused to expand upon that initial approximation, and there was no-one who could fill in the blanks of her mother's story. So this sister lingered over Ruth's childhood, the eternal excuse for her mother's desperate love. According to the essay, the sister made Ruth feel like a replacement, never quite measuring up.

Why was this all news to me? It didn't tally with the image I'd always had of Ruth, the one who seemed destined for greatness from the moment we'd first met, who seemed so preternaturally sure of herself. Had Ruth kept this part hidden, or had I just not known where to look?

Through the wall I heard her coughing, or maybe sobbing, and there was nothing I could do to stop it. I was on my own, and she was too.

TWELVE

I had nothing more to write, except what really happened, and I wasn't that dense. Plotless, I was left to tinker with the character I'd created, Brenda's beatific biographer performing his literary good works. How tedious I found him, how eminently *worthy* (of a kick in the teeth, or permanent deletion), and to stop me doing something I shouldn't, I repaired to Mercy House. Two days had passed since our last meeting, time enough for Brenda to catch her breath, plan the next chapter. More importantly, Brenda would help me forget about Ruth.

She was not alone. I spied Brenda on the far side of the dining room, next to Miralem and Edna, the pair I'd met on my last visit. Brenda was stroking the former's back, her head resting on his shoulder. I found myself balling my fists as I stalked across the room, nurses flitting likes shades between the tables, wiping this or spooning that. Brenda still hadn't noticed me, even as I stood, arms folded, at the end of their table, my back to a flat-screen blaring cricket, the Gabba's roar, and the sound of cutlery, the slurp and squelch of two dozen mouths.

—Oh, it's you, Brenda said finally. I don't recall you making an appointment.

She sounded terse, though she gestured for me to sit, and then turned back to Miralem, talking softly in his ear, staring into the middle distance with wired, rheumy eyes.

—Would you please take something off my plate? Brenda said, addressing me. You could do with fattening up.

Brenda indicated the glutinous globs on her plate, one a rusty brown, the other pale green, a fjord of gravy flowing between them.

—We must get it down the hatch, or it's the feeding tube for us. Now tell me, dear son of my son, in your expert culinary opinion, what in the world would you call this dish?

—Palliative gumbo? I said, taking the tiniest mouthful, which was easily more than enough.

—The technical term is texture-modified sustenance. Roast beef and three veg, pureed to a pulp, but who knows what's actually in it. Last week I saw a vat with a label saying Essence of Chicken. Make of that what you will. It's a shame, because here, as in penitentiaries the world over, meals are about the only thing we inmates look forward to. Occasionally there's a spate of hunger strikes, and the regime gives us steak and frozen calamari, often paid for out of the pockets of the kinder-hearted staff. It's none of their faults, but they are the only ones we can complain to – the tip of the spear, as it were. But I'm forgetting my manners. Edna, Miralem, you remember my grandson. He's here to interview me for a school project. A book, actually.

—A book? Edna said, sounding alarmed. What's it about?

—Search me, Brenda said. I haven't read a word. Perhaps he's worried I won't like how I come off. Or maybe it's his character he's not happy with.

I didn't care for Brenda's tone; mocking, ironic, it spoke of troubled waters ahead.

—It's about Brenda's life and career, I said, at my placatory best. The books she wrote.

—Sounds enthralling, doesn't it? Brenda said, clapping me on the back. A real page-turner. He's assured me my story's in the public interest, though I beg to differ. I would have thought that the ramblings of a geezeress do not a bestseller make.

With a surreptitious glance at the staff, Brenda scraped her plate into a pot plant beside the table, before turning to Edna, talking as if I wasn't there.

—Yes, I was a writer, and a feted one at that, until the pricks ran me out of town. I'm sure that's what his book's about: my tragic downfall, how and why I was brought so low, *victimised* in his mind. I suppose I shouldn't begrudge him his inheritance, I just wish he'd warm his hands up, so to speak. He steals into my room under the cover of night and pumps me full of drugs. Then the interview begins. He might seem a man of few words, but you should hear him behind closed doors. He's even quieter.

Edna fixed me with her best principal's glare. I tried to read Brenda's expression, but she seemed focused on coaxing the spoon between Miralem's lips. I thought I'd understood the terms of our arrangement: my presence in exchange for her secrets. But she seemed to resent me being there, to see me as an intrusion.

—Can you take over? Brenda said, chucking the spoon in my lap. My wrist is about to drop off and I fear Miralem hasn't managed to get much down. It's hard to witness all this terrible senescence, to watch a person like Miralem lose everything that's lovely about him. If it were up to me, I'd dope him to the gills and smother him with a pillow, rather than let him linger like this.

Miralem's lips were firmly pursed as I strafed the spoon towards his mouth, twisting his neck away and batting at my arm, first softly then with more vigour, sending the spoon skittering to the floor, the strap of Miralem's singlet slipping down and exposing a patchwork of scars on his shoulder.

—They're from Miralem's bear, Brenda said, with a phlegmy cackle. Bouboulina. Named after the Greek freedom fighter. Heroine of the revolution.

We were back on terra firma, Brenda's attention turned back to me. As she went on to explain, Brenda had been forced to watch Miralem dementing over the course of the last eighteen months. As his grip on reality had begun to slip, he'd told her stories about his upbringing in Bulgaria, lucid at first and then progressively more fragmentary, switching between English and his native tongue, leaving Brenda to fill in the gaps in the narrative.

—Don't put this in your book. As far as I know, Miralem grew up in a village in the mountains on the border between Bulgaria and Greece. He described it as a place out of time, which had barely changed for hundreds of years, even when the communists came to power. His father trained brown bears, trapping them as cubs and chaining them to the wall of their barn, forcing them to stand upright to avoid choking. Eventually they learnt to walk on their hind legs, dance and perform tricks.

One of the bears, Bouboulina, was particularly intelligent. Through a very bloody form of trial and error – which is how Miralem got his scars – his father trained Bouboulina to give a sort of massage, stepping daintily on the villagers' backs. Miralem said the pressure was immense, as if his bones would break. Bouboulina's skills drew people from miles around, peasants who swore that only the bear with the magic paws could heal their aching muscles.

Miralem left home at fifteen, heading across the mountains towards Thessaloniki and a ship bound for Australia. He told me that the night before he left, he stole into the yard and tiptoed over to Bouboulina's cage. She'd grown skinny over the years, her fur thin and waxy. Miralem opened the cage, and she cowered in the corner, covering her eyes with her paws. He had to hit her hard before she trundled off, upright, into the woods.

—Is that what Miralem told you? Edna was shaking her head. I seem to remember he got those scars in the army.

—Maybe it's bullshit, Brenda said. It's not like there's any way for me to verify his story. He was probably trying to get in my pants.

Miralem spat a mouthful of food straight into my lap.

—This seems like something a nurse should be doing, I said, dabbing the stain with a serviette, unsure what to make of the story Brenda had just told me.

Brenda outlined the latest round of budget cuts, a fresh staffing shortfall, resulting in Mercy House's administrators asking its more able-bodied residents to help out at meal times.

—A war-time mentality. One for all and all for one, to stave off the enemy at the gates, barbarians of the worst kind, time and money. I don't mind, really I don't, it's nice to feel useful. Now I must repair to the ladies; this food tends to play havoc with my guts. I'll be as quick as possible, but truth be told, I might be some time.

The plate was finally empty, but most of Miralem's food had ended up on his lap. I wiped his mouth with a wet serviette, surprising myself with my delicacy.

—We all love Brenda very dearly here.

Edna's voice caught me by surprise; I'd forgotten she was there. After shaking Miralem's jumper free of crumbs she arranged his cutlery neatly on his plate.

—Mercy House is not a nice place to live or work, as I'm sure you can tell, but we try to make the best of it. I first met Brenda during the care worker strike three years ago. The staff was down to a skeleton crew and could only deal with the most pressing emergencies. There was often no-one to cook or clean, so we were more or less left to fend for ourselves. It was a scandal.

A few days into the strike, there was a knock on my door. It was Brenda. I'd just moved in, and was feeling very blue. I was ready, if you'll forgive the theatrics, to give up. I'd seen Brenda striding around the halls, having a go at the nurses. She was quite formidable. Without any preamble, she told me to stop feeling sorry for myself, that the other residents needed my help. She organised a cleaning roster, did a stocktake of the kitchen. She put Miralem in charge of cooking. He'd been a cook in the army, and what he came up with was a marked improvement on the usual fare. I doled out the medication, while Brenda did everything else. She made sure everyone got three square meals, walked them down to Stony Creek. She even called the families of the residents who'd passed away. Sometimes she'd stay on the phone for hours, talking about these people she'd only known passingly, if at all. She made these perfect strangers feel comforted, loved.

Edna stood, leaning hard against her Zimmer frame, waving off my offer of help.

—I didn't know Brenda was a writer, let alone a famous one, but it makes sense. She is brilliant and a tough cookie, but not as tough as she makes out. She's very taken with you. Please promise to be careful with her.

Too late, I thought, though I would be careful not to get caught. Too late, too, to chuck it in. Brenda was attached, and the only responsible thing was to give her what she wanted. Me.

It took Edna two minutes to reach the door of the dining room. I stayed at the table, waiting for Brenda to return, reading from *The Widowers*, trying, failing and eventually succeeding in distracting myself from what Edna had just told me, swept up by the procession of gibbering voices, the husbands whose wives had disappeared into thin air, dense, muscular paragraphs pulled from the reptilian corners of the male psyche.

Should I just cut it off? Would that be preferable? Pop down to the abattoir, ask them to attend to this nasty thing between my legs [. . .] That's what my mother used to call it. *Nasty little thing.* Touching it will make hair grow on your palms. She hit me if she caught me with my hands in my pockets [. . .] *Just like my mother.* That one really got her going. [. . .] Have you ever fought with three children sleeping in the house? Everything whispered and hissed. You fight in shorthand. You pig. You dog. It's much harder to insult a man than a woman. [. . .] I earn a wage. I pay my taxes. Sometimes I wish I would come home and [. . .] I just wish she would see me [. . .] It was even worse when she gave me what I wanted. We did it in the dark because her face made me feel like a murderer. The worst kind of man. [. . .] Never again, I'd think afterwards. It was onanism from then on in. I would let my palms grow out [. . .] But after a few days I was at it again, wearing her down [. . .] Was this really what marriage was, this exchange of goods for services?

I don't know why I started keeping a diary. It seemed important to get my thoughts down. [. . .] I really took to it, writing at the office, in front of the telly, a few pages here and there, sometimes just a word or two. Eventually I was filling up a notebook a month. [. . .] I never re-read them. I've never been much of a reader. [. . .] Things were better for a while. Suddenly my problems seemed manageable. We started talking, making love, a phrase I came to adore, as if love was not a property one possessed but something created by two people, day in and day out. [. . .] One day my notebooks weren't in their usual hiding spot. And then there she was at the dinner table, the diaries open in front of her. When she saw me she started reading aloud [. . .] Had I really written all that? It seemed impossible that one man could have so much self-pity. [. . .] I truly have no memory of writing the ledger, a list of the exact times and dates I initiated sex, and her excuses for refusing it. Headaches, tiredness, colds. It was very comprehensive.

This was one of the tamer entries. The anecdotes were stitched together with minimal narration by a woman who never utters a word throughout the course of the novel, who does little more than sit in silence and refresh the pot of tea. A cold and spiteful book. No wonder critics had presumed Brenda wasn't who she said she was – or, rather, didn't say. These vignettes were so repulsively male, each page steeped in sweat and semen. Inconceivable Brenda had dreamt it all up. But I would find out soon enough, and then I would ask for forgiveness.

Miralem was clenching his fists, knuckles white, his jaw making a frantic, mashing motion, eyes glinting with malice. The room had darkened, as if a cloud had passed over the sun. The TV was off, the plates cleared, the dining room was empty, save for me and Miralem, the two of us silent in our cells of unknowing.

—I have something to tell you, I said, my voice clear and pure. I am deceiving Brenda, your friend and lover. I'm not her grandson. I'm a nobody who saw my opportunity and struck. I'll never write a novel that will make my name; I need someone to make it for me. I'm telling you this because I don't know what to do. And yet there's only one thing I *can* do. Nothing.

Footsteps coming from the doorway. I spun, expecting to see Brenda. But it was a man, a stranger, followed by the nurse in the cast who'd started everything.

—Good afternoon, he said, holding out a fat-fingered hand. I'm the director of this facility. We were wondering if we could have a word?

The director's office was as rundown and chaotic as the rest of Mercy House, files stacked precariously, a drooping ficus in the corner. He must work from home, I surmised, for no sane man could stand that clutter. The director ushered me to a chair across the desk from him, while the nurse perched on the far corner, her body angled away from me. I was terribly anxious, though I knew I shouldn't show it. Instead I went on the attack.

—What's this all about? I said. Has something happened to Brenda?

—It's been brought to my attention that you've recently started seeing Mrs Shales.

The director sounded wary.

—Seeing? What on earth do you mean by that?

I sounded outraged, the right tone to hit. But inside I was aghast, the edifice crumbling to reveal the foundation of shit beneath it. Had they heard what I'd said to Miralem in my fit of hubris and self-pity?

—I said it first, the nurse said. That you were Brenda's grandson.

—What am I being accused of exactly?

Somehow, I'd put myself in the shoes of Brenda's flesh and blood, the *real* me, I felt as irate as he would.

—Nothing, the director said. As yet. Far be it for us to separate residents and their families. But we have to do our due diligence. So you are Brenda Shales's grandson? The result of a forced adoption in 1967?

—If that's what the file says. My father has always been sketchy on the details.

—And how did you find Mrs Shales?

—I haven't done anything wrong.

—That is very likely the case, but we're conscious of the need to protect our residents.

—From what? It's not like Brenda has any money. Have you talked to her about this?

—Of course, said the director. She has no doubts as to your identity, but unfortunately we need to seek some assurance. It's not every day a relative turns up out the blue who doesn't want *something*. I'm sure you understand.

I understood alright. This was where it ended. I'd have to leave Mercy House and never come back, leave Brenda alone, the story unfinished. To do anything else would be too risky. Unless . . .

—I have exactly the proof that you need, I said, offering my hand. It's just not immediately accessible. I'll call you this time tomorrow, and we can clear everything up. Thank you for taking such great care of my grandmother.

They followed me out of the office, watched me take the corridor that led to the entrance. Once I was out of sight, I stopped, waited a few breaths, before doubling back and taking a different turning.

Brenda didn't seem surprised to see me, nor did she object when I suggested we take a walk. We followed a trail through a thicket of scrub down to the backwash where Stony Creek flowed into the Yarra. The boardwalk spanned the inlet, the water still as a sheet of glass as we walked along the sun-bleached boards towards the strip of land stretching out from the oil terminal, rotten pylons jutting from the water. To our right, the Westgate curved like a writer's sclerotic spine.

—You don't seem your usual self, Brenda said. Something you need to get off your chest?

It would have been one of the many perfect times to tell Brenda that I couldn't maintain the deception any longer – though that too would have been a lie.

—I just spoke with the director.

—Odious creature, isn't he? I suppose he had some tricky questions for you. Checking if you were here to steal my loot.

—What did you tell him?

—Nothing. What could I tell him? I gave birth to a son who was put up for adoption, and then you turned up. Am I missing something?

From somewhere deep inside me I found a reserve of strength to lie even more fluently. For this might be the last time I saw Brenda, unless my moon shot came off. So I'd have to take what I could get. To deflect Brenda from what I was really thinking, I began talking about the last two days with Ruth, her drinking and disappearance, the essay and the strange incident in bed, where Ruth had seemed to perceive me as the ghost of boyfriends past.

—I had to get away. She's not present. Or maybe she's too present. On edge. Not like her at all.

Brenda gave no sign of hearing, staring out at the sun glinting on the water.

—Much as I'm enjoying this stroll, she said, my brains are being bouillabaissed. I think we need to find some shade.

We turned back in the direction we had come, Brenda stopping every few metres to lean against the railing, me standing sentry to keep the sun off her neck. How real and vivid she seemed in that shrill afternoon light, the dense hair on the back of her scalp, her shoulders stippled with sun spots, the sweat stains on the hem of her singlet. How much I was going to miss her.

We followed the water to the memorial for the disaster of 1970, beneath the struts of the bridge. Twisted steel girders mounted on pedestals, a list of names. We sat on a bench and Brenda rubbed her hip through her jeans, then rested her head on my shoulder, the cars on the bridge thrumming far above our heads.

—Did your father ever talk about me?

Her voice was offhand, though she was gripping my wrist quite hard.

—No, I said truthfully. He never said word.

—You know, when you first appeared at my door, I thought you'd been sent by him, an emissary from my long-lost son, looking to reconnect. Did he ever tell you I sent him a letter? That was decades ago. A social worker got in touch to tell me about the change in state policy. They were trying to reconnect parents with the children taken from them. At first I wanted nothing to do with it. I'd left that all behind me. It was a regrettable incident, and my troubles were small potatoes, knowing what other women of my generation went through. But eventually I cracked and wrote something short, introducing myself. He must have been about your age at the time. The social worker told me your father replied, said very politely that he wasn't interested in meeting, too much time had passed. Of course I understood, but still, I was devastated. It felt like I'd lost him all over again.

Brenda looked stricken, and I surely didn't look much better; I looked, presumably, like I felt: as if I'd sniffed a bin full of rotten meat. And yet sitting off to the side was my writer's self, rubbing its hairy paws in glee, welcoming the opportunity to bind us ever closer.

—He kept it, I said. The letter. I found it in a cupboard the last time I was at his flat in Geelong. I took it to social services and they helped me to track you down. I still haven't told him I've been seeing you, but I will, I promise. I know it must be hard to stir everything up. I want you to know how much I appreciate you letting me into your life.

It felt good to get my story straight, to flesh things out. Active, *declarative*.

Brenda sat up straight, suddenly composed, as if my words had confirmed something she'd long suspected.

—What is he like?

I have always been good at telling people what they wanted to hear. With lovers, friends, mothers, I was the person I thought they desired, a provisional me, a temporary mistake. I didn't know what version Brenda wanted to hear. Did she want my father to be sinner or saint, absentee or devotee? The bad or the good? Or something in between? What was the least cruel thing I could tell her? Nothing, that was what, and that was what I said. Nothing. Instead, I extracted my phone from my pocket and began scrolling through my photo album, a wasteland of screenshotted receipts, passages from novels, the photos I'd taken of Ruth as Brenda. Eventually I came across my selfie with the American novelist who gave his characters disabilities. He looked vaguely pissed off, arms folded, upper lip curled away from his teeth. Brenda studied the screen, closing one eye and then the other, holding it millimetres from her face.

—A face only a mother could love, I said. Sorry, that just slipped out.

—Indeed, Brenda said, and then began to laugh as if she would never stop.

When enough time had passed I placed *The Widowers* on the bench between us, feeling very much like one of the men between its pages.

THIRD INTERVIEW - STONY CREEK BACKWASH - 22 FEBRUARY

This heat is ridiculous, you might have to carry me home. Now, what were we talking about last time? I seem to recall discoursing on my university years, my parlous living situation, my long-distance relationship with Maria and the way I got *Anchoress* into my editor's hands. Stop me if I've missed anything.

The first year of my studies passed in a blur. They threw us in at the deep end, a gruelling schedule of pracs and tutes. I was particularly ill-suited to teaching; I couldn't project my voice, nor stick to a lesson plan. But you're not here for my professional disappointments – at least, not that kind.

All that year I was corresponding with my editor, sending drafts of *Anchoress* back and forth through the post. He called me his *mystery woman*, imploring me to put firmer ground beneath the reader's feet. *Stet*, I wrote in the margins. *Keep as is.* Not through any writerly pride, I did not think myself capable of following his instructions. Though the book was going to be published, I was the last person to know what it meant, what it was doing and why. I was curt with him, which lent me an air of authenticity.

I'd kept Maria abreast of developments, speaking from the offices of my publisher under the cover of night. She listened with an attentiveness that seemed forced, or else she didn't listen. Despite her reticence, I managed to extract a promise to let me stay in Sydney for a week or two in the summer holidays. But then, the day before I was due to leave, she called to tell me she'd come down with the flu, though she didn't even pretend to sound sick. I offered to nurse her back to health, like in the old days, cursing myself for how pathetic I sounded. She wouldn't budge, so I spent the summer alone.

It was around that time I saw an ad tacked to a noticeboard at Union House, among the call-outs for roommates, announcements of strikes. It said that a young woman was needed to assist with certain private investigations. All very vague, but the price quoted was nothing to sneeze at. I called the number and arranged a meeting the following day at Jimmy Watson's.

Arnold was a blustery man, with a fleshy, Irish face which always looked to be recovering from a hideous sunburn. I took an immediate dislike to him, perhaps because he resembled my father – though in fairness, Arnold was a prick in his own right. Standing at the bar, schooner in hand, he spent a few seconds sizing me up before ushering me to a table in the courtyard.

Arnold got straight to the point, explaining he worked as a private dick and that his bread and butter, as he put it, were affairs of the heart and loins. You must understand that, back then, divorce was reserved for the most wretched lechers and lepers. Since Federation, the state had decided it was preferable for unhappy couples to stay together whatever the cost, and more or less the only way to dissolve that pact was to prove adultery or alcoholism to a court of law. *But how can unhappy couples separate*, Arnold asked me, *if they have no desire to cheat?* Wasn't it unfair that the morally corrupt could slip the surly bonds of matrimony, but the miserably faithful were consigned to spend their lives together till death did them part? Arnold was a Catholic and a rationalist. He wanted the greatest sum of happiness for the greatest sum of people, and if divorce was the way to achieve that, who was he to stand in its way?

Much of his work consisted of what one might expect: stake-outs, tailings and telephoto lenses. But Arnold provided an extra service to couples who had agreed to separate but didn't want to cheat. They paid Arnold to photograph one of them, almost always the husband, in compromising situations with young women who weren't their wives – women such as me. The wives could then present these photos to the court, prove fault, and they would finally be free of each other. Whether those judges believed the photos were authentic was beside the point; it was a piece of necessary theatre to save the state's face.

Arnold assured me my identity would be protected, and my modesty too. A photo on the arm of a man; perhaps the two of us lying fully clothed on a bed. Nothing salacious. He entreated me to think of it as a sort of public service, helping unhappy souls to move on from situations which had brought them nothing but pain, offering fresh starts to people who had married the wrong person.

I didn't know what to say. The job sounded awful, the money great, and I was in desperate need of it. My cleaning shifts had been cut, I was behind on rent at Cumberland House, and there was only so long I could put Carmel off. I thought of what Maria would do in my situation, what *Brenda Shales* would do, the two of them somehow fused in my mind, and I made my decision.

Once or twice a week, I'd meet Arnold at the Oasis, where we'd collect the keys from the owner, who stared at my chest as if he could see the face of Christ in it. We'd repair to a room, where Arnold spent the next hour doing my make-up and fitting me with wigs, a different colour each time, though they all looked the same when the photos came out, colour film still being a luxury back then. Arnold took great pleasure in fussing over me like a mother hen, never letting me peek at the mirror until he was finished. I suspect he was a secret fetishist, that he wished it was him being prettified, but he was entirely professional. I was usually impressed by the final results, the smoky eyes and carmine lips so thoroughly unlike my own. I had a believable, homely beauty, that of a starry-eyed secretary seduced by her boss.

When Arnold finally deemed me ready, we would return to the reception, where the client, as Arnold insisted on calling them, was waiting. I signed the reception book, using the client's surname, which, along with the photos, would be used as evidence in the divorce proceedings. Most of the men didn't acknowledge me, clearly ashamed by the seediness of the business. Instead, they looked at Arnold or their shoes, nodding like chastened schoolboys as Arnold explained how we would proceed. Others went a little overboard, shaking my hand and thanking me in that high-flown, Pommy-inflected Australian that I've always loathed. Some men were determined to bring me down a peg, cracking jokes to Arnold about what other services I provided, saying something along the lines of: *May as well get my five bobs' worth.* To Arnold's credit, he always came to my defence, assuring them I was a good, upstanding girl, and a uni student to boot, and any impropriety would result in the termination of the operation.

I vaguely recognised the politician – a Labor man and staunch unionist, it later transpired, as they all were back then. I remember his softness, the heat of his body radiating through his shirtsleeves as we lay beside each other on the bed. Arnold spent half an hour curating the mise en scène: the half-empty bottle of whisky on the nightstand, clothes strewn about the floor, the man's homburg hung on a bedpost. The politician talked in the tone of a wireless compere, apologising for entangling me in this messy business. He felt great shame, he told me, at having to resort to this. But life was too short to live a lie. He seemed to be working up the courage to tell me something more, but before he could, Arnold interrupted with a clap of his hands, entreating us to look at the camera.

The photo was splattered across the newspapers a few weeks later, the bedclothes pulled up to my chin, the crook of one elbow covering my eyes, the other arm flung out, palm upwards. As Arnold had assured me, there was no way I could be identified, though my bed mate was perfectly visible, the now dishonourable Mr John Higgins staring down the lens as if the camera was in the process of stealing his soul. The photo needed no explanation, we'd been caught red-handed, this man of the people tending to the needs of a 'local constituent', as the journalists referred to me archly in the series of articles which triggered Mr Higgins's resignation and the divorce from his wife of two decades, painted as a long-suffering martyr of her husband's unspeakable peccadilloes.

Don't you just love adultery? Arnold crowed, as he flicked through the tabloid with his stubby fingers. *The sin so bad they had to command against it twice.*

Arnold maintained he hadn't the foggiest how the photograph had made its way into the papers. Perhaps it was a court official with an axe to grind, he suggested, or the owner of the Oasis, but I suspect it was Arnold himself, who wanted a wider audience for his handiwork, who couldn't bear to see it wasted on a handful of law clerks.

When I saw my visage in print, covered up as it was, I felt so ashamed to be part of this man's disgrace. I told Arnold he could find another girl for his seedy business.

But he managed to talk me down off the ledge. He'd been looking for someone to take minutes at certain meetings which he refused to describe unless my discretion was assured. Normally Arnold was a terrible gossip, and the fact he was being so coy made me think with a certain writerly intuition that these meetings would be of interest to me, which indeed proved correct.

I suspect very little good has ever come from secret meetings of men, and the ones I attended with Arnold were no exception. They were held once a week at a community centre in Fitzroy, a dingy space with a trestle table with sandwiches and urns of coffee and tea. There were a few dozen regulars, with drop-ins week to week, married men, all white and comfortably middle class, judging by the cut of their suits.

They called themselves the Husbands Emancipation League, a private interest group formed to resist the Family Law Act which would bring about no-fault divorce, if Gough Whitlam got his way, allowing women to leave their husbands without providing just cause. As I came to learn over the few months I attended those meetings, there were similar groups sprouting up all over Australia, the names of which I still remember: DAD (Dads Against Discrimination); DARL (Divorcees Always Regret Leaving); FORCE (Fathers' Organisation of Revolutionary Custody Entitlement). All of them were threatened by what these laws symbolised: a loss of power and prestige. This feeling was reflected in the media at the time, endless articles framing Australia as teetering on the lip of a precipice, with anarchy at the bottom of the drop, women's rights taken at the expense of men's.

Arnold was chairman of the Melbourne chapter. For the other men, the proposed laws were affairs of the heart and loins, to use Arnold's lexicon, while for him it was an affair of the wallet. He was a pragmatist and knew private investigators would be on borrowed time, professionally speaking, if spouses were simply allowed to up and leave.

He was exceedingly good at telling people what they wanted to hear, beginning every meeting with the Lord's Prayer, following it up with a homily on the institution of Christian marriage. Arnold presented himself as a mover and shaker, with connections in the media and parliament. The other men paid membership fees, which Arnold pocketed, after doling out my wage.

My job was to take minutes. The husbands believed themselves to be part of a revolutionary vanguard, patriots whose exploits would be extolled from some glittering masculine future. My notes, which I typed up back at Cumberland Place, would act as proof for the generations to come that there had been some men brave enough to swim against the current. Quite why they needed *me* to take minutes was a trickier question, as many husbands seemed to resent my presence, glaring at me as if I were their footloose wives, on the verge of leaving them. I think my presence gave their meetings a patina of legitimacy; it allowed them to believe their crusade was enacted in the name of women as well as men. Strangely, it often seemed as if the husbands were speaking directly to me, as if I were their confessor, allowing them to say things they never normally could.

Each man would stand and give his two cents about the new law, their speeches quickly transforming into maudlin stories about the trials of marriage and the many reasons their wives wanted to leave them. All they wanted was the opportunity to be better fathers, lovers and husbands, to fulfil their obligations to the women they professed to love now that their unions were imperilled.

Their speeches were remarkably intimate, the husbands confessing to the things they'd done and those which had been done to them. They told me their unnameable desires, their hopes and fears. It was a form of therapy, I suppose, disguised as politics. But mostly what they talked about was sex, conducting performance reviews of their wives' desire and ability to satisfy them. They framed sexual dissatisfaction as a fate worse than death, even worse than womanhood. They talked about sex as if it were an algebraic equation, a mountain to be climbed. Satisfaction as something which had to be ripped from between the legs of their wives.

Yet though they seemed so resolutely unhappy, the husbands were steadfast in their belief that staying together was preferable to separating. The thought that their wives might be happier without them was so unpalatable they would prefer wedded misery.

At the time, their words struck me as little more than banal, but I've come to know those meetings had very dire consequences. You're too young to remember the Family Court attacks in the early eighties, when judges and lawyers involved in divorce cases were shot dead or blown up. These acts of terrorism were designed to intimidate the legal professionals and also the women whose rights they protected. Those crimes for the most part went unsolved, but I knew deep in my bones that whoever planted those bombs must have attended meetings just like those of the Husbands Emancipation League.

The irony was enough to make me weep. Women were meeting all over the country, planning for a more equitable future, and here I was, diligently scribing for the men who wanted it to remain the same. And though I was appalled by what they said, I'd never heard men speak with such frankness, and I realised this afforded me an insight very few women had. These men wanted to wring so much from that little word *wife*: they wanted them to be mothers, maids, ingenues, sluts, confidantes, accountants, liberated women. No wonder they all were so disappointed.

You probably think me a dead-eyed journalist, sharpening my pencil while these men made nooses of their words. Their testimonies, as they insisted on calling them, did eventually inform

The Widowers, but at the time that was the last thing on my mind. Despite my better judgement, I pitied those men who felt nothing but pity for themselves, these sore winners whose worlds began and ended at the tips of their cocks.

I can't go on anymore, I'm feeling a bit poorly. Now help me up. I need to get back. Chop chop. What are you waiting for?

Don't pout – this is not the last time we'll see each other.

THIRTEEN

I was in deep, the lies piling up, but this next one would be my most audacious yet, more likely to fail than not – but what choice did I have? If this didn't come off I was out of options. One more, then no more, as my mother would say when reaching for the bottle.

My father hugged me like he was about to commit a hate crime, thumping my ribs with the flat of his palm at the entrance to Magma, a cheerless steakhouse on Pakington Street, in the centre of Geelong. In the years since his business went belly up, he'd become fit to the point of sickness. With his gaunt cheeks and shaved and gleaming skull, he looked like he'd just returned from the oncology ward rather than the ocean pool at Eastern Beach.

I had long ago stopped asking what he did for a living, for it was either nothing, or nothing good (last I heard he was soliciting donations for a charity that I was fairly sure was fake). Exercise had replaced entrepreneurship as his one abiding passion. He was usually in bed by seven, and that night he was all but nodding off across the table, before slapping himself sharply on his cheek, flapping his arm to get the waiter's attention. Inspecting the wine list as if proofing it for publication, he reminded me of a pigeon with a broken wing, puffing his chest to ward off predators. He eventually settled on the same bottle he always ordered at our quarterly meetings, a humble Pepperjack, the cheapest on the menu.

—Tonight I want something with a bit of body, my father said, as he had so many times before. In lieu of someone. My shout, of course.

I loathed this charade of bourgeois prosperity, he the provider, me the cringing mendicant, though it sure beat a meal suited to a man of his means – or to mine. Tomahawks ordered, we hacked valiantly through the catch-up. He was fine. I was fine. Ruth was fine too. Nothing of note to report. He yawned and fiddled with his Fitbit. My V/Line back to Footscray seemed aeons away. The only person he didn't ask after was my mother, who *was* fine, as far as things went, chained to a tree in Swan Hill, raging against the final act of a life with its share of misfortunes, my father chief among them. I got the impression that he genuinely didn't think of her, this woman he was married to for the better part of two decades. She was long in the past. To his credit, my father had never once complained about the loneliness he'd inflicted on himself. Things had hardly worked out for him, but he seemed infuriatingly content with his lot in life. *This* was the man I was hoping would save me?

—What's your position on NFTs? He asked me, almost dreamily.

I was saved from answering by a thrum from the slabs of volcanic stone beside our plates as they began to heat up, slowly at first, and then with great ferocity. Magma specialised in 'hot rock dining', where steaks were cooked at the table, lending the restaurant a charnel air, the sound of sizzling flesh punctuated by customers' yelps of pain as they glanced the stones with their hands. My father took his steak cremated, and I was already halfway through mine by the time he was ready to tuck in, field stripping fat from the meat, our faces sheened in sweat.

—Let's get another bottle, he said threateningly. We're having a good time.

—There was something I wanted to talk to you about, I said, when he was good and drunk. I'm working on a new book. It's about a woman called Brenda Shales.

He looked wary, picking meat from between his teeth with the tip of his knife.

—The name rings the vaguest of bells. Wasn't your mother a fan?

Ironic it was my mother's copy of *Anchoress* that had, in a sense, started all this. To take it one step further: my father left, and I became my mother's reader. I drew a deep breath and asked for my inheritance.

—Brenda Shales was very famous. And then she disappeared. Recently, I stumbled across her, and she told me her secrets. But there's a problem . . . How do I put this? She thinks I'm her grandson. She thinks you're her son. Or someone along the lines of you. It's a long story.

—I'll bet it is.

This was my confession, trialled on a more forgiving audience, practice for the mea culpa I'd likely have to make with Brenda, Ruth and – who knew? – the reading public at large.

—Needless to say, I wish it were otherwise. But to get what I want from Brenda, I need to maintain the fiction, which is where you come in. Staff at her nursing home are becoming suspicious.

They want proof I am who I say I am. I'm not, but you get where I'm coming from.

I wanted my father to teach me not to care, not to feel the need to think myself good, to think only and forever of myself. I slid the script across the table, the fleshed-out story of my father. Him adopted into a family of thin-lipped disciplinarians, never knowing who his real mother was. Then Brenda had tried to contact him, decades later. It had all been too much. He hadn't been able to face it, but he'd remembered her name, had known she was a writer. Then his son – me – had caught the writing disease; must be something in the blood. He'd found the letter. Though it was too late for him, he was happy his son could have a relationship with Brenda. Happy for Brenda, too.

—They want to believe me, they just need some convincing. If you read that to them, I'm pretty sure they'll lay off. No-one would go to such great lengths to keep the lie alive. No-one except me.

My father looked like something had herniated. He appeared totally unconvinced.

—Have I ever asked you for anything? I said.

—No, he said, with a great sigh. And that was always a great regret of mine. Besides, I'm not much of an actor.

—No, I said. But you are a salesman.

My father had bought the Freedom Furniture franchise in the arse end of the Howard years, and it was a huge success, until it wasn't. My high school graduation coincided with the recession no-one saw coming, my father least of all. Sales targets weren't being hit, KPs un-Indicated, and head office was reconsidering the viability of every franchise in the Freedom Furniture family. I worked there the final summer, just before I left Geelong for good.

My father was a mystic who believed in a golden ratio of settees and modular sofas which would bewitch any customer. At his direction, I rearranged the shop floor displays in French provincial and gaucho hacienda, neocon pomp and hippie chic. He shrieked at me to lift with my legs, to wipe my fingerprints from anything I touched. Occasionally a customer was foolish enough to enter the store. My father would corner them and deliver his patter.

—Are you living your ideal life?

They looked at him with hostage eyes as he explained his theory of flatpack living, a noxious condition of modernity that favoured disposability over permanence, surface over depth.

—Our furniture is an antidote to that way of life, he told them. It's all in the name: Freedom.

That night, he stuck to the script, adding flourishes of his own. Kind and curt, he spoke to the director of Mercy House as if he was an agnostic customer seeking reassurance he hadn't been had. It was a consummate performance, though I shouldn't have been surprised; my father had been lying a lot longer than I had.

Geelong slid by through the train window, past the strip malls of North Geelong, the former site of my father's store on the shoulder of the Princes Highway. Soon the houses gave way to the industrial zones of Corio, the woodchip mill and the Shell refinery, a spire of flame belching into the night. The train slunk through Lara and out into the paddocks eroded by the suburbs' creep, the You Yangs blotting out the stars. I had a sudden vision of my father as Brenda's son, ripped from his mother's breast, carted off to a family of strangers. In a way it sort of fit. It would provide a neat explanation for the way he was, but he had no excuse, just as I didn't. No, the story of my father was nothing to write home about; he better resembled one of the wifeless men in *The Widowers*, and so did I.

The train was pulling into Deer Park, the lights of Melbourne glittering in the distance, and for a moment I glimpsed my face in the window of the train, shifty and insubstantial. I saw, too, the reality of the situation, pretending to be someone I wasn't to steal a stranger's story, profiting from Brenda's labour and life. How would Brenda feel if she were to discover I wasn't her grandson, that she'd lost her family all over again? Not great, one would imagine. I thought too of Brenda's real son, the one she'd given up. Giving birth, giving up for adoption – they could have picked a better expression. And then there was Ruth, allergic to duplicity and doubletalk. If she found out what I'd done, I couldn't see a scenario in which she declined to kick me to the kerb.

A steep price to see my name on the cover of a book: a *biography*, of all things. I thought back to when I'd confessed my desire to be the next great Australian writer, a notion which struck me now as ludicrous overreach. I was risking everything for what would likely amount to very little, a slim volume politely reviewed, a tidbit of literary arcana. But what else was I to do? Pull out? Fess up? That would achieve nothing, save to salve my conscience. No, I wouldn't stop pretending; instead, I would stop pretending to care.

*

I arrived home to find Ruth scrubbing the skirting board in the bathroom, a cry for help if ever I'd seen one. It was clear something had happened. She looked a little dazed when she saw me, her face red and shining, as if she'd been expecting someone else. She gave a weak wave and returned to the job. With a feeling of trepidation, I brewed a pot of tea, invited her to drink it with me on the back step.

—Helen visited while you were in Geelong. I'd been thinking about her nonstop, and then suddenly there she was with a bottle of chardonnay.

—And did she read it? The essay?

—Oh yes, Ruth said, with a rueful laugh. She'd read it all right. But that's the least of my concerns. She told me something tonight which amounts to nothing at all or something completely unforgivable. It depends how you look at it. I don't mean to sound coy, but I'm still trying to make sense of everything.

Ruth was inviting me to press for more, her face latticed with light through the flyscreen door, but I was preoccupied, wondering whether the director had believed my father's story. I feigned a yawn, stood. I'd had my fill of confession; I was tired of the truth.

FOURTEEN

For a little while at Linh's, it was like nothing had happened. Brenda, the story of my father, the growing distance between me and Ruth. Things had settled, if only for a little while, the deception and dissimulation now in the past. I didn't see those few hours of calm for what they were: the eye of the storm.

It had just gone eight in the morning when Ruth and I arrived at Linh's unit in Seddon to look after Aloysius while Linh was at a conference. Linh was his emotional support human, and the little runt lost the plot if left alone for more than a few minutes. We let ourselves in with the key in the letterbox, our footfalls loud on the polished floorboards. The living room was spotless and got the morning light. We stood on the threshold, while Aloysius eyed us warily. I felt a sort of release, like a window had been opened in the stuffy room of my soul. How cooped up I'd felt since meeting Brenda, existentially speaking. The stress and strangeness seemed to lift and float away, spores carried off on a breeze.

Ruth and I thumbed through the bookshelves, raided the fridge, Aloysius nestled between us as we lounged on the suede settee, a Sorrento, a Freedom model, I recalled with a certain fondness. We chatted about nothing much, but to me it felt like everything, proof the thread between us hadn't been severed. Ruth rested her head on my shoulder while she scrolled on her phone.

—This feels nice, she said, sounding half-asleep. Shall we see something at the Sun?

Then I felt her stiffen. She passed me the phone with the film listings. Among the remakes and blockbusters, the Sun Theatre was screening the film adaptation of *The Widowers* as part of a month-long showcase of Australian cinema, 'Oi! Oi! Oi!': well-worn classics like *Wake in Fright* and *Muriel's Wedding* and commercial flops like *The Widowers*, which had been rightly panned when it was released in the early eighties, reborn as kitsch in the decades to come.

—It's probably time to get to work, Ruth said, pulling out a package of study drugs. I have a lot on my plate.

The drugs made Ruth grim and affectless, chain-smoking on the back porch with her laptop on her knees, fielding requests from editors to engage in further daughter-boarding. It seemed a terrible effort to speak, as if she were drawing the words up from a cool, dark lake. Ruth's withdrawal was down to her mother's visit, I knew, but still I was reluctant to ask what had passed between them. Better not to make a fuss. It would only upset her to talk about it. Like the rest of the world I'd find out how she was feeling in the next piece she wrote.

I had work to do as well, transcribing Brenda's monologue under the Westgate Bridge, fleshing out the parts between her confessions with the narration of a prim and prissy good boy, grateful for the gift of Brenda's words: my shadow self, or perhaps its opposite, a man not much like me basking in the glow of the approved biographer. My narrator's rectitude was just as fake as the conditions I'd inflicted on him in previous iterations of my binned autobiographical novel. The Ruth character was even worse: a Ruth without the ruthlessness; a noble, sober puritan who wholeheartedly endorsed the book about Brenda. The two of them spent their scenes walking along the canal to Coode Island or the Heavenly Queen Temple, cooking dishes of extreme complexity, watching slow and stately cinema, making love like sombre procreators. I hated every word of them.

Aloysius was quite taken with me, scooting his bony bum against the top of my foot while I worked. He cajoled me to the backyard, cavorting across the grass, bullied me into tug of war with a festering rubber chicken. He wouldn't let go, even as I lifted his skinny body into the air, Ruth filming on her phone. Perhaps I was a dog person, despite the allergies. Maybe I needed to take care of someone who couldn't take care of me. As I spun Aloysius, I felt my phone buzzing in my pocket, a call I was tempted to ignore, but now was not the time to drop the ball, though I did drop the dog, losing my grip on the chicken as I levered out my mobile, Aloysius sprawling on the grass with a mournful yelp.

—Duty calls, Ruth said, rolling her eyes.

It was the director, calling to offer his apologies, to formally invite me back into the fold. Instead of relief, I felt resignation.

The show would go on and on, and there was nothing I could do to stop it.

—Well, he said, when I didn't answer, I'll pass you over to Brenda.

My heart was so loud I was sure Ruth could hear it. I scuttled down the side of the house.

—Brenda? How are you?

—That was the first thing you asked me, the first words out of your mouth. Can you make a wild guess how I'm feeling? You let him call here without speaking to me? My son. Your *father*.

She said the last word like a curse, and that's how I felt: cursed, doomed to be forever on the verge of being found out, dangling over the edge of a cliff, lacking the guts to let go. It was exhausting, living in this hysterical register, in which every word I said was a weapon I turned upon myself. I couldn't keep this up much longer – but then again I could, because it would be infinitely worse to have sunk this low and have nothing to show for it.

—Let me make it up to you, I said. What are you doing tomorrow night?

Linh returned just as it was getting dark and made straight for the dog.

—I've missed you, you beautiful, beautiful boy.

They garrotted Aloysius, raining kisses on his snout, until he whined in protest.

—I hope he wasn't too much trouble. I know he can be a little clingy.

Simon was holed up at his parents' farm outside Hamilton, reworking the ending of his novel. In his absence, Linh seemed altogether lighter, and who could blame them? With grace and good humour, Linh launched into a story about the travails of the nine-to-five pet owner. In the six months they'd had him, Aloysius had filled a hole in Linh's life they hadn't known existed. Thankfully Linh could bring him to the Docklands arts precinct where they yawned away the work week, assessing grant applications for climate change-themed musical theatre and trans vampire romps in a disused commercial precinct on the windswept marina. It was a far cry from the world Linh had written about in their short story collection, *The Morning After*, a book of pregnancy scares and text message break-ups, stories cadged from friends and fuck buddies. Back then Linh was more designer drugs than designer dogs, and it was this reputation that had precipitated the job offer from a savvy arts institution. Linh was wary of accepting, though eventually they did, telling themselves they'd find time to write in the morning, they'd be the same writer they'd always been, except with super and savings. They took the job in part to please their parents, who despite the success of *The Morning After* had told Linh they hadn't emigrated from Ho Chi Minh City so Linh could write about broken condoms and butt stuff. But since then, they'd barely written a word, published nothing, and when their parents stumped up the down payment on the unit in Seddon, Linh resigned themselves to the life of a mortgaged young professional.

—So, what are you two writing?

The sentence was dripping with the resentment of the frustrated former artist, who'd traded time for money. Linh was fond of telling us we were the last real artists they knew, meaning we had no dependents or impediments. No money either. It often felt like Linh wanted us to apologise for the way we'd chosen to live, and sometimes we hammed it up, claiming to desire security and stability, though most of the time we didn't. Other times we told Linh to quit and join us in a life of noble precarity, though Linh's family had different expectations from ours. They expected more. We resented Linh's resentment, their jealousy of a life which was available to them, should they choose it. So when we talked about what we were writing, we were talking about our lives, the blood sacrifices in lifestyle and earning capacity.

—Now that I'm the poster girl for filial hit pieces, Ruth said, a British magazine wants me to write about the symbol of the monstrous mother-writer through history: Doris Lessing and Muriel Spark, leaving kids with dickhead husbands in colonised countries. Jean Rhys, whose baby died while she was out on a bender. Products of their time, victims of history and circumstance.

We discussed her progress over a single ciggie shared between the three of us, beneath a woolly, smoke-filled sky.

—They want me to look at the contemporary iteration of motherhood writing. A thin excuse for me to further bag out Helen. These motherhood novels are interesting, though, in that the writers are almost expected to loathe it. It's all about the strictures of domesticity, the effect on an artist's ability to work. Weirdly, it's blokes who seem more passionate about parenthood.

—Penance, Linh said. An acknowledgement the world doesn't need more novels about troublesome men. A sound business decision, too.

—Dadbod literature, I said. Most straight male writers seem like they've been fixed by a vet. Like they've never had an erection in their lives.

—Speaking as an arts administrator, Linh said, men writing about their erections does not play well with funding bodies – nor readers.

While Ruth was on the toilet, I gave Linh the elevator pitch for the book, the biography of a once-famous writer overlooked by the vicissitudes of history and culture.

—You're telling Linh about Brenda?

Ruth was standing in the doorway, wiping her hands on the seat of her pants.

—Brenda? Linh sat up straighter. As in Brenda Shales? As in the writer no-one's heard of for half a century? Are you saying she's *alive*?

I clutched an imaginary microphone and said, after a long pause:

—No comment.

Then I told Linh the whole saga: the chance encounter at the pool, my visit to Mercy House, where Brenda had admitted me into her life. For the past few weeks she'd been telling me how her novels came into being, which was proving quite the story. The book was coming together alarmingly quickly. When it was finished, Linh, with their network of professional connections, would be the first to know.

—All of this sounds very mysterious, Linh said. And, might I say, exceedingly fundable. So, what are you waiting for? Show me what you've got.

Linh and I had been each other's first readers since we'd met in an undergrad writing workshop, The Story of You, exposing each other's fatal flaws over jugs of Carlton Draught and the Lucky Strikes Linh had smuggled back from La Paz at pubs and cafes around Melbourne Uni. Linh's metier was infection, orifices and discharge: *auto-erotic fiction*, as they'd described it in class, to a resounding silence. The consensus was I couldn't write women. They strolled with great poise through the fetid rooms of my stories, trying not to gag.

—Make your women cringe when you sit at your desk, Linh had said.

I was adept at writing male dysfunction, but couldn't bring myself to have a female character do anything bad, feel anything wrong. In later years I hit on a solution: write the male unravelling, then change his pronouns. Abjection hung better off women, I came to think; rage and frustration became transgressive when bellowed from their mouths.

That afternoon, as the three of us sprawled around Linh's living room, I played the recording of the interview beneath the Westgate Bridge, traffic whirring in the background. Brenda confessed to that strange job with the private investigator, those terrible meetings of men. Immediately I was drawn back into her story, the strange confluence of history and incident.

While Brenda talked, Ruth googled, tallying Brenda's confessions against the public record. With an intake of breath, she passed around her phone, showing us an article about the spate of terrorism incidents in Australia in the eighties, fuelled by the changes to divorce law. Beneath a black-and-white photograph of the Family Law Court of Australia, its facade a pile of rubble, the article detailed the murder of judges and lawyers who had overseen no-fault divorce cases, the bombings of cars and houses and finally the court itself. Despite a half-million-dollar reward, the cases remained unsolved until 2020, when a man in his seventies was charged with some of the crimes. As Brenda had observed, the cases had been characterised at the time not as a trend of domestic terrorism and intimidation, but rather as the consequences of a law which had gone too far, rending the fabric of the nation.

—Am I right in saying that the men in those meetings are the ones Brenda wrote about in *The Widowers*? Ruth said. The reason *The Widowers* is so raw is because it's real, those words ripped from men's unsuspecting mouths.

—Unethical, I said. But necessary.

I hoped one day people would say the same about what I'd done.

—So presumably they're the ones who brought the suit against Brenda, Linh said. This is all very timely. Angry men are quite the rage in the discourse.

—I get it now, Ruth said. Your book, I mean. It's not just a who, what and when. It actually has something to say.

—But when do we get to meet her? Linh asked.

—Yes, Ruth said. It's not fair you're keeping Brenda all to yourself.

One more lie to add to the agenda. Now I had to find a way to keep Ruth and Brenda apart, for the two of them meeting would bring everything out in the open, which was the last place I wanted it.

FIFTEEN

It had been three days since I'd last seen Brenda, and I'd missed her in a way that felt dangerous. I was in her thrall, and she was in my mine, if she could get past my latest betrayal. I'd kept my father from her, which needed some explaining. But I would win her back, seduce her, figuratively speaking, to find out what happened next. Brenda would be my salvation or damnation, there was nothing in between. I used to think the same about Ruth, about salvation, at least, but now I wasn't so sure.

I saw Brenda, but she couldn't see me. She was standing before the Sun, dressed up for the occasion in a charcoal smock and cowboy boots, hair combed into some kind of order: dressed up to say goodbye? I peered around the trunk of a gum on the corner of Canterbury Street, watching Brenda scanning the crowd for my face. She looked stiff and awkward, out of place in the sea of millennials streaming into the theatre. I made my approach with confidence, slow-striding and chest out, as if nothing had happened. Relief when I saw how relieved she was to see me, a crackle of electricity when we hugged, crushing the posy of dried perennials I'd brought as penance. I had her just where I wanted her.

—I can't believe I'm doing this, she said, as the usher scanned the tickets.

Toting popcorn and post-mix Cokes, we took our seats in the front row, the theatre surprisingly full. Some moviegoers clutched well-worn copies of *The Widowers*: bespectacled men with Hapsburg chins, birdy women with gender studies haircuts. *Writers.* Little did they know greatness was in their midst. I tried to shield Brenda with my body, as if she were at risk of assassination; I wasn't quite ready to share her yet.

When the houselights dimmed, I leant in and began whispering my apology, the story I'd been practising the whole way from Footscray. Before I'd really got going, she stopped me with a hand placed on my thigh.

—I've been through worse. Let's be good colonial subjects, and pretend nothing happened.

The Widowers was a sanitised version of Brenda's novel, a tonal mess. It began with tracking shots of a rural township in the style of Terrence Malick: winnowing wheatfields; wide, empty streets; a bones-and-feathers voiceover, which made Brenda squirm in her seat.

There's a widower in all of us, she simpered, as the camera zoomed in on the trunk of a ghost gum. *We're all lonely travellers, walking down this road called life, looking for a special somewhere, someone, to call home. When I first arrived in town I thought I was there to help the widowers, but in the end, it was the widowers who helped me.*

At first Brenda watched through the fingers of a hand over her eyes, the other manacled around my wrist.

—Let me know when it's over, she whispered.

—Which part?

—All of it.

After the languorous opening, the film performed a ridiculous about face, shifting to an office in inner-city Melbourne, where the plucky protagonist, Gina, a busty blonde who wore nothing but jumpsuits, worked as a marriage counsellor. Gina hears of the epidemic of women who had upped stumps from a rural town on the border of New South Wales, whose left-behind husbands were known colloquially as the Widowers. Gina is dispatched to help them win their women back, teaching the finer points of husbandhood in a series of jaunty montages which brought a hail of laughter from the audience. Gina demonstrates the correct technique for sweeping and washing the dishes, tying aprons around the bellies of the sunburnt farmers. She conscripts a mincing stylist to give each widower a proto-*Queer Eye* makeover, entreating them to trade in their flannies and shapeless jeans for bell-bottoms and loud floral shirts. There was something off about all their accents, they were too broad to be believable.

The only true widower in the film is a shearer called Harry, a flaxen-haired stud who looked pulled from the trenches of Gallipoli, forever riding a white horse through the town, shirtless and glistening. He comes to Gina for grief counselling after the loss of his wife, one thing leads to another and Gina offers herself on the barn floor in the middle of a storm, in a series of sex scenes so graphic they seemed to belong to a different film entirely. The audience was in stitches by the time the women all returned, giving a lusty cheer when each wife walked through the door, ready to give their blokes a second chance. Brenda was laughing too, a hacking, cacophonous sound, soaring above the maudlin strings of the soundtrack.

The bar was standing room only, though Brenda snagged us a table outside on Ballarat Street, pointedly rubbing her hip while a couple fell over themselves to vacate their seats.

—I have to say I quite enjoyed that, she said. I've always thought a strong negative reaction preferable to a blandly positive one.

We recapped scenes from the film, marvelling at its magnificent ineptitude. Of all the bizarre interpretations enacted upon *The Widowers*, the film ranked as the strangest, reducing the novel to a simple love story, and a tawdry one at that. Brenda explained that she had signed away the rights in the first few glorious months following publication, before the backlash had begun. An Australian production company stumped up for location scouting and B-roll of the Victorian countryside. The money ran out and shooting was repeatedly delayed, until the option was bought by an English studio who recast the film as a sort of romantic comedy, shooting on a back lot outside London with a cast of British actors putting on dinky-di accents. When the film was finally released, years later, to unanimous opprobrium and non-existent ticket sales, Brenda was mired in the court case, just beginning to comprehend the mess she was in.

—More on that later, she said. If you're a good boy. But don't look now, we seem to have been rumbled.

I swivelled and saw Ruth and Linh on the other side of Ballarat

Street, Aloysius slinking between their legs. Ruth was waving uncertainly, head tilted to the side. How long had they been standing there? I noticed how close Brenda and I were sitting to make ourselves heard over the drinkers' din, leaning over the table, foreheads almost touching. I didn't want Ruth getting the wrong idea.

—Someone you know? Brenda said, with a grim little smile.

—Ruth, I managed to squawk, trying to keep my face in check.

So this is how it ends, I thought, and then felt, a pall of dread draped over me as the two of them loped across the road. An ambush, plain and simple, and no doubt Ruth's idea. She'd known where I was going, and was trying to get between me and Brenda – why I didn't know, but it couldn't be anything good. And then they were flanking our table, as if cutting off all means of escape, Ruth radiant in a bamboo pyjama suit, her skin golden in the bar's lamplight.

—My god, Linh said, with a smile that showed each of their clean, white teeth. It's true. You're Brenda Shales.

Brenda gave a pained smile and cupped a hand around her ear.

—Could you speak up, dear? I think some people inside didn't hear you.

I gave a hollow bark that could have been construed as a laugh.

—Brenda, I said. Meet Linh.

—Charmed. And this must be Ruth. It's nice to put a face to a name after all this time.

Brenda spoke with a cheeriness that struck me as completely false, though Ruth noticed nothing amiss, crouching over the table and enfolding Brenda in a hug.

—Brenda, how lovely to meet you; I was worried I'd never have the chance.

—Will you join us for a drink? Brenda asked. I'm sure I can rustle up a couple of extra chairs.

—I don't think we will, Ruth said, perhaps seeing something in my face. But why don't we have you over for dinner – say, the day after tomorrow? Linh can come too.

—Two outings in one week, Brenda said. I don't know if my heart will take it. But yes, that sounds lovely. Now, do you mind if I borrow your boyfriend for a couple more hours? I still have a few things I'd like to get off my chest. We won't be long, I promise.

As my world crumbled, Ruth kissed me on both cheeks, her hair smelling faintly of cinders, then walked off into the gloom. If Ruth and Brenda spent any time together, my deception would come crashing down. Brenda would realise I was not her grandson, and Ruth would realise Brenda thought I *was* her grandson. I had to find a way out.

—What's the matter? Brenda said. Your face looks positively cubist.

—You can't come to dinner.

—Why ever not? I promise I'm house-trained.

—I need to tell you something. I haven't been completely honest about the circumstances of our meeting. With Ruth, I mean. I haven't told her I'm your grandson. She made an assumption which I failed to correct, and then it seemed too late.

Could Brenda see through me? This was skirting dangerously close to the truth, but it was my last resort.

—Sounds like quite the pickle. Why have you been so cagey? You can tell your nan.

I pictured all the possible lies hung like garments on a rack. Brenda stared with obdurate blankness, for all the world like the photograph on the back of her books. Then, in a shocking turn of events, she smiled.

—You *are* my grandson, aren't you? You haven't been telling me porky pies?

That mouldy old chestnut. Hadn't we moved past this? My cheek began to throb; I was clenching my teeth quite hard, angry to still be in this ridiculous position, angry at Brenda for never correcting the nurse's mistake. Unfair as it was, I couldn't forgive her for what I'd done to her.

—Yes, I said. Yes, I am your grandson.

—That's all I needed to hear, Brenda said. She smiled sadly. If you don't want me to come, I won't. But what are you going to tell dear Ruth?

Despite the pain in her hip, Brenda insisted on walking back to Mercy House, leaning heavily on my shoulder as we trudged along. Even though I'd warded off the most immediate threat, the evening had an air of finality. I had a feeling I wouldn't be returning to Mercy House.

By the time we'd turned onto Beverley Street, Brenda was clutching my arm, her breath coming in ragged gasps. It took five minutes to walk the final few metres to Mercy House, but we eventually made it, me half-carrying her through the entrance, past the deserted reception desk, and down the corridor to room twenty-seven. I helped get her shoes off and laid her on the bed, her heart hammering against my belly, slowly slowing, until she had recovered enough to sit up. I gave her a pill, and a second for the queen. And then I waited for her to tell me everything.

FOURTH INTERVIEW - MERCY HOUSE - 25 FEBRUARY

Can you feel it? We're getting close. Very soon you'll have squeezed this lemon for all it's worth. For what use is the confessor once everything's been said? So now you know how *The Widowers* was made: I nicked the words of those men and twisted them to fit my purpose, though they still saw themselves in them. But we're not up to that quite yet.

Anchoress was published at the end of 1973, just in time for Christmas. My editor told me to ignore the reviews and he didn't have to ask twice. There was a second printing and then a third but still the sight of it in a shop window or on a commuter's lap brought me nothing but shame.

I hadn't spoken to Maria for months, my calls and letters unanswered. Eventually I got hold of one her housemates, who told me she'd moved out long before, that she still owed them rent. It was the same story with the abortion clinic. Maria had stopped turning up for work, had even left a pay cheque uncollected. Neither of them seemed concerned; Maria disappeared all the time. And yet she was never far from my thoughts. It was just like me to worry about Maria during my moment of triumph.

I scraped through my exams by the skin of my teeth and accepted a position in Tatura, a town in the Goulburn Valley. I dreaded the move, despite consoling visions of writing on the verandah overlooking the wheatfields, a blue heeler lazing at my feet. The crucial court date was approaching when no-fault divorce would become a reality and the men from the Husbands Emancipation League were reaching a feverish pitch. Increasingly they had the air of men condemned, making final pleas for stays of execution, which I dutifully transcribed in duplicate. From the beginning I'd kept copies for myself, without quite knowing why.

The husbands directed their vitriol at me, their native informant, stand-in for the women whom they needed and resented in desperate, equal measure. It was almost as if they knew what I had in store for them. And then one night I couldn't bring myself to leave the house, the prospect of spending another second in that smoky room filled me with an unnameable dread. I skipped the meeting, then another. My book was selling after all; I could put that world behind me.

One night, I was just drifting off to sleep when Carmen yelled from downstairs that there was a man was on the phone. It was one of Maria's housemates. He sounded frightened, told me Maria had rocked up out the blue, though none of them had heard from her in months. She couldn't string a sentence together, seemed confused as to where she was. They'd thought she was drunk or tripping, but as the hours wore on and there was no change in her they'd started to get worried. They were on the verge of calling the hospital when Maria had begged them to call me instead.

I borrowed Carmel's guttural Kingswood and drove all night from Melbourne to Sydney, reaching the city's outskirts just as dawn was breaking.

Maria answered the door, arms folded, face impassive, studying me with that piercing look of hers, as if she could see beneath my skin. Ignoring my outstretched arms, she turned on her heel and padded back inside.

I followed her down the darkened hallway to the kitchen, bathed in the cool, blue first light of the day. After opening the window, she lit a joint, ashing into the kitchen sink, while I prepared tea, her housemates nowhere to be seen.

Maria had lost weight, the skin stretched tight over her face, the tendons in her neck and forearms picked out in sharp relief. Her features seemed to have shrunk, save for her eyes, which loomed from their sockets like the lanterns of some deep-sea fish. But it was her hair which had undergone the most precipitous change. *I've been pinked*, she said, gesturing to the red, raised skin on her scalp. It was a shearing term, she explained, meaning the closest shave possible without drawing blood.

And then she began to tell me about the shock therapy courses she'd submitted to once a fortnight for the past few months. Depression she could handle, but the periods of frenzied activity between her depressive episodes, when the world seemed to speed up and she was so restless her bones felt on the verge of bursting out of her skin, absolutely terrified her. These manic periods were accompanied by black holes in her memory, in which she'd try to piece together exactly what she'd done and with whom. She'd find her bedroom filled with crap she had no memory of buying, waking up in the beds of strange men and women with no idea how she'd got there. She eventually sought help, though help seemed the furthest word from what the treatment entailed.

Every fortnight she'd attend the Chelmsford Clinic in Pennant Hills, where she was sedated, shocked and kept under observation. The doctors administered *psychosurgery*, as they called it, barbiturates and invasive procedures in lieu of the dreaded talking cure. Maria felt like a different person when she awoke, her self floating free above her, the past a series of loose threads that never seemed to knit together. She hadn't told anyone what she'd been going through; it didn't tally with the image of the *empowered* woman she was so desperate to project. Some of the more hopeless cases at Chelmsford underwent an experimental procedure called deep sleep therapy, in which they were placed into a coma and shocked and shocked again without ever being brought back to consciousness. Maria wasn't that far gone yet, she assured me, but listening to her story I knew that if she continued down this road, I would lose her forever. I told her I wouldn't leave the house unless she came with me.

She slept the whole way back to Melbourne, as I blasted down the Hume Highway, past Goulburn, Yass, Gundagai, Tarcutta, Albury, Glenrowan, Seymour, stopping only to refuel or stuff my face with roadside meat. I watched Maria out the corner of my eye, her shaved head pressed against the window. I had the childlike fear she'd never wake again. It was all I could do to keep my eyes on the road.

*

The book was selling better than I could ever have expected, my PO box stuffed with letters fair and foul, requests for interviews, all of which I ignored. I had only Maria on my mind. Since she'd returned from Sydney, Maria had put on weight, her skin browned in the sun. She'd kept her head shaved, enjoying the reaction it produced in others, especially Carmel, who sucked her teeth every time they crossed paths. It seemed the worst of it, whatever it was, had passed.

As the new school year approached, I sent Arnold a letter of resignation and arranged for Carmel to pick up my mail and forward it to my new address in the country.

It was stinking hot the day we visited Nell and Vince in Balaclava to say goodbye. Maria was coming to live with me in Tatura, and we didn't know when we'd be back.

When Nell saw her daughter standing on the doorstep, she went white as a sheet, clutched her chest, and seemed to swoon back into the arms of her husband, who carried her to the living room settee. All quite Victorian.

It took a long time to understand why she had responded so dramatically, Nell and Vince talking in Italian, Maria translating laboriously. As far as I could make out, Maria's appearance had reminded Nell of something that had happened just after they immigrated to Australia, before Maria was born. One day in 1939, an army platoon had arrived at Nell and Vince's St Kilda tenement. They had a list with Vince's name on it, and made it clear Vince was to pack a bag and come with them. He was driven to a prisoner of war camp in Murchison, a small town on the Goulburn River. Vince had been naturalised before the war began, indeed he was a *White Australian* who'd fled Mussolini and the Blackshirts, but in the eyes of the Australian government Vince was a potential fascist sympathiser and saboteur.

He whiled away the war years with other denizens of Axis countries, the Germans in one compound, the Italians in another and, later, the Japanese in a third. The camps were hastily built on a tract of red dirt ringed by razor wire, a windswept nowhere a few kilometres from town. The men slept on camp beds in huge canvas tents, terrorised by mosquitoes in the night and flies during the day. They ate spam or strips of kangaroo meat so tough they had to soak it in water in order to get it down. The soldiers treated the prisoners with benign indifference; it was obvious from the first these bewildered men weren't enemies of the state, instead just poor souls with unfortunate surnames in the wrong place at the wrong time. The men picked peaches and cherries in the orchards surrounding the camp. For Vince the work wasn't all that different from the summers he'd spent picking tomatoes in the countryside outside Bologna as a teenager (although this time he wasn't getting paid, a fact that didn't escape the local fruit pickers, who resented the free labour the inmates provided). The prisoners weren't allowed to send letters in their native language, lest a fascist code was embedded in them. Vince had attempted a few missives in English, though Nell couldn't make heads nor tails of them. Then she'd moved, and the letters stopped coming, and Nell had given her husband up for dead. In Italy, when soldiers came for someone, they seldom returned.

Towards the end of Vince's time in the camp, a recruiter arrived from a football club in Melbourne. With the help of a translator, he spent the afternoon explaining the strange game of

Australian Rules, a name which seemed appropriate for the ordeal the prisoners were enduring. The league was facing a shortfall of players, as most able-bodied men were fighting on the other side of the world. The recruiter had been given permission to fill the team sheets with the most athletic prisoners, their one ticket out of the camp. The prisoners were given a few hours to practise kicking and handballing, then were taken to a sun-baked oval in town and separated into teams, and the game commenced. The prisoners were playing for their freedom, and the game quickly descended into an orgy of violence, packs of men descending on the Sherrin, a tangle of knees and elbows, while the townsfolk cheered from the sidelines. Vince stayed on the boundary, praying the ball never came his way, as he watched his fellow prisoners scrap and pummel. The barracks resembled a field hospital by the end of the game, broken ribs and limbs, terrible concussions. In the decades since, the sight of a football had filled Vince with terror, which had made it difficult to truly assimilate, as the most sacred thing in this country was its precious Australian Rules.

Once the Italians had surrendered, and Mussolini had been strung up by his feet, the Australians finally permitted the Italians to return home. The camp's doctors shaved Vince's head and rubbed him down with delousing shampoo. When he turned up at the boarding house where Nell had taken a room, Vince looked like a ghost back from the dead. And it was this image she'd seen when she'd opened the door to Maria, the deathly version of the daughter she loved. On our way out the door, they hugged us as if we were shipping off to the front.

Before leaving Melbourne, I drove to my parents' house. It looked the same as ever, large and sullen, though the trellis was back, tacked to the struts of the balcony. I thought of my mother laid up in bed, a book in her lap, my father bristling in the bank. I placed a copy of *Anchoress* on the front step, closed the front gate and didn't look back.

Tatura was deep in the Goulburn Valley, a strange name, as the land is flat as a sheet. The minute I stepped into the classroom, I knew I'd made a terrible mistake. Rows of jug-eared dullards, slit-eyed sadists. Children. What had possessed me to think I could be a teacher?

Maria and I were the only people in Tatura between the ages of sixteen and thirty, and I was glad to have her there, even in such diminished condition. The able-bodied had left for greener pastures, and the leftovers consisted of sad, wiry men who ogled us in the pubs, and plump women in pinafores who glared at us in the shops. After a few such encounters, we took to staying home in the evenings and on weekends, holed up in our draughty worker's cottage, a low-slung thing with a wraparound verandah and floorboards a foot wide. It was on the edge of town, overlooking the wheatfields, which at first light looked like a great, grey sea.

We were able to go weeks without men, though occasionally our loins got the better of us and we drove into one of the neighbouring towns – Shepparton or Kyabram, Echuca or Nagambie, a different one each time – and did the rounds of the pubs. Despite a few hair-raising experiences, we usually found what we were looking for.

Maria managed the correspondence forwarded from Carmel, the only person in Melbourne who knew where we were. Letters from readers, positive and negative, missives from my editor announcing this success or that. He was pressing me about the next book, a prospect I had hardly considered.

Maria and I merged together in a way I now find difficult to explain. She was brash and I was the steadying hand; I was the kindling and she was the fire. Together, we made one perfectly functional human, and that was what it felt like, strange as it sounds. It felt like we were the same person. And though she still suffered from the occasional bout of dolour and delirium, as we called them, they were fewer and further between, and during them I treated her exactly the same as I did when she was fully herself: not as a sick person who needed tending to, but as my friend. She said my presence was better than any drug; it gave her something to hold on to when she felt her sense of self slipping away.

When the Family Law Act was ratified, Maria and I got stonkingly drunk at the pub in town. The victory felt personal, the perfect exclamation point to the hours I'd spent at those meetings. At home we picked through the transcripts from the Husbands Emancipation League, which I still had with me, cackling at their plaintive words. We had just got stuck into the sherry when Maria said I should write a book about my experience. The idea struck me as mad on the night, but it began to grow on me over the next few days.

By the time the holidays rolled around, I had very little else to do but write. I spent the summer redrafting the testimonies, resisting the temptation to make them too neat, preferring the rawness and banality of speech verbatim. I imagined they were speaking not to me, but to their wives, revealing themselves at their most unvarnished. Finally, I knitted the testimonies together with the barest of narratives, a woman living at the ends of the earth, an empty vessel for the men to project themselves into. It was a quick process, remarkably quick, the words pouring out in a sort of controlled fury, all of it finished by the time school went back. My editor had begged for an author photo for the latest reprint of *Anchoress*, so before I sent off the new manuscript, Maria and I spent an evening fooling around with her camera, sometimes she behind the lens, sometimes me, taking ridiculous author photos, staring sternly into the lens, chins in hands, cigarettes smouldering between our knuckles.

My editor wanted to know where the stories had come from, and I told him the same thing I told the prosecutor: nothing. He rushed *The Widowers* into print, timing its publication with the day the Act took effect. Before I knew it, it was out in the world – and that was when my trouble truly started.

I shouldn't have walked to the cinema. I think I might have overextended myself. Could you find my pills?

There, that's much better. Now, where was I?

The reviews were so savage they took my breath away, and in letters from readers I was called every name under the sun. Maria thought it the highest praise to produce such visceral reactions, though I was thankful for the anonymity of that name, Brenda Shales, *la belle dame sans merci of the Antipodes*. How utterly ridiculous! I was able to convince myself it had nothing to do with me.

The prize from Switzerland came like a very lucrative bolt from the blue, which I deposited in an account in both our names. Maria popped champagne at the bank and sprayed it over my head. I lived in fear of another letter informing me that there had been a mistake and I'd have to give the money back, that all of it was a very vivid dream.

Oh I don't feel well at all.

The men from the Husbands Emancipation League launched their suit eighteen months after the book was published. There was no denying I'd violated the non-disclosure forms Arnold had made me sign a lifetime before. I'd stolen the men's words, impugned their reputations, if not their names, and they were coming for every dollar I had. Though it wasn't a matter of money, they assured my publisher; they were standing up for the rights of men, of man. I didn't have a leg to stand on, legally speaking. My publisher advised me to settle before brushing me off for good, he wanted nothing more to do with me. Maria wanted me to fight, go public, name and shame Arnold and his not-so-merry men, but I knew Arnold could do the same to me. He knew my real name, and he had those incriminating photos. It was mutually assured destruction.

In an out-of-court settlement, the Husbands Emancipation League was awarded the royalties from *The Widowers*, though I managed to hang on to the prize money. I promised to keep quiet about what I'd seen and heard in those meetings, though really the cat was out of the bag. They could have got the book pulped, but it was in their interest to keep it in print; Arnold was a pragmatist to the last. They even got my publisher back on board. The book kept selling, though I never saw another dollar from my writing.

Ironic, isn't it? I stole these men's stories to make a name for myself, and now you're here stealing mine. A male reclamation project, is that how you conceive of it? Half a century of come-uppance? Tell me, what is it you think we're doing here? What do you *want* with—

PART THREE

SIXTEEN

I'd imagined many different endings during those restless weeks. Tossing on the sweaty mattress, staring at my computer, I'd imagined all the ways it might unravel, variations on a theme of shame and humiliation. I'd stuff up, slip, Brenda or Ruth would find a discrepancy in my story, in me. Mercy House would dig a little deeper, or my father would suffer a crisis of conscience, make my confession for me. The threat was so omni-directional it was hardly worth worrying about, because there was nothing I could do to prevent it. Yes, even then, I still believed it was out of my hands.

Most likely, I'd get what I wanted from Brenda – a book with my name on it, beneath or above hers – and then the risk would multiply like a virus, every reader another person who might unmask me, the critics emerging from their garrets to take me to task. It was sure to come out, the hoax, the scandal, my name forever tarnished. But that would all come after the writing world had trained its eyes on me. Yes, the other writers would hate me for my success, and I'd welcome their hatred, even if it proved to be my undoing. I was resigned to losing everything, suffering for my art, a synonym for career.

But in fact the end, when it came, was nothing like that. Of all the scenarios I'd imagined, this one had never occurred to me. It was, truly, the last thing I expected.

When Brenda collapsed, my first thought was for the book. Her face changed, like a cloud had passed over the sun, then her eyes flickered shut and she slumped forward – slowly enough, thankfully, that I could stop her from sliding off the bed. Since the second pill, (or was it the third?), her breathing had grown progressively slower, more laboured, and she had to pause between sentences just to get the air in. But I had been determined to get to the end, ignoring Brenda's silent entreaties, looks which said, clearer than any words could: *MERCY*.

It was past two in the morning, Mercy House silent as the – it didn't bear thinking about. I remembered to switch off the recorder before I yelled for help, jabbed the panic button, even as I fretted about how I'd find an ending.

I wrestled Brenda into a seated position, checked her wrist for a pulse, but all I could feel was the spastic rhythm of my own. Her skin was ashen, waxy, her lips troublingly blue. I held my palm under her nose and felt nothing, so there was nothing for it. With shaking hands I removed the pillow from behind her head and laid her flat on the mattress to begin CPR, the mechanics of which I vaguely remembered from school (chest pumps to the rhythm of 'Staying Alive' by the Bee Gees). I was still clutching the pillow when the nurse burst into the room and clamped her arms around me, smelling of tiger balm and cheap shampoo, her grip surprisingly strong.

—No you don't, she hissed.

I bucked and wriggled, trying to get free. Then I realised what she'd seen: a ghostly figure looming over Brenda's prone body, pillow in hand.

—Please, I said, beseeching. She needs help.

Begrudgingly the nurse let me go and performed the vitals checks.

—Her pulse is weak, she said, inspecting the pill bottle. Jesus, how many of these did she take? And how did she get them?

The nurse injected something into Brenda's shoulder.

—Is she going to be alright?

—That remains to be seen. She's overdosed, but I've given her naloxone to revive her. Though truth be told, if she doesn't wake up in the next few minutes, she may not wake at all.

The nurse was speaking on the phone now, but all my attention was on Brenda, willing her eyes to open and find mine, as they had that first day, peering beneath my skin to the black flower blooming in my heart.

Suddenly her body stiffened, as if electrified, every muscle taut then slack. Her eyelids fluttered open and she gave one great wet loud gasp. She didn't look my way once, not even for a second, before the nurse descended, started asking her questions. I wanted to cry with relief even as I knew it was over between us, that I had to leave and never return.

*

I only had myself to blame. Myself and maybe Ruth, because it was her ambush that had precipitated my confession to Brenda. To continue lying to Brenda I'd been forced to tell her I was lying to Ruth. And so I'd pushed Brenda further than I should have, given her one pill too many, desperate to get the story out of her.

I'd been waiting all morning for Ruth's apology, but she was mooching in bed, still in the grip of her essay and whatever her mother had said to her, too caught up in her own problems to even ask how things had gone with Brenda, though it was the last thing I wanted to discuss.

As the day wore on, I began biting my nails (fingers then toes), making cuts around the cuticles. Then came the bald patches in my crotch and underarms as I tore the hair out in tufts. That afternoon, my shits were frequent and floury, and I had a permanent stitch in my side. Pure psychosomatics, the likes of which I never would have believed had it not been happening to me, mirroring the conditions I'd given my novel's narrator. My symptoms were surely no less than I deserved.

I was starting to comprehend that last night's material was the last I'd get, the story of *Anchoress* and *The Widowers* with the final act missing, an ambiguous ending I wanted to rewrite more than anything in the world.

There would be no consequences, no side effects, but just to be safe I kept my phone firmly on aeroplane mode, to avoid the director, the police, Brenda. I'd leave Brenda in situ, undisturbed; I'd reconnect – or was it reattach? – with Ruth, though things still felt stretched taut between us.

I was seething over the trick outside the Sun, but also at her literary malingering, bedbound from success and attention, crippled by her lucky break. Nevertheless, I maintained my equanimity, shuttling cups of coffee and snacks to her bedside, a service she acknowledged with the slightest of nods. Why couldn't I just ask her what was wrong? Or else tell her of my own woes, inform her it was over between Brenda and me; that would be sure to perk Ruth up. But instead I found myself imagining a life without Ruth. How clearly I could see it, the future me in his scabrous digs, mind occasionally stretching back to the exact point in time I was now living, the wilting of his salad days, as he would come to think of them, in which he observed Ruth slipping away in slow motion.

The only thing left to do was write. I started with the previous night's interview, trying to focus on what Brenda had said instead of how she'd said it, her voice growing progressively fainter while her breathing grew louder, until I could barely understand her, which was perhaps for the best. The story confirmed what Ruth and I had suspected: the widowers' words were stolen straight from the mouths of those angry men who'd eventually enacted a spectacular revenge. At least I had that, the story of *The Widowers*, the nadir which Brenda never crawled back from. The remaining blanks I could fill in well enough, Brenda consigned to penury and obscurity, exiled to the Goulburn Valley. Perhaps the rest wasn't anything to write home about, though I'd never know for sure. Better to pretend I had everything I needed.

Linh had been pestering me to send them the manuscript, which currently consisted of the conversations with Brenda, alongside a potted history of my life with Ruth – real life, just heavily redacted, biography with the bad bits taken out. Linh would tell me what I had, help me make it into something sellable. But that afternoon I found I couldn't let go, scanning the document, the words barely registering, deleting then replacing phrases almost at random. The problem was the ending. The final scene was so unsatisfying, Brenda's recitation cutting off mid-sentence. Fitting, perhaps, too: Brenda keeping one last secret, which would never be revealed.

With Brenda out of the picture, I could at long last give Ruth my full attention. The water was scalding but I slid in gingerly, knees drawn up, taps digging into my shoulder blades. It was terribly uncomfortable. We'd often bathed together like this, me curled at the end of the tub, toggled like a Tetris block around Ruth's body, Ruth's feet chocked either side of my head, close enough I could kiss her corns, which I did that night, just the way she liked, until she flicked her toes irritably, hitting me in the nose.

—What's going on with you? I said, in the voice of a stranger. With us? It feels like you haven't been very present lately, and I suppose I haven't been either. I know I've been caught up with Brenda.

As I spoke, Ruth slid deeper into the brackish water, until she was submerged entirely.

—Brenda, she said, when she finally surfaced. Brenda, Brenda, Brenda. I am so looking forward to talking about something other than Brenda Shales and the manifold ways the world has wronged her. I've had a lot on my mind lately, as you know, or perhaps you don't. But this has nothing to do with you *or* Brenda, for that matter.

I prepared myself to explain that Brenda and I were no longer, that for better or worse, Ruth now had me all to herself. But before I could say a word, she said:

—I want to tell you what happened with my mother. That night you were in Geelong, she arrived unannounced. I could tell as soon as I opened the door that she was there to talk about the essay. She wanted to explain why she'd been such a mess when I was a kid, what really happened to my sister.

Ruth refreshed the water with her foot, hot gushing down my back.

—She told me about Ruth, the *first* Ruth, who died a year before I was born. At first, I thought I'd misheard; Helen was crying quite hard – for protection, no doubt. But eventually I understood what she was trying to tell me. I had been named after my dead sister.

Ruth's voice was calm and cool, but I could perceive the control she was exerting. I felt frozen, struggling to keep my head above water.

—Apparently my sister was very attached to my mother, always hiding in the folds of her skirts. The opposite of me. It feels strange even calling her my sister, because I've never thought of her as a real person. She was just an alibi invoked by Helen to explain why she was too much or too little. Anyway, Ruth didn't die in infancy as I'd always thought. She drowned at the age of three, in a neighbour's pool. An unlocked gate, Helen lost sight of her just for a moment, and that moment was enough.

Ruth was mushing a sliver of soap between her fingers, staring at a point above my head.

—It explained so much: the swimming lessons she'd inflicted on me; her terrified, terrifying love. It also confirmed something

I'd always suspected. I was a do-over, a make-up. The price of my existence was to make Helen feel less broken. To save her because she couldn't save my sister. I was conceived a few weeks after the other Ruth died. My father had begged Helen to get rid of me; he even gave her an ultimatum: him or me. Another price I'd paid without knowing it. Helen couldn't abort, but she told me that *the pregnancy*, as she called it, felt like a betrayal of the other Ruth. So she compromised, gave me a necronym, a tribute to this stranger I'd never know. Later on she regretted it, saw my name as an act of violence, though it was too late to change it. She tried to treat me as if I were my own person, but she couldn't; she was always weighing me against *her*. That's not to say Helen didn't love me; she did, her love was like a pillow held over my face. And now all her worst fears are being realised: she's losing her daughter again. At least I'll have some premium material for my next essay.

Ruth's joke sounded like one of mine, terribly misplaced. I very much wanted to transmit comfort, but it was hard to do in such a confined space. I settled for a kiss on her left big toe.

—She left and we haven't talked since. I suppose I got what I'd always wanted, the truth. Now I have to decide what to do with it. It was a relief to finally be rid of her, to have my version of my childhood confirmed in such concrete terms. Nerd that I am, I've been reading about necronyms, which were common back in the days when everyone lost a child, though that doesn't make it any less tragic. I read about the theory of replacement children, understood Helen was following a script as old as motherhood itself. The mother of stone and water, at times as distant as another solar system, at others so close it felt like I was being subsumed.

It wasn't difficult to put myself in her shoes, to comprehend that impossible bind.

Rationally, I know the story changes nothing. But these last few days I've felt a sort of existential terror. My life suddenly seems provisional, a yawning abyss of the self, if that doesn't sound too wanky. I started to think about all the big decisions I'd made and hadn't made over the course of my life. Maybe I rejected professionalism to make having kids materially impossible. I didn't want to make the same mistakes as Helen. Maybe I was drawn to writing to process the shame I've felt for as long as I can remember: shame for being born, which has changed into shame about who I am, a usurper whose life is built on the bones of another.

My toxic self-image is probably news to you. I have been very diligent about keeping that part of myself to myself, for fear it might change the way you see me. I know how you look up to me. It's one of the reasons I was first attracted to you. It feels – felt – so nice to be admired. When I perceive myself through your eyes, I largely like what I see. But your love is so easy. Soft and slobbery, like a dog's. No strings attached.

—Isn't that good?

—In a certain sense, yes, it's the best thing in the world. But it feels like a lot of pressure. It means there are certain aspects of myself I can't show you.

—You sound like you're talking about your mother.

She nodded slowly.

—Perhaps I am. Your love reminds me of hers. An impossible love I can never live up to. A few days ago I felt a great release, as if a terrible weight had been lifted. It feels like I have an opportunity to build a self from the studs up. I still don't know who I am and what I want, but that is starting to feel liberating rather than terrifying.

—And what does that mean for us? I asked. For me?

—I'm not sure yet. Small is the gate and narrow the road that leads to life, and only a few find it.

Immediately I felt the need to comfort Ruth, though her words showed that she didn't need me for that. My desire to handle her feelings was a way for me to exert control, to avoid the messiness of life. If I could manage her emotions, I could stop her, and by extension myself, from feeling anything at all.

She let me towel her dry and lead her to the bedroom, already looking half-asleep, leaning on my shoulder as we moved through the house. I didn't think of Brenda once as I tucked Ruth in and lay beside her, picked up *The Golden Notebook* from the bedside table and began to read.

Within minutes she was asleep, and I was alone. All I could do was wait and hope Ruth came through the other side loving me as much as I loved her.

Later, much later, I slipped out of bed and tiptoed to the front room, where I booted up my computer. My manuscript glared at me on the screen. Ctrl + A + Delete. That was all it would take. Easier than book burning. Better for the environment, too. And then, I finally had it. I wrote what had happened the night before: Brenda collapsing before the finish line, while the writer – her acolyte, amanuensis, leech – knelt beside her bed, weeping with a conviction I could never muster in real life. I channelled the angst of the last two weeks, the hateful feeling of not getting everything I wanted. I thought of Ruth lying in bed, as I wrote a scene of wrenching pathos, Brenda drifting off, pulse slowed to nothing, while the writer raged against the unfairness of it, Brenda dying so her story could live on through him. It was a full stop. An ending.

It was the best thing I'd ever written.

SEVENTEEN

It came upon me in the shower, as I was scrubbing behind my ears: the knowledge it was over. All the knots I'd tied myself in, all the lies I'd told. Finally behind me. Brenda was alive and alone, as she had been before I'd arrived to ruin her life, a guilt I'd carry for the foreseeable, though hopefully not forever.

A subtle difference between guilt and shame. Guilt was feeling bad for my behaviour towards another, shame bad feelings towards the self. I behaved wrong versus I *am* wrong. I'd felt ashamed for a very long time, thanks to my years of pigging, among other things. I wrote about myself in the third person, I gave myself diseases and disabilities, tried to make myself eminently unlikeable, because that's how I saw myself, because I'd lost my love for literature, because I had nothing to say. Shame, too, for the way I was with Ruth, copying the way she went about things, Ruth and I, two peas in a self-hating pod, unbeknownst to me until last night. And all that shame had stopped me feeling guilt for what I'd done to Brenda, and then it came to me that morning in the shower, leaning against the tiles, a gout of guilt welling up as the water cascaded down my lie of a body. I had everything to feel guilty about but nothing to be ashamed of; I was a man capable of bad, just like any other, capable of good too (in theory at least). Who needed a priest or a shrink to get this sense of closure? I was the self-absolving subject, more than capable of forgiving myself. Everything was going to be fine.

I stepped out of the shower to see Ruth on the phone, picking at her toenails on the back step. Maybe it was a trick of that thin morning light, but Ruth looked different, her face fuller, skin brighter. Our talk in the bath had changed something. Though I was still unsure where we stood, we were back on solid ground.

—It's Linh, Ruth told me. Is dinner at eight too late for Brenda?

The dinner party. How had I forgotten? Obviously Brenda wouldn't be coming; she'd promised as much even before the overdose. It was too late to call it off, tell Ruth and Linh some approximation of the truth, so instead I said:

—I'm sure it'll be fine; Brenda's quite the night owl. I'll give her a bell now to confirm.

Trying to contain my panic, I walked to the other end of the house, held my phone to my ear, even spoke into it, ridiculously, unbearably, in case Ruth was listening.

—Hi, Brenda, it's me. Thanks again for yesterday. Just confirming you're still on for tonight . . . Yes, eight o'clock. Any dietary requests?

What other choice did I have? I could pretend Brenda had been taken ill, but that would necessitate a raincheck, more lies and explanations. No. Better to participate in the sham (sham, shame, what was the connection there?). Pretend to be surprised when Brenda didn't show later that night. One last lie, then I could finally pack it in.

I would handle everything. It was my mess and I'd clean it up, once and for all. I stole a shopping trolley from Coles, performed a knight's tour of Footscray, taking pleasure in taking action, blowing the last of my blood money on a leg of lamb and a case of pinot, chop-chop and chrysanthemums – funeral flowers, Ruth informed me balefully on my return. She was off to the gym, legs jiggling in anticipation, positively bursting with energy, back in the game.

I had nothing to worry about. A nice meal with Linh and Ruth, a few drinks . . . I was almost looking forward to it, imagining my feigned consternation when Brenda didn't show up. It was probably good for the fiction I would concoct: Brenda had given me everything she had, and now she wanted to be left alone. But it seemed vitally important to keep moving, not think, so I cleaned the house like I was expecting a visit from the health inspectors, until the bleach made me light-headed; I prepped the meat and got it in the oven, which was when Ruth returned from the gym, pink and sweaty, with a glint in her eye I hadn't seen for weeks: Ruth there to save me.

She led me to the bathroom and ordered me to kneel, to keep my eyes on the ground. She peeled off her gym clothes and put them in the hamper, save for her underwear – floral-patterned Bonds – which she draped over my face, the crotch lined up with my nose.

—Something to remember me by, she said.

I continued kneeling while she showered, mad with desire and dread, trying not to read too much into what she'd said, telling myself things were back to normal, the fever broken, even as I felt a sense of foreboding, a male intuition something terrible was about to happen.

Linh arrived just as evening was coming on, the sky bleeding out, a hilarious pink. They were toting a bottle of Hendrick's and a marked-up manuscript, which they fluttered in my face as soon as I opened the door. Aloysius greeted me with a paw placed on the toe of my boot, head angled so I could chuck his sinewy chin.

My manuscript. Evidently I'd sent it last night, though I had no memory of doing so. I'd killed off Brenda and the project with it, but yet again my ambition had got the better of me, the shadow self that wanted success above all else. Deep down, the only thing I feared more than being abandoned was being ignored.

—I stayed up all night, Linh said, as I busied myself with the drinks. I have many thoughts, oodles of feels. Where's Ruth?

—Just shaving my legs, Ruth bellowed through the bathroom door.

—That's okay, Linh said. Depilate away, we've got business to attend to.

The gins were tongue-tinglingly strong and we drank them in the backyard, my mood mellowing with every sip, the sun setting in a dazzle of light.

—Did you know people from the western suburbs are called squinters? Linh said, shielding their eyes with the back of their hand. I always thought it was some racist thing, but apparently it's just a word for workers who face the sun during their commutes. So let's talk turkey, or whatever textured vegetable protein you'd prefer. I'm getting distinct oral history vibes. Alexis Wright or, even better, Alexievich – you know, without the radiation.

I couldn't help but grin. Despite everything, I still had something to show for these weeks of intrigue and hoax.

—Now, I'd love to know a bit more about your agreement with Brenda. Do you envision the book being published under your name or hers? Have you discussed a division of advances and royalties? What about promotion? Is Brenda finally planning to show her face in public?

Linh's hard-boiled talk made me realise how little thought I'd given to the practicalities of publishing. Even before the overdose, my deception was a highwire act, but eventually there would come a point when the book would exist in the world, and I'd have to explain the circumstances of our meeting to Ruth, Brenda and every rotten reader. I tried and failed to picture Brenda stalking onstage to read the story of my father, Brenda empanelled with some white-teethed professionals. All moot now, but still, it was inconceivable I hadn't looked that far ahead.

—Because if you're planning to be the frontman, Linh went on, be prepared for some curly questions. For instance – and I'm just playing devil's advocate here – why are you the right person to tell this story? And by you I mean –

—A poorly published bloke, assuming squatter's rights of Brenda's story. I get it. I suppose I would answer by saying: *because I found her.*

Found. Like blood in one's stool.

—That answer will need some workshopping. I wonder if we might discuss the other parts of the book, the sections not in Brenda's voice. On first reading, I feel something's not quite working there. I've been trying to put my finger on it, and I think – forgive me if this sounds blunt – but I think you're still struggling to write women.

I tried to explain. I'd only met Brenda a handful of times. With so little to go on, how was I expected to create a vivid portrait of the artist?

—I don't mean Brenda, Linh said. I mean Ruth. Or at least the character who I presume is based on Ruth.

Though it was a subplot, my novel was a declaration of love for this Ruth-like character, framed as its red, beating centre. I had left out Ruth's distance and difficulties, her relationship with her mother. But wasn't that what love was? Unconditional admiration? The blurring out of the messiness, which had no place in my novel?

When eight rolled around, we were pretty well drunk. The roast was resting and the house smelt like blood and fat and tobacco. For decoration, I'd plumped for a sort of share house chiaroscuro: shawl thrown over the painter's lamp, bathing the room in bars of buttery light and inky shadow; beeswax candles guttering between the plattered roast, the kale a deep purple.

The knock was so soft that at first I thought I'd imagined it. We were sitting in the living room so as not to muss the dinner setting, Linh recounting Aloysius's toilet schedule in minute detail. There was a scrabbling at the front door, a frantic sound, like an animal caught in a trap. If it wasn't for the fadeout of the track – 'What's Going On' – there was no way I would have heard it. I skipped to Kate Bush and cranked the volume, asking Linh in a loud voice whether Simon had had any luck shopping his novel.

—Shush, said Ruth. I hear something.

There was no denying it now. It was knocking.

EIGHTEEN

I tottered to the front door as if to the gallows, Ruth and Linh close behind. It was stuck in the frame again, but I managed to get it open. I peered into the darkness, and to my relief saw nothing. But once my eyes had adjusted to the gloom I saw Brenda at the end of the garden path, back to us, fumbling with the gate, as if she'd had second thoughts. *Keep going,* I urged silently. *Save us both from myself.* But Brenda turned and gave a ghastly wave, her wild, white face swimming in the dark.

—I thought I had the wrong house. Don't you all look lovely, while I must look a sight.

As it happened, she did. Her hair was lank and tangled, eyes heavy lidded, mouth agape. She looked like someone who'd very recently overdosed.

—I'm terribly late, and I'm terribly sorry, I'm in a bit of a tizz. My nana nap went longer than planned.

She gave a stagey wink which turned my stomach, then bustled past me and down the hallway to the living room.

Had I dreamt the last few days? Had she forgotten? Forgiven?

Fat chance. She was here to exact her revenge. But it seemed that first she wanted to drag things out, and I had no option but to play along, to assume the role of host.

She ran her fingers over the objects on the mantel, the vitrines and figurines and the sickly spider plant.

—Look at all these lovely *things*. I shudder to think how long it's been since I set foot in a bricks-and-mortar house, a space for living instead of dying. On average, we oldies last nine months in a nursing home before we give up the ghost, even less in a joint as rotten as Mercy House. There's a certain elegance to that, don't you think? Nine months in the womb, and nine months in a facility waiting for the end.

Linh was nodding along, while Ruth's jaw was set, eyes wide, communicating something along the lines of: *Is this woman alright?*

Brenda was in character, scourge of social niceties, all diatribes and non sequiturs. I felt sick at a cellular level, recalling what I'd told her about what I hadn't told Ruth. Brenda knew too much.

—I've been there four years now, Brenda continued, lighting up and gesturing for an ashtray. And before you say anything, I'm still in relatively fine fettle, my mind and body still feel like my own, which is more than most can say. But listen to me shitting on; I'll just get dosed up and I'll be right as the proverbial.

Brenda dumped her handbag on the living room table, tufts of tobacco and a pharmacopoeia of blister packs and bottles.

—I have uppers and downers, tranqs and barbs. Plenty for everyone. My contribution to this lovely spread.

—Is that a good idea? I squeaked.

She grinned at Ruth and Linh, pointed a bony finger in my direction.

—Florence Nightingale is my self-appointed dispensary, but he's a bit of a soft touch, especially when I give him what he wants. When we're on a roll, he's a veritable pusher.

—Shall we get stuck in? I said, maniacally cheery. The food's getting cold.

—Where did you disappear to after I conked out? The staff were all very interested to know. We all wanted to thank you for raising the alarm.

She stepped towards me, arm outstretched. I flinched, thinking she was going to strike me, but instead she stroked my cheek, almost tenderly, then pinched it between her brittle fingers, cooed:

—My hero.

Over Brenda's shoulder I caught Ruth's eye. She was looking at me as she had a few days ago, when she'd taken off the eyemask: as if she didn't know me at all.

Brenda was enjoying herself, which spelt trouble for me. She wriggled at the head of the table as if her bum was aflame, eyes fixed on mine, a fact I was sure Linh and Ruth must have noticed as they picked through their lukewarm dinners. The food was plenty edible, each spud an oily chrysalis, the carrots sweet and tender, the lamb still pink in the middle. A banquet with me as the main course.

—What a pleasure it is, Brenda said, to chew hacked flesh and swallow the juices of dead wounds. I can't for the life of me remember who said that. Now, could I trouble you for some Phar Lap? My tastebuds have been thoroughly institutionalised, alas.

Ruth and I looked at her blankly, but Linh rose, grinning, and padded to the fridge. They returned with a bottle of tomato sauce and Brenda proceeded to sozzle her meat.

—Phar Lap, Linh explained. Dead horse. *Sauce.* When my parents first moved to Melbourne they were diligent assimilationists. They taught us all this ridiculous rhyming slang, even though it was long out of fashion. The phone was the dog, as in the dog and bone. Ham and eggs for legs. You get the picture. The kids at school thought we were nuts.

—Doesn't that take me back, Brenda said, with red-rimmed lips. A language for drinking, fucking and fighting. A piss a snake's hiss. A four-by-two, a Jew. Scotch tape for rape.

She mashed out her cigarette in a half-eaten spud.

All this chitchat was setting me at ease. For the first time since Brenda had arrived I permitted myself to think that things might turn out alright, that I would get through this night with my lies intact.

—You know, it all reminds me of that clever name the nurses were calling you behind your back, Brenda said. What was it now? Rhys?

—What is she talking about? Ruth asked, curious.

Not quite sure how I'd ended up there, I told the table about the incident with the night nurse, Siobhan, which had precipitated this pig taking myself off the market; Siobhan's slip of the tongue, which had sent me shame-spiralling to the pool, where I first laid eyes on Brenda.

—I didn't know that, Ruth said, with an air of confusion.

I'd relaxed too soon. I now foresaw more courses of pure excruciation, the unravelling of all my untruths and occlusions.

—So you two met at the pool? Linh asked.

What would I do without Linh and their impeccable manners? But equally, why couldn't they keep their mouth shut? For in a field of strong contenders, this was the moment I'd been dreading the most, the one in which Brenda spoke directly about how we'd met, who she thought I was, and how I'd wormed my way into her life.

—You make us sound like lovers, Brenda said, blowing me a kiss. Do you want to tell it or shall I?

She lit another cigarette and then resumed.

—We still don't really know why we get old – scientifically, at least. There are theories, of course: shortening telomeres, DNA lesions, death by a thousand cellular cuts. But we still don't really understand why our bodies conk out, this planned obsolescence. In 1967, when I was a young woman, a doctor performed the world's first successful heart transplant. The patient died a few weeks later, but that's beside the point. We thought people would live forever, trading an organ here and there, our bodies endlessly renewed. Not quite, as it turned out.

Brenda talked in that torrential style I was so familiar with, perfect for an interview, but hardly dinner party fare. As Brenda talked I kept my eyes on Ruth, but she seemed concerned with a morsel of lamb which she continually brought to her lips then replaced on her plate.

—Sometime in February, I'd just completed my weekly aquaplay with the other ambulant residents, when I noticed a sallow paparazzo at the end of the access road, gawping at me from behind his phone. He was the first person to recognise me in years. Decades. Old age is the perfect disguise, a foolproof way to blend in. I never resented losing my looks, as for the most part they'd brought me nothing but trouble. Nowadays nobody gives me a second glance, let alone takes my photo. But I knew, even before he trained his phone on me, I'd seen that look a thousand times before.

News to me Brenda had noticed me noticing her that first time – little more than three weeks ago, though it felt like aeons longer. Clearly, Brenda knew more than she'd been letting on; she was trying to tell me something I'd been too dense to pick up on.

—He looked like a son without a grandmother – sorry, mother. Where on earth did that come from? And there he was the following morning, and then again the week after that. A writer, a fan, an acolyte. A man with a plan to tell the world my story. I was sceptical at first, but eventually he wore me down. Now, could I trouble someone for a top-up? Preferably something stronger if you have it.

I exhaled so hard I thought I'd spurt up a lung. I'd flown across the face of the sun and barely singed my wings. I was struck by how easily Brenda had spun a lie out of nothing – a lie from her perspective, that was, because what she'd said had just happened to be the truth.

—Now this is what I call service, Brenda said, once Linh had returned, draining her drink and gesturing for another.

—Have mine, Ruth said. I suddenly don't feel in the mood.

—Very sensible; we all need some time off now and again. A little birdie told me that you'd been overdoing it a smidge.

We all winced. Brenda was messing with Ruth, and by extension me: punishment for the role I'd forced her to play in this farce. I wasn't sure what Brenda was up to, but I was sure it was nothing good.

—I wonder if it might be germane to pop on my publishing hat, Linh said, just for the teensiest second. I've had the great honour of reading the manuscript from start to finish, and what we have here could be big. *Big* big. The jacket copy writes itself: recluse re-emerging after half a century's silence to set the record straight.

—That's certainly one way to put it, Brenda said, swallowing another pill. Eminently blurb-worthy. How I wish I'd had you in my corner back in the bad old days.

—Well, it's never too late.

Linh snatched a card from their clutch and slid it across the table. I was suddenly struck by a vision of one possible future for the book. Linh running the show, me written out, the silent partner I always should have been. I saw a profile timed for the fiftieth anniversary of *The Widowers*, the whirlwind world tour, the crowning glory of one of literature's forgotten mothers, finally enjoying her day in the sun, a heart-wrenching portrait of a time when women's lives weren't their own. The bidding war between the big houses, the movie option, the reprints of Brenda's back catalogue. Brenda in listicles ('10 Notable Literary Recluses', 'Women Writers Who Deserve More Attention'), Brenda claimed as feminist influencer, as avatar for the lost idealism of the Whitlam years, as Nobel dark horse. The bonfire of Brenda, the cultural capital she had accrued over the last half-century going up with a whoosh.

—Tell me, Brenda, Linh said. It must have been hard to open up after such a long time.

Ruth gave a contemptuous snort, which she managed to disguise as a sneeze. Linh's question belonged to another domain entirely, the realm of softballs and easy-won truths, Brenda's story repackaged as a feminist parable of fortitude. Not whatever *this* was.

—I have always reviled confession, Brenda said. The penitent in the box, the analysand on the couch. A problem named is a problem solved. Better out than in. But I was surprised how easy it felt, and, please forgive the simile, how like a glorious evacuation after fifty years of being backed up. It's been unpleasant at times, but he's been very patient with me. Neither pushy nor needy. But everyone's a gentleman when you have something he wants. Although I never expected it, I'm very taken with him. He's the grandson I never had.

Brenda was getting off on my evident discomfort, dangling the disclosure I didn't want Ruth to hear. I'd invited this barbarian into the city, this other woman hellbent on disruption. A part of me just wanted her to come out and say it, get it over with – but a bigger part of me didn't.

—That's the third time you've mentioned grandsons and grandmothers, Ruth said.

—A sage observation, Frau Doktor. Probably just the misfiring of a faulty synapse. But I'm all ears if you have another interpretation.

This was what it must be like to see your parents fuck. Scratch that: grandparents, worse yet, your parents fucking your grandparents. Brenda was rubbing her hands like some malevolent sprite. Things couldn't keep going like this. It was literally impossible. But still she droned on, implacable, a king tide sucking me closer to the rocks.

—I'm trying to remember how he put it, legs crossed on the end of my bed, a blushing bride with an embarrassing request. He wanted to be the next great Australian writer. He wanted to be me. Greatness through association, a transfusion of talent. It's all a touch Oedipal, don't you think? He's been pouring honey in my ear, telling me how I'll finally get my respect, recompense and revenge. But really he just wants to be my heir apparent, my executor and executioner. I've often thought it would be better if I were dead – for him, at least. He nearly got his wish a couple of nights ago. The dead have no right of reply, though fear not: this is not a case of literary scotch tape. But there's no denying biography's a grubby business, and one can't help but feel a tad despoiled.

The hostility in the room was something physical, a great black wall. Even Linh's smile was beginning to waver. As the silence dragged on they rose and went to tend to Aloysius, licking his arsehole on the living room couch.

—And what about you, dear Ruth? I'd love to get your two cents on our little undertaking.

Brenda's voice was measured, but I could sense the malice in it, the challenge, which Ruth was the last person to shy away from.

—I'm very sorry all that happened to you, Ruth said, very carefully. Your child taken, your work taken. It's terrible. Unforgivable. I don't understand why you unburdened yourself. Neither do I know what he did to compel you, but now I'm sure it must have been something quite nasty. But he's a big boy, and he's made his bed. Clearly you have some sway over him, and I find that quite disturbing. You know, for the longest time, I didn't believe a word you said; I thought you were just telling him what he wanted to hear.

—And what would that be? Brenda said, through a gust of cigarette smoke.

—A digestible story of a white woman in peril, like all those wretched podcasts I rot my ears with. But I can see that you're not a victim. You're the furthest thing from it. You've known exactly what you're doing the entire time.

It had never occurred to me to assess the veracity of Brenda's story. I had been so caught up in tricking her into telling it, I hadn't stopped to think whether she was actually telling me the truth.

Brenda put her hand to her heart and slumped theatrically in her chair.

—Got me. There's no point denying it. I haven't been completely honest – at your boyfriend's behest, actually. He asked me to lie to you about *the exact nature of our relationship*: his words, not mine.

—That's enough, Brenda.

My voice was that of a stranger, reedy and contemptible.

—Now he speaks. Brenda grinned. What's the harm in telling her?

Brenda was asserting her authority, making a claim on me I only dimly knew she had.

—She makes it sound like you two are fucking, Ruth said, her voice even.

—Don't get the wrong end of the stick, dear Ruth. I'm a bit long in the tooth for all that. No, your boyfriend only has eyes for you. Never has there been a young man more in love. More in awe.

—Why aren't you using his name?

It was the last thing I expected to hear out of Ruth's mouth.

—You keep saying boyfriend, young man. But you've never used his name.

Brenda looked at Ruth, then at me, and then she smiled. With a sort of dawning horror, I tried to recall whether I'd ever actually told Brenda my name. It seemed impossible, but it also felt true. Yes, I was almost sure of it. Brenda didn't know my name.

Not even the truth could save me now. Only more lies, the one thing I'd forgotten to bring to dinner. Better to have a lie and not need it than need a lie and not have it. We sat frozen in the candlelight, a tableaux of ill-feeling, each of us waiting for the other to speak.

—This pooch is pooped, Linh called from the living room. Endless thanks for a lovely evening, and Brenda – what can I say? It's been an absolute pleasure.

I expected Brenda to follow suit, but she was sunk in stony silence, sitting *harder* in her chair, hands gripping the edge of the table, eyelids fluttering ever so slightly, as if on the verge of sleep or stroke. Ruth was standing behind her, glaring at the back of Brenda's head and then at me, while Linh struggled with the door, Aloysius whining to be released.

It was high time to manhandle the situation, march Brenda down the corridor and out the front door, requisition a lift from Linh, assume the penitent's position at Ruth's feet. It would mean the book wouldn't get the final chapter it deserved, Brenda's disappearance explained once and for all, and maybe that was for the best. The fact I was fretting about the book did not reflect well on me, under the circumstances, but still, someone had to.

Ruth called out to Linh that she was coming with them, and stalked down the corridor, me following a few paces behind, almost begrudgingly. Outside the pressure had dropped, a skittering, kinetic energy in the air, a southerly whipping in from the bay.

Ruth turned when she heard me coming, as she had when I'd first got out of the hospital. I recalled watching Ruth watering the rosebushes as if viewing the scene from a fractured future.

Well, the future was now, or then, and I needed to address the affair with Brenda, for that's what it was, though an affair of the head and the heart rather than the body. Let her go. Yes, I remember thinking that. But was I referring to Ruth or Brenda or both? The truth was: I didn't know.

—Let's skip ahead, Ruth said, sensing my hesitancy. You never were a convincing apologist. Mistakes were made. A regrettable incident. Et-bloody-cetera. But what do you have to be sorry about? Brenda was a cow, sure, but you're not responsible for what she says. The dinner party was my idea. So what is this thing she thinks you need to tell me? Be real with me.

I felt the bolus of truth trapped in my throat, which I could neither swallow nor spit up. Lightning lit the sky, though the real tumult was still a way off, and for a moment I could see Ruth clearly. I remembered then, as if hearing it for the first time, everything she'd told me, the story of the glow-worms and the story of her sister, me forever bearing witness (a strange phrase, as if the intimate parts of other people's lives were a terrible burden); Ruth asking me to see her in a different light, not as an antidote to all I hated in myself, not as someone invulnerable to the world, nor as someone vulnerable. Linh had been right, of course: I did have a problem with women. I had wanted Brenda to save me from writing and Ruth to save me from myself. I admired Ruth so much I didn't really know who she was. How had it taken so long for me to see her? Brenda, that's how. Even now Ruth was trying to tell me something, as the rain began to fall, looking up at me with confusion, resentment and, worst of all, hope.

—I'm as real as I'll ever be.

I WANT EVERYTHING

I think I was trying to make a joke, but I sounded so sad when I said it.

—That may be true, Ruth said. And that may well not be enough.

NINETEEN

I must have stood in the rain for quite some time after Ruth left. When I finally returned inside, I was soaked through, my bare feet flecked with grass and dirt, teeth chattering, though cold was the last thing I felt. My footprints looked silver in the candlelight as I walked to the living room, where I found Brenda slumped on the couch, trying and failing to get a cigarette lit with a candle's guttering flame.

—Jesus wept, what happened to you? A drowned rat doesn't begin to describe it.

The rain was working its way through the roof, as it always did during storms, steady drips on the floorboards. I hated Brenda then, glowering at me in triumph, her face distended by the drugs.

—You'll have to give me the recipe for that lamb. 'Twas simply to die for.

I wanted it all over with, or else to return to the beginning, that clean, well-lit room of utter uncomplication. I shouldn't have been surprised. It was always going to turn out this way. At a certain point, one of them would have found out what I'd done.

Eventually I would have had to choose. But in truth, I'd already chosen. This was what the entire evening had amounted to: me choosing.

—I know I wasn't the epitome of tact tonight. But I kept the cat in the bag, didn't I, deep down in the depths of a sack? I'm sorry my lies weren't to your liking. But good things come to those who wait. You wanted an ending, so now I'm going to give it to you.

This was it. The centre of the maze, where all my lies had led. More than the book, more than the fame and notoriety, this was what I'd wanted. To know.

Brenda stood and walked to the dining room table, returned an eternity later with my phone. There were missed calls from Linh. From Ruth too. My finger hovered over the banner with her name emblazoned across it. But instead I opened the recording app.

—Now before we begin, I was wondering if you might do me a favour. My feet are killing me. An absolute slaughter. Why don't you give them a quick rub, there's a good lad. I promise I'll give you what you want as soon as you've put some feeling back into them. Pretend for a minute you're dear Bouboulina.

I thought at first she was joking, but no, there was her bare foot flexed, nails gnarled and yellowed at their distal edges; they hadn't been cut since our first meeting. Not quite believing what I was doing, I knelt before the couch and took them in my hands, and I rubbed for all I was worth, feeling the weight of Brenda's presence. I was the reader, the confessor in his final form, crushed beneath that foot I'd first seen, all those years ago, on the back cover of *Anchoress* and then *The Widowers*.

The first kick landed on my shoulder; an involuntary spasm, I thought, a pressure point pressed too hard. The second hit me full in the face, pain spiking up through my nose. I knelt while Brenda kicked and kicked, the blood running hot into my mouth. So this was what forgiveness felt like.

Brenda fixed me with a glare of cold fury, communicating the message clearer than any words could. There was no need for my confession. Brenda knew. She'd known the entire time.

FINAL INTERVIEW - STIRLING STREET - 27 FEBRUARY

And so it's you and me again, just what you've always wanted. I must admit that felt very restorative. A kick is worth a thousand words. I imagine you're going to be quite sore in the morning; I shudder to think what Ruth will say. Sorry! I keep putting my foot in it, don't I?

I'm fine by the way. Thanks ever so much for asking. No ill effects in the end, though I slept for a whole day and night. They didn't even pump my stomach, though apparently I was on the verge of carking it. It felt pleasant actually, drifting off; the rude awakening less so. I remember the look on your face when I woke, the grim resolve, like a captain going down with his ship. You'd decided to give me the boot. I suppose you thought that was the honourable thing to do. After everything, you thought you could get away with your dignity intact. But for better or worse, it seems we're stuck with each other.

If I were you, I'd stay away from Mercy House. They're on the warpath, half-convinced you tried to bump me off. Elder abuse.

That's what they're calling it. I'm going to be in deep shit when they realise I've snuck out. I didn't mean to ambush you tonight, by the way. I did call. Multiple times. So we could get our stories straight. I wanted to see you one last time.

Now I think we can finally dispense with the preliminaries, don't you? If I'm going to go the full monty, I'd prefer to keep the audience as small as possible.

I know you're not my grandson. I mean *quelle* bloody *surprise*. When I saw you standing at my door, I pieced it together in a second. You'd recognised me at the pool, seen the name on the bus, come to rubberneck. The nurse mistook you for a shiftless relative – an honest mistake – which you were in no hurry to correct.

Go on, tell me how things got so out of hand. Give me your mealy-mouthed mea culpa. Or on second thought, don't. My grandson! What a ridiculous idea. You didn't have to go to all the trouble, you know; I probably would have given you what you wanted, if only you'd known how to ask. Yes, after all this time, I think I was ready to unburden myself.

Call it Stockholm syndrome, call it whatever you want, but despite myself, I've grown fond of you these past few weeks, though I have a funny way of showing it. I think it's because of the fact that, like you, I've been pretending for a very long time.

It happened on a Sunday in '78, months after the lawsuit had concluded, in the doldrums of the school holidays. The house felt like a penitentiary. I had been at her to take a trip, but she had demurred, as we didn't have a pot to piss in. We decided not to fight the bastards; we didn't want to drag things out. Probably for the best, there was nothing we could have done.

That day was a stinker, the heat radiating through the floorboards, a haze over the wheatfields. I was making breakfast when I heard moaning from her room. From beneath a bedsheet, she told me the light was too bright, it was pulsing behind her eyes, even with the shutters drawn. I tried to make a game of it, poking and prodding, asking where it hurt. *Everywhere*, she said. *It hurts everywhere.* And then she began to sing.

Her voice was slurred, but I recognised the song as one the nuns made us sing back in St Kilda, an anthem about the noble pioneers who'd made this country their own. I peeled back the sheet and saw the right side of her face was slack, one pupil dilated to a terrible size. I couldn't see any white at all. The sheets were soaked. Sweat, I thought, but when I took her in my arms I could smell that it was urine. She couldn't even form words by that point, was mumbling strange, drowned sounds in my ear.

At the hospital in Shepparton the doctor explained there'd been a haemorrhage in the subarachnoid mater, a thin membrane between the brain tissue and the skull. It was called that because it looked like a web and protected like a mother. They'd done everything they could, but by the time the ambulance arrived she was already too far gone. There was no way to know what caused it: she could have bumped her head in just the wrong way, or perhaps it was a tangle of vessels just waiting to burst. The doctor told me that when the brain was on its way out, it often went to strange places. And in her final moments of what you might call consciousness, she'd returned to those years in school, back when we first met.

*

It was months before I rejoined the world of the living; in fact, I don't think I've ever fully rejoined it. I hope you never experience that type of grief, like your heart's beating outside your chest. In those three years in the country, we had become the same person, and then that person was gone. I barely left the house those next eighteen months, as one decade rolled into the next. Grief for the most part, but there were practical considerations too. Even the gentle Taturans knew my face from the papers, that idiotic author photo plastered over their *Chronicles*, *Heralds* and *Stars*. It caused quite the stir, even in the badlands of the Goulburn Valley. *The authoress and her tragic friend*, I could almost hear them saying behind their melanomaed hands. *Terrible what happened*. I could never tell whether they were talking about me or her.

I ended up in Sydney. With the prize money I rented a beautiful unit in Randwick, overlooking Coogee Beach. Coogee, I came to learn, is a Dharug word meaning the smelly place, referring to the mounds of kelp and wrack that washed ashore on the king tide. I was into my thirties and the most vital chapter of my life was over, my one chance for safety and security snatched away. I lost all capacity for self-protection, if I'd ever had any to begin with. No. From then on, I didn't care what happened to me.

I tried to blend in with the crowd, but I just felt more conspicuous. A twist in the faces of passers-by, startled incomprehension, as if they'd just seen a ghost. *Don't I know you from somewhere? Weren't you that woman who?* Women wanted to shake my hand, congratulate me on a job well done, a finger in the eyes of the blokes who'd made their lives a misery. The men were like pigs in shit, jeering, leering. To all of them I would always be the writer, though writing was the furthest thing from my mind.

When my savings began to dwindle, I decided to get a job. One afternoon, I went for a trial shift at a social club in Newtown, a dreary place off King Street, empty save for a couple of lunchtime drunks. The owner was rangy, shy to the point of imbecility. Through a complex system of grunts and gestures, he made it clear he wanted to observe me pour a pony, carry a keg from the cellar, buff the pewter trough at the foot of the bar, which still smelt faintly of piss, though the six o'clock swill was long gone by that point. With his glasses off he looked like a turtle without its shell, rubbing the lenses on the hem of his singlet, his gaze travelling up my body, stopping at my neck and descending again. *I'm a prawn*, I thought, as I poured and polished. *Toss the head and keep the body.* Finally he ushered me to a windowless office and sat behind the desk. He produced a box of matches and a paperback. My photo staring up at me again. The matches fizzled in his stubby fingers as he detailed the many deaths he'd imagined for me.

There is a lovely quote in the *Book of Revelations* I've thought of many times over the course of my life. *Because you are lukewarm, and neither hot nor cold, I will spit you out of my mouth.* For all of us sinners a state of holiness is to live between God's lips, like colonies of microbes. Still, it seemed to describe my life in the years to come perfectly. I was either hot or cold, but never, ever lukewarm. But watching that man trying to get the book lit, sighing in frustration, I prayed for the lukewarm. I realised I'd never be free of *The Widowers*, that it would follow me for the rest of my life. Needless to say I didn't get the job.

What is it about that book that so gets men's collective goats? I hardly imagine it a matter of prurience and propriety. It was not the message but the messenger, *Brenda Shales*'s Promethean theft. I suppose it showed men how they didn't want to be seen, biologically fated to wreck and ruin, no more than their fetid drives and desires. Is that something you can relate to?

Leaving the man's office I took a wrong turn, ending up in a smoky alcove, lights flashing on the opposite wall. Pokies, fruit machines, one-armed bandits. I stood transfixed on that sticky, threadbare carpet, watching the spinning wheels, listening to the chirps and trills, a murder of tropical birds. It's difficult to describe the feeling that came over me, as if the room had suddenly brightened, and I could perceive everything with a lover's attention. The heat of the men perched on the stool, the erotic chunk of coins fed into the slot. It was as if a shard of black glass had lodged in my brain, kicking it into overdrive. I thought for a minute I was having a stroke, that it was happening to me too. But no. This was something else.

The game was called the Luck of the Irish, reels showing clovers, spuds and pots of gold, a portly leprechaun swimming in a sea of coins. A tsunami of currency was cresting behind him, and he seemed to be swimming for his life, trying to outrun the money that would eventually drag him under. I'm not sure how long I sat there, but it was dark when I found my way out onto the street, my head and pockets lighter than air. It was the first time in forever I hadn't been thinking of her.

Everything moved quickly after I found the machines. I could sense the commotion coming from afar, rumbling towards me from a great distance, the light suddenly brighter, sounds louder.

My brain moving at an incredible speed, a godly strength coursing through me, as if I were Atlas tossing the beach ball of the world between my palms. There was never enough time or stimulation, never enough of anything. I had to be around people, things, to gorge on the viscera of life. The commotion, that was the only way to describe it, the bustle of numinous life imprinted on my skin, a black wave cresting inside me. *The Commotion*. Sounds like *The Widowers'* sequel.

I never knew how long those episodes lasted, nor what I did during them. I'd often wake with bruises all over my body, in strange beds in Parramatta and Lane Cove, with the taste of blood and I don't know what in my mouth. Face down in a toilet stall or lying on the sand, water lapping at my feet. Time passed in a terrible blur. I bled money. Pissed it away. I hid my wallet and chequebook, but I was never a match for that woman under the influence. I worked in pubs and cafes around the city, but I'd usually get the sack as soon as the commotion appeared. I'd stop showing up for work, or I'd show up in a state that was anything but professional.

I wish I'd had someone to tie me down. Literally. Someone to keep me bedbound by force, like dear Iphigenia, to prevent me being drawn inexorably to the slots, when the commotion came on, the worst part of me determined to explode my life for good. The lights and sounds. The near misses. The jackpot forever dangled. Gambling's seldom exhilarating; in truth, it is frightfully dull. There's not much to say. Once I sat at the slot, losing money felt just as good as winning. Even better, for it meant it would be over all the quicker. I barely registered the wins or the losses, or time passing at all. It was pure disappearance. The only pain one can avoid in life is the pain of trying to avoid pain, but back then avoidance seemed preferable to facing up to what my life had become, trading a large pain for a smaller one. Yes, strange as it sounds, I look back on those years with a certain fondness.

When there was nothing left, I hitchhiked back to Melbourne, staring out the window as the truckies stared down my top. My father was clutching a cricket bat when he answered my knock in the middle of the night. His hair was thinner and waist thicker, while my mother looked much the same, skulking behind him in the entrance hall, haunted, hunted. She looked very much like me.

It was hardly a heroine's welcome. They seemed perturbed by my arrival, my father stroking the edge of the bat as if it were the nape of a child's neck, my mother pecking my cheek then bustling me to my old bedroom, stopping at the threshold as if she could go no further.

My room had the air of a mausoleum, the bed and desk still there, the clothes of my girlhood hanging in the wardrobe, the school uniform moth-eaten at the hems. I heard them murmuring through the wall. I felt like I was young again, knocked up and locked up. Did they regret how things had turned out? Did they perceive – as I was beginning to that night, my feet dangling off the end of the mattress – that the slow process of my unravelling had begun not with the death of my friend, nor the lawsuit, but right there on that bed, all those years ago?

*

My father did his best to avoid me, leaving the house at dawn and not returning until after dark, drunk as a lord. At home, my mother followed me about like a shade, too polite to ask what had happened. When I next felt the commotion coming on, I endeavoured to make myself scarce, but instead spilt the beans at the kitchen table, telling her everything, making up for those years of silence.

Eventually she convinced me to see a shrink, an odious man forever sniffing the tips of his fingers, as if I might infect him. I was a rare specimen, he told me: a woman who'd survived in the wild without medication or institutionalisation.

He wrote a script for lithium. The drugs did their job, though the side effects were nothing to sneeze at. I pissed constantly and shat rarely. I lost my hair and libido and finally all sense of myself. Things became hazy and formless, time passed like a slow-moving river. My face grew puffy from the meds. On the few occasions when I ventured out of the house, people no longer recognised me as the famous author; instead they saw a doped heifer trotting around the bay, her long-suffering mother in tow. If I didn't take my drugs, a jagged peak of pain would rear up, unassailable. No, it was easier to do what I was told.

I saw another side of my mother during that time. She was softer, more forthcoming, prone to flights of regret and remembrance. She told me of her own grandmother, whom she'd never met, a woman always dressed in mourning. Though she'd never married, she did bear a hutful of children, sired by the local menfolk. My great-grandmother would stay awake for days, visited by angels and demons, wandering the town babbling to herself, weeping. During one such episode she jumped into the river, was never heard from again. My mother told me that, despite all outward appearances, she had always wanted a better life for me, one devoid of sadness and suffering. But it was not to be, it seemed. That was the closest I would get to an apology.

Ten years passed in the blink of an eye. Ten years of nothing much, eventless, incident-free. I was cooked and cleaned for, I was heavy and dull and dumb. Not sad, not afraid. Nothing much of anything. My father died as he had lived: on the job, on the piss. My mother went six months later. That one hurt more than I'd expected. Not long after, I woke with a pain in my guts, as if I were about to give birth to an octuplet of octopuses. At the hospital I was diagnosed with lithium poisoning, my gastrointestinal system on the verge of shutting down. They pumped my stomach and tore up my script. I was left to fend for myself, pharmacologically speaking; it was too dangerous to try anything else. I convinced them to release me by telling them I had a son at home to look after me.

When the commotion returned, I was bouncing off the walls, completely insensible. I lost the new money in much the same way as I had the old, holed up at Crown Casino, expanding my repertoire to blackjack and roulette. I refinanced, remortgaged, lost it all again. In a few years, I was back where I'd started, penniless and alone, running from creditors, moving houses and jobs.

Eventually I found the right balance. New drugs were invented – mood stabilisers and the like. Eventually I felt borderline normal, but by that point everything else was gone.

*

In the early 2000s I had my bright idea. It was in the bitter depths of winter, and I whiled away my days among the other untouchables at the Footscray Library on Paisley Street, where I could sit all day in the warmth without disruption. I was not exactly homeless, though I spent the odd night prowling the streets, waiting for a bed at a doss house, an experience I would not altogether recommend. Without a fixed address I couldn't claim government benefits, let alone find a job. I'd long ago declared bankruptcy, but still, whenever I raised my head above the rampart, so to speak, signing a lease, getting on the books, my creditors hounded me for money I didn't have. For interest. It was a dark time, even by my standards, and one I don't care to dwell on.

I read all day, there was bugger all else to do. I didn't take much in, at least not at a conscious level, the words washing over me, book after book of them. But at night, listening to the screams of the damned in the beds beside me, I felt the words I'd read become lodged within me. Yes, I read more and I read better in those years than at any other point in my life.

One day I read an article about a government cock-up involving the digitisation of government files. Clients were arriving to find their identifying documents had been deleted, lost in the changeover. A cavalcade of disappearing records. I began to daydream: what if I became someone else, with a new name, a new identity? A fresh start. I could become anyone I wanted, even Brenda Shales, that nom de plume which had more or less ruined my life.

I used it sparingly at first, almost as a game or a joke. Brenda Shales to bus mates and the staff of my new rooming house. I began to dream bigger, started to see that my name could help me to achieve some things I'd been lacking since my parents died.

Security. Solvency. On the treacle-slow library desktop, I read about breeder documents, the small proofs of identity which could be used to fake bigger ones, and I started then and there at the library, giving my new name to the tow-headed attendant, who didn't bat an eyelid. I signed up for anything and everything: loyalty cards and local clubs – anything I didn't have to pay for.

During my first interview with the Footscray housing services I had my great stroke of luck. The officer was a bespectacled, bookish-looking woman in her late thirties, and when I told her my name was Brenda Shales, her eyes widened in recognition. I explained that I wanted to check on my application for public housing; I'd had an interview a couple of weeks ago at which I'd submitted my important documents, so they should have everything on file. The housing officer tapped away and told me nothing was coming up, but that was no surprise; the system was having teething problems. Could she have a peek at those documents again? I'd handed them over in our previous interview, I said, and I hadn't made copies, but I showed her my sheaf of identity cards, showed her the cover of *The Widowers*. Upon seeing the photograph, she couldn't contain herself any longer: she'd written an honours thesis on my work, she said. At the time she had wanted to be a writer; still did, if she was being honest. She took pity on me, and signed me up for the public housing waiting list while they tried to track down the missing documents, a torturous process in that newly digitised world. My story wasn't uncommon, she told me. Women over fifty were the fastest-growing homeless population, women who'd been dependent on men their entire lives who suddenly had to fend for themselves after an ill-timed divorce or death.

At first I lived in terror I'd be found out, dreading each ring of the telephone, every knock at the door of my unit on Droop Street. But once I'd been living under the name of Brenda Shales for a few years, I calmed down. It was all remarkably simple. When someone looks at a woman like me, they see grandmother, they see invalid, they certainly don't see someone with something to hide. One old woman looks just like another.

So there you have it. You could use this information to expose me, but then again, I could do the same to you. What would the authorities say if I told them about your heartless impersonation? That's not a threat. Yet. I merely point it out to demonstrate we both have skin in this game.

Is that your phone ringing again? Ruth, I suppose. Persistent thing. Now, I am going to tell you what happened, the part I left out, which I've never told anyone. This is an exploding offer, so think very carefully before taking the call . . .

Good. She's gone.

She was right before. Ruth, I mean. What I told you was neat: a how, a what, a why, a when. Everything in its place. Trust but verify is that how that saying goes, although Ruth doesn't trust me a whit. Not like you. You believed the novels were mere biography, real life by another name, and in a sense they were.

I have something to show you. Let me just get my bag.

There you are. This should clear everything up. Now, tell me what you see.

TWENTY

It was a photograph, *the* photograph, shot from below, the author peering down at the camera, at me. I held it close to the candle, my future contained in that single faded frame. Everything was familiar, the dramatic lighting from below, the shadows cast on the ceiling, the boot eclipsing the bottom of the photo. But the woman wasn't who I expected. Her face was round and full, freckles dusting her cheeks. She had straight, blonde hair flowing down her back. The picture of health, save for her eyes, which were sunken and ribboned with burst capillaries. It was the face of a stranger, but with a dawning horror, I realised who she was.

Outside the storm was easing, the rain barely a whisper on the roof. I felt the weight of my body sprawled on the sodden floorboards, the weight too of what I'd done, and what had been done to me. I wanted to swallow my tongue with shame. Laugh a lung up. All of it had been for nothing. A case of mistaken identity. My mistake.

My hand was steady when I held the photo up to the candle, allowed the flame to scorch the stranger's face, to make it a secret once again. The woman on the couch gasped, as if it was her skin singeing. It took forever to crawl from the table to her feet, but I made it eventually, tasting blood caked on my upper lip.

    I lay my head on the woman's lap, a terrified child, eyes shut tight like curtains drawn over the world. She worked her fingers through my hair, traced figure-eights across my scalp, told me it was going to be alright, like I was someone she loved, like I was family. When I could bear it no longer I looked up and saw the face which I'd allowed to ruin my life. I finally recognised who she was. An impostor. A nobody. She was just like me.

FINAL INTERVIEW - STIRLING STREET - 27 FEBRUARY (CONTINUED)

You look a bit like her. Especially in the dark. A slip of a thing. Sickly. I've often wondered whether she was already sick when I took that photo, if it was the beginning of the end. We were two sides of the same coin, she the head, of course. She was just getting started. But she was my loss. Mine. One I guarded for the rest of my life. I wanted to forget her, but the world wouldn't let me; people would forever see her in me.

I'm not Brenda Shales. I never have been. I didn't write those novels, I didn't write anything. Knowing her was as close as I ever wanted to get to the messy business of literature. *Brenda Shales*. My best friend and betrayer. Brenda wasn't her real name, of course, just as it isn't mine. Maria's not my name either, though you're welcome to think of me as such. My friend, the author of *Anchoress* and *The Widowers*, died that sweltering afternoon in 1978. I might even have killed her. You can be the judge of that.

I was her lackey and confidante, her gift horse, and now I suppose I'm her biographer, in a manner of speaking. Perhaps you can give me some pointers. It was never my intention to take things so far. At the beginning, I was curious. I wanted to see how low you would go. Horizontal, as it turns out. Was that really your father who called the director? A for effort. How on earth did you manage to wrangle that?

I've taken great pleasure in watching you try to keep the plates spinning. We oldies must keep the grey matter active, and I've had fun making my lies fit and cohere. It gave me a sense of purpose. I enjoyed myself as much as you did. I saw your face when I told you all my dirty secrets, like all your Christmases had come at once.

I have always been good at spinning a yarn, but in this case I cleaved as close to the truth as I could. Everything I described really happened to me: the pregnancy, those horrible meetings of men. *The Widowers* and *Anchoress* would never have been written without me. I was their inspiration, my friend's reluctant muse. It's just that I'm a different person from who you thought, I'm truly nothing to write home about. I must return now to the beginning, just when we are so close to the end. Everything from here on in is God's honest, though. Honestly.

I met Brenda – for clarity's sake I will continue to use that name – at school, back in St Kilda in the sixties. I was the daughter of the penniless Bolognans, she the bank manager's daughter, head girl, the choicest of the chosen, and for some reason she chose me, the hairy-shinned charity case, who represented a sort of rough-and-ready otherness, which I played up to as best I could. My trick with the eggs, the story of the Beatles and my father being beaten, everything calibrated to attract and appal, to impress upon her that I was someone worth knowing. At the Tolarno, she was a woman possessed, a swot by day and a lady of the night by – well, you get the picture: bedding a new bloke every week, partying with reckless abandon, as if the rules of propriety and, indeed, biology didn't apply to her. She slept with half of St Kilda, yet it was me who fell pregnant from my single dud root with the art dealer's assistant, my wog womb finally getting the better of me.

When I told my parents the bad news, I expected understanding, for as far as I knew they'd left Italy in such a rush they'd never even tied the knot. But my mother wailed like a fire truck, while my father cursed in dialect that would have made a stevedore blush, the two of them possessed by their ancestors, virgin's bedsheets hung from windows, blood feuds and honour killings. All in all, it was a disturbing about face; they were pinkos, for Christ's sake. Sometimes I worried I'd slipped when I was talking to you, given the game away. The story of my father in the internment camp was so very detailed, I was surprised you didn't question it.

Anyway, you know what happened next, more or less. They kept me locked in my bedroom for six months, the window boarded over from outside. I knew I wouldn't keep the child, even if I'd wanted to, and so I thought of it as a foreign body which had to be removed, like a tumour. I thought of the baby, *your father*, not as life but death.

My only respite were Brenda's daily visits. My parents agreed to lock her in with me for a few hours after school, ostensibly so I could keep up with my studies. They saw Brenda as an avatar for the staid respectability which had forced their hand, stumbling over their English as they laid out their reasons for keeping me hostage, all of them news to me. They believed that as the daughter of immigrants I would be scrutinised in a way that other girls weren't, they said, and perhaps they were correct. *A regrettable set of circumstances*, I remember my father saying, a phrase he'd clearly practised.

When we were alone, I was full of questions about the outside world, but Brenda gently prodded me back to how I was feeling, asking me to describe the flushes and flashes, the pangs and pains of pregnancy. She wanted to know about what I thought of my pitiable situation, to cease holding my tongue and let the bile and self-pity pour out. You know these last couple of weeks remind me of talking to her.

She was there with me in the receiving room, while Vince and Nell waited in the corridor. Hers was the last face I saw before they doped me up, so that I wouldn't struggle, when they came to take him away. I remember her staring down at me with the attention of a lepidopterist, itching to pin me to a board.

He's called Ian, of all things. My son, I mean. A name only a mother could love, though I don't love him; I don't know him well enough for that. He's the publican of a bar in Bangkok, which is probably a euphemism for something I don't care to know about. Before that I believe he was in the mines, FIFO from Bali to Karratha. We've met a handful of times, and he occasionally gives me a bell on my birthday, not that he's much of a talker. He's had a nice life, as far as I can tell – more of a life than I could have given him.

*

The first time I saw *Anchoress* was at Cumberland Place, just before I dropped out of my teaching degree for good. One of the girls had left a copy in the living room. I remember thinking *what a hideous cover*. I read a few pages, then I read a few more. The name Shales rang a distant bell, then I remembered the nun from our schooldays, whose eggs I'd drank, and who'd beat me so savagely. At a certain point I realised the book was not written for me but *about* me, and there was only one person who could have written it. Brenda had transposed the story of your father to fit her life and family, and she'd transmuted it too, into something brutal and beautiful. Some sections seemed ripped straight from my lips, and yet the character – dare I say *my* character – saw the world more clearly than I ever could, with an almost saintly attention. It was as if Brenda had clothed my story in stiff brocade, sutured up the wound of my life. She had talent, there was no two ways about it. I told you the story of my pregnancy filtered through Brenda's version of events; hiding behind her words allowed me to speak honestly.

I didn't allow myself to feel betrayed, for without Brenda, what would I have had left? No, I didn't resent the theft, for a story is not something you own. Besides, she'd been with me through it all; it wouldn't have been hard for her to put herself in my shoes. But how had she not told me during those marathon phone calls from the offices I cleaned in Melbourne to her Sydney share house? I didn't even know she was a writer! She enjoyed keeping secrets, from me more than anyone. Deception is just as addictive as any other drug. You should know. Assuming a pen name, Brenda Shales, had nothing to do with shyness or propriety. No, my friend simply loved being two things at once.

Perhaps you think I'm trying to draw a parallel between you and her? She was ruthless, but it always served a purpose: she needed raw material, but she did something with it. I suffered for her art, but at least some art came from it. You didn't even ask questions. Didn't take notes. You just wanted information. Data. You have the soul of an engineer.

But where was I?

Oh yes: it was the time of dolour and delirium. I dropped out of school, lost my cleaning gig. The sporadic work with Arnold and the husbands was all I could handle, though it was far from a fulfilling vocation. I never told Brenda about the sporadic visits to the shock doctors. It was not an era which rewarded disclosure, even between bosom buddies like us. Stiff upper lip and all that. Besides a few grim flashes, I truly don't remember what those doctors did to me. And that's probably for the best. So when I was spilling the beans to you, I made my friend the headcase, a narrative convenience to save me the bother of making things up.

During those phone calls, I told Brenda about the men at the meetings, their self-pity and hatred for the women they called their wives. I even pretended I'd gone to bed with the worst of them – field research, I called it – still as desperate to impress her as I had been in high school. She was interested in the husbands' testimonies, though I was vague about the details, nor did I tell her about the minutes I'd been keeping. I knew what she wanted from them and me. A sequel.

And then one morning Brenda was standing at my bedroom door. It was the first time I'd seen her in years. I found out later that Carmel had called Brenda in a state of panic, telling her of my erratic behaviour, my return from the hospital, head pinked, semi-vegetative, not making a great deal of sense.

The house in Tatura had been in her family for generations, the last vestige of a sheep station parcelled up and sold, a rickety farmstead where I was to recuperate while she wrote the *great Australian novel*, as she referred to it ironically, though she was deadly serious. Her parents had even put it in her name, an early inheritance. If the history books were to be believed, her venerable ancestors had been on the wrong side of the Frontier Wars, and Brenda wanted to write a doorstopper reckoning with the sins of her fathers, narrated by a woman out of time, living alone in the threadbare family seat. Occasionally she talked about her writing as like being possessed by a force outside herself, in a trance, not responsible for her actions, her very own commotion. I suppose this was her way of saying sorry.

While she tapped away, I became a sort of secretary, dealing with the mail flooding in to the post office box I'd set up in Shepparton. By dealing with, I mean disposing of. Letters of love but principally hate, which I'd read to Brenda at the end of a day, her toes curling in pleasure. I cooked and cleaned, like one of the widowers' wives. As if to make the arrangement official, she even altered her will to leave me the house in Tatura, if anything were to happen to her.

Sometimes, when she'd had a few too many, she let slip her high opinion of herself. She believed that, unlike other writers, she didn't have to answer for her words; she thought that she could remain inaccessible. But more often than not she railed against her critics' dimness, reciting sections of their reviews by heart. She saw herself as above the ruck and fray, but she was just as thin-skinned as the next writer, scuttling about for praise and attention.

I can't deny it's me in that ridiculous author photo, included on every reprint till kingdom come. It captured the *idea* of Brenda Shales she'd created, a marauder trampling the vegetable patch of Australian letters. Or perhaps she just wanted plausible deniability. It was a sort of joke, though in the end the joke was well and truly on me.

When the commotion came on, she hid the car keys and left me to my own devices. I couldn't do much damage to myself, seeing as we were so far out of town. I ran naked through the fields, drank myself silly, and eventually the symptoms passed. I presumed I'd end up in her next novel, the madwoman in the attic, or the granny flat, as it were. But thankfully there were no questions; she didn't seem the slightest bit interested in getting under my skin, nor knowing what went through my head when I lost control, and I loved her for that, her careful inattention.

We could have gone on like that indefinitely, living rent-free with only her royalties and pocket money from her parents. I don't know how I managed to spend so much time doing not much at all, but I've seldom, if ever, been happier. Besides, Brenda had ambition enough for the both of us. But her family saga was not coming together, judging by the sighs coming from her bedroom. Six months of false dawns, she confessed to me one evening, leaving her with little more than an opening scene: a woman driving into a nameless country town. The pressure was getting to her, her editor's letters growing increasingly pointed as he asked for news of the manuscript she'd promised. She started to grow dissatisfied with me, huffing about the state of my cooking and the house, treating me like the help – like her wife.

One day I was cleaning her room while she was at the town hall archives, digging up dirt on her family. I found the dictaphone tapes in her underwear drawer, neatly labelled with dates and times, each one a recording of my voice while I was in the grips of the commotion, stark-raving, nonsense for the most part, punctuated by moments of coherence, in which I summed up my life with surprising precision. She must have followed me around, or else secreted the recorder wherever I happened to be going mad. She never spoke up herself; it was as if she didn't want to leave evidence of her presence. Now who does that remind me of? She couldn't help herself, just as you couldn't. Even your lovely friend Linh had an ulterior motive, looking at me like I was dinner. And Ruth with her little essay, burning her mother at the stake. Never let your finer feelings get in the way of a good story.

I couldn't believe Brenda was at it again, sifting through the detritus of my life, threshing me through the fine-toothed machine of fiction. I saw then what I was to her: subject matter. She kept me around to assist in her brilliant career, handmaid and helpmeet, bearing witness to the gruesome trick she was playing on the world. That afternoon, I wanted to destroy her – so I did.

I'd kept the transcripts from those meetings of men. They were the only record of that time in my life when things were unspooling, when I was in and out of the hospital. They were catnip to a writer like Brenda, primary documents that appealed to her desire for gendered retribution, though as far as I could tell the men in her life had been nothing but nice to her. I'd been very careful to keep the transcripts out of her clutches, though it wasn't like I had any great plans for them. No, I never wanted to be a writer. Nor was I concerned with upholding the reputations of the men from the Husbands Emancipation League. I wanted to protect Brenda from herself.

But I was angry that day I found the recordings. And so I left the husbands' transcripts on her desk. In her vainglory, she interpreted them as a sort of offering, as if I were signing over their lives to her, to do with what she would. She drank the poisoned chalice in a single draught, including the transcripts verbatim, as I knew she would – just as I knew the husbands would recognise their voices stitched together with the offcuts of her still-born novel. I'd wanted to get back at her for using my life as fodder for fiction – or, to put it in simpler terms, for using me.

Once I'd cooled off, I tried to convince her to modulate, modify, protect her backside. But she refused to change a word, declaring that any intervention would dilute the brutal realism of the husbands' voices. She explained this to me very slowly, as if I were too dense to comprehend such a subtle literary concept. *Besides*, she told me, *blokes don't read books.*

She wasn't the same after the lawsuit, once the public well and truly turned on her. At first she insisted I read every piece of hate mail, and she scoured the papers for mentions of her name, but at a certain point the fight went out of her, and it was all she could do to get out of bed. Now I was the ministrator, drunk on the power of care. I've never felt more in control of myself than when she was sick. It was grief for the life she thought she deserved, which surely would have passed, had fate not intervened.

She'd been complaining about her head for days, migraines and a pulsing behind her eyes. I could tell something was seriously wrong by the way her speech was starting to slur, her terrible pallor, her sensitivity to the light. The good was always given to her – brains and friends and men and charm and money and talent – while I was left with the dregs. I walked around the beautiful old house, which, the thought burst in on me unbidden, might one day be mine. As her symptoms worsened I waited on her hand and foot, feeding her when she was too weak to lift the spoon, bathing her in bed, cleaning up when she had an accident. I didn't have a plan, not consciously, but when I finally made the call to the hospital, I knew it was already too late.

Has the price of admission been worth it? All those lies and dissimulations, for *this*? I'm sorry everything got so convoluted – *my bad*, as the kids say. This is my first attempt at the whole authorship shebang, but all things considered, I think I've made a decent fist of it. And I've enjoyed telling things in my words, being the centre of attention.

Would you have wanted to tell my story if you'd known it was mine and not hers? The biography of the great author's friend doesn't have quite the same ring to it, does it? My slings and arrows were no more outrageous than those suffered by most women I knew. Barely worth mentioning. What happened was only legitimised when it became literature, when she took it for herself.

Despite it all, I felt a duty of care towards that name that never was, *Brenda Shales*. Oh, how she'd hate me for showing how the sausage was made, far from cruelty-free. She, like you, was a talented thief, and the world takes a dim view of such figures these days. We are more on the eggs' side than the omelette's.

I never asked to be involved, with her lies or yours. You spoke once of revenge, and perhaps that's what all this amounts to: my revenge against the world which saw her in me.

What is the plan for your granny's will and testament, now you know its suspect provenance? Will you wheel me out onstage to read the story of your father? Subject me to the public at large? In truth, I don't know how many lies I have left in me.

On the topic of truth, wouldn't that be infinitely more interesting? For our book, I mean. Your grubby unmentionables hung out for all the world to see, your confessions interspersed with mine. I can see it now: the slip of the tongue that snowballed, the good lad gone bad, the deceiver deceived. For some people it's better to be hated than ignored. Yes, that's a book I'd be happy to put her name to: one where you come off as badly as I do.

Is that thunder, or is someone fumbling with the front door? I'm sure I'm the last person Ruth wants to see, so I should make myself scarce. Tell Ruth what you need to tell her, but I'd suggest you start with the truth. Think of it as practice. The only way out is through. This need not be the end, but before I go, I'd like an answer. Just a word will suffice.

So, do we have a deal?

ACKNOWLEDGEMENTS

This book took the better part of five years to write, and I owe a great debt to a great many people.

Endless thanks to the dream team, Grace Heifetz and Jane Palfreyman, for taking a chance on me, and for your guidance, brilliance and friendship. This is only the beginning!

Thanks to the peerless team at Summit Australia and Simon & Schuster and the people they work with, particularly Anna O'Grady for her PR wizardry, Sandy Cull for the sexy and singular cover, Ali Lavau for her sagacious edits, Fleur Hamilton for the masterful marketing, Tricia Dearborn for the eagle-eyed copy-edits, Reilly Keir for the audiobook magic, and Rosie Outred for bringing it all together.

Thanks to Sophie Missing at Scribner UK, and particularly Ella Fox-Martens for her supreme editorship. Thanks too to John Ash and Julie Flanagan at CAA.

To all early, middle and late readers. Without your insight, grace and tenderness, this book would be nothing to write home about:

Leonie Amerena, Luke Brown, David Carlin, Laurence Cummings, André Dao, Naiose Dolan, Ben Eastham, Panagiotis Kehagias, Ruth Gilligan, Ella Křivánek, Lauren Oyler, Catherine Rush, Ronnie Scott, Nick Tapper, Anders Villani, Francesca Violich-Kennedy.

Thanks too to all those who did favours, made introductions, and wrote letters. It's so very appreciated: Octavia Bright, Rita Bullwinkel, Paul Dalla Rosa, Gregory Day, Elena Gomez, Melinda Harvey, Luke Horton, Samuel Rutter, Lynne Tillman.

Residencies, institutions and prizes gave vital support along the way, in particular: Creative Australia, the Hawthornden Foundation, the Speculate Prize, RMIT University, and Vil A Joana.

Thanks to my family: Leonie, John, Massimo and Donna.

And thanks most of all to Ellena Savage, without whom my book and life would not be worth a damn.

ABOUT THE AUTHOR

Photograph by Anna Tagkalou

Dominic Amerena is an Australian writer whose work has been widely published and anthologised. He has won numerous prizes, scholarships, fellowships, and grants, including the Vil La Joana Residency, the Hawthornden Fellowship, the inaugural Speculate Prize, an Australia Council New Work Grant and the Alan Marshall Short Story Award. He has a PhD from the University of RMIT and he lives between Melbourne and Athens, Greece. *I Want Everything* is his debut novel.